Timeless:

As the World Stands Still

Allan Marks

PublishAmerica
Baltimore

ISBN: 1-4137-5541-0
PUBLISHED BY PUBLISHAMERICA, LLLP
www.publishamerica.com
Baltimore

Printed in the United States of America

September 16, 2003

This book is dedicated to those people who stood behind me no matter what. Most important, my mother, Fawn; my wife, Jessica; and the friends who knew that, no matter what, I would finish what I started. Two special notes to two very special people in my life, Jason and Pati. Jason, I cannot leave you out of this dedication. You are by far the best Game Master I have ever known and without you the character of Rowan would have never become such a detailed creation. Last but not least, Pati, how can I ever thank you enough for realizing that I could not resist a challenge even when I was near the point of giving up for good? I'm sure that this is one challenge that you are happy to lose. You truly are a best friend.

Chapter One

December 15, 1998

Dear Diary,

It's me again, just in case you have forgotten, I'm Rabecca. But how can you forget me? After all, you're the only one I can talk to openly without worrying about stepping all over your emotions!

Okay, okay, with all joking aside we've finally made it! It only took countless hours to get here in the middle of Hicksville, U.S.A, also known as Heritage Landing, and now I know why Rachel decided to leave home for college. I know that's mean, but even she says the only thing nice about being out here is the scenery.

I find it hard to believe sometimes when I wake up in the morning that I actually trust these people this much. If you would have told me nine months ago that I was going to be traveling with people I haven't known that long I wouldn't have believed it. But here I am staying in a house I do not know, meeting Rachel's mother with her boyfriend and mine. It's kind of scary thinking about Brian and myself being in a relationship this long, especially knowing that I have some feelings for him, yet at the same time thinking that we are not going to make it last much longer. And to think that I am still talking to him about marriage!

I can't explain what I am thinking, but don't get me wrong Brian is a nice guy sometimes. Yet when I am with him I feel like I am alone.

I don't want to lead him on, but he is so nice at times that it is hard finding the right way to let him down easy. Every time I think about trying I start picturing Brian with tears running down his face totally heart broken. I'll think of something, I have to, otherwise it seems like wedding bells are in my future.

I hate to cut this short, but I've got to get ready. Everyone is wanting to check out a night club that opened last year one city away from here. Who knows if the night will be interesting, perhaps I'll tell you all about it later.

Rabecca

"Come on, Rabecca, if we wait much longer for you then we ladies can't get in free."

Rabecca casually slid her diary under the mattress of her guest room bed as she answered Rachel's call. "I'll be out in a minute, guys."

Slowly she checked her makeup within the full-length mirror upon the door of the guest room that leads to the hallway before undressing. Her blouse and jeans landed upon the bed, sending a rush of cool air over her body, causing goose bumps to rise along the length of her pale skin. A hook on the closet door held the dress for her evening out. The deep violet and black velvet molded to her pleasant frame made her pale skin look more radiant and the raven black hair that spilled over her shoulders looked like fluid in motion when she moved.

The designs that she had painted around the corners of her eyes swirled, causing the green and yellow within her iris to glow as if it had the aid of some unnatural light. Her lips curled to give a sly smile as if she were a lioness preparing to stalk her prey.

Her voice became deeper and more seductive as she talked to herself, "Now for the finishing touch." Rabecca sat upon the bed as she pulled knee-high boots that were the color of wet black leather onto her legs, and as she stood the high heels made her appear much taller and intimidating than what she truly was.

Rabecca opened the guest room to find Rachel, Porter, and Brian all awaiting her with impatient looks upon their faces that faded rapidly as they noticed each other's choice in clothing.

Rachel was outrageous with her personal thoughts and hair, which had been cut closely since she was a teenager to make her full face appear more slender, and was dyed a fluorescent red. She attempted to hide her body behind a midnight blue blouse and black skirt that extended to her ankles.

Porter and Brian stood at her sides and were both dressed similar. They both wore tan slacks and a pull-over sweater vest that covered their white, pressed shirts and ties. The only subtle differences between their dress and appearance was that Porter was slightly taller than Brian and kept his light brown hair long enough to touch his collar. Also Porter was more fond of bright colors, such as the red vest that he wore.

Brian kept his fiery red hair cut very short, and, while wearing his thick glasses with the black vest, he looked as if he were a pre-law student.

Rebecca studied each of them and could not keep a grin from creeping across her face. "Okay, you three, are we going to a night club, bible study, or a funeral?" Rebecca laughed softly after her question.

Rachel quickly responded with a slightly harsh, sarcastic tone, "Well, I think I speak for everyone in saying that I'm wondering if you have risen from the grave."

Rebecca gazed at Rachel's eyes as she gave a seductive smile. "You know, Rachel, not to sound vain, but there may be some truth to the expression: drop dead gorgeous."

Music rolls into my ears like thunder crashing in harmony with wind and rain. The sound acts like the heart beat of all who move on the dance floor, filling them with life. As I mingle with the shadows, thoughts of having the life they all have fill my mind, yet the desire for the perfect prey still burns hot within the very fiber of my body.

Should I choose a blonde, brunette, or one with fake hair coloring? Male, female, innocent or impure? Should I make my choice from those who have not yet noticed me, or the few who have been watching my movements for hours?

No, it is still too soon to find the one for my passion of hunger this evening. Perhaps as I take my normal seat within the back of the room someone will volunteer themselves for my dark lusts. Yet as I await my prey I cannot stop my mind from drifting amongst memories of the past.

I can still hear her voice, smell the sweet perfume that she wore, and feel the warm touch of her slender fingers against the cold skin of my face.

Though they are memories of joy and love, I cannot stop depression from soon setting in with the cold facts of reality. I continue to exist within the past, knowing the pain of truth will always linger there, though I still hope that someday, somehow, Kyra will return to me with open arms. But unlike those who put faith in higher power, I am forced to look upon the harsh truth that I can never forget.

I have learned to force back the tears of sorrow well, but heartache still resides where the greatest of all loves once grew, for unlike most life true love is forever. The music stops momentarily and my ears fill with conversations from the span of the room. Within the few moments for the change of music I allow my eyes to fill with the images of those who are around me.

The new generation has filled this room, those who claim they long for death and view it as being romantic. They wear pale makeup on their face with black lips and sometimes designs about their eyes that match the clothing upon them.

The music begins again with its rhythmic, dark pulse, which causes bodies to sway as if it entrances them to do so with no will of their own.

I have had my fill here on this night. My lusts will be fulfilled later, perhaps tomorrow or the night after.

Sometimes I do wonder why I stay around these three. I can't believe the way they are dressed and they are expecting to have a good time looking like Young Yuppies of America coming to recruit new members.

The car crept to a halt in an available parking space within the crowded lot as people and shadows move toward the illuminated front of the building.

"Rabecca, Brian, Porter, welcome to the Club Unknown." Rachel opened her door as a sign for the others to follow. Porter quickly walked around the car to catch up with Rachel and began to escort her, trying to appear formal as they walked along arm in arm. Brian moved closer to Rabecca to offer his arm as they walked close behind them, trying to mock both Porter and Rachel and to show that Brian is with her.

Rabecca stopped and looked Brian over from head to toe once again. *I can't believe this,* she thought, and with some hesitation takes his arm to be polite.

With each step toward the line leading to the entrance of the night club the appearance of the figures became clearer. People from all walks of life had gathered there awaiting to gain entrance. Some were in their teens and dressed quite casual and with hair almost non existing to extending to their waist. Yet there were some there who appeared single and approaching their prime in the middle of life who hoped for a younger catch to make themselves feel more alive.

But there were those who were scattered amongst the line who chose to dress as Rebecca, leaving Porter, Rachel, and Brian being the ones oddly dressed.

The line did quickly thin as the large doorman with a shaved head began asking for identification. He stood there wearing his black suit, turning away groups of teenagers for being under the legal drinking age, yet some were because of their attitudes, but they did not wish to question him much for politely telling them to leave.

"I need to see some identification on everyone." For being the most properly dressed, Brian, Porter and Rachel were the least prepared for the stop, and as they scrambled to find a proof of their age Rebecca stood there patiently awaiting them to hand him the information that was being asked of them so that they could continue on. The three each found what they were desperately searching for and joined Rebecca who was with identification in hand, to show the doorman the verification of their birth date.

His eyes glanced one by one at the rectangular cards matching faces with picture. "The preps are okay, but I'm not too sure about you."

Rebecca's anger began to grow into rage with each breath that her lungs took. The doorman looked her within the eye as the other three tried to contain their laughter.

"Don't take it personal, sweet cheeks, but I get too many kids playing dress-up like you with the heavy makeup, trying to pass off a fake driver's license, especially a license from out of state."

Anger had caused Rebecca's face to flush and show through her white makeup. "Now listen up, you gorilla look alike." Her words were cut short as the doorman looked behind him and opened the door for a shadowy figure approaching. Her eyes were locked upon the man who neared with this smooth face looking downward, showing no regard of someone or something in his path.

He dressed as if he were from high society, and each graceful step that he took caused the ankle-long black coat that draped over the fine-tailored black suit to catch the passing air, causing it to flare backward almost like a cape. The blood red shirt was accented by a highly polished black gem that pinned at the collar in place of a tie.

He raised his head only after reaching the doorman to look at him before calling him by name, "Hello, Norman." His dark brown hair spilled over his shoulders like waves and came to rest at the middle of his chest.

"Leaving us so soon, Mr. Rasland." The tone within the doorman's voice had turned from sarcastic to a deep respect.

"Yes, Norman, I do believe I am through here this evening." The pain within his voice and eyes was very subtle and almost unnoticeable unless one looked and listened carefully.

"Should I call for the limousine, sir?" Norman shut the door as Mr. Rasland stepped out under the night sky.

"No, Norman, I believe I will walk for a while." He began to walk away within the embrace of the cool night when his ears were filled with Rabecca's voice.

"As I was saying, Norman, is it? I think I would like the chance to speak with your manager."

Norman looked at Rabecca as if she were trying to pull an elaborate joke upon him. "I'm sorry, little lady, but the managers are very busy this evening."

Mr. Rasland turned around and gazed at Rabecca with his black, reflective eyes. "Yes, Norman is right. The managers here are also the bartenders and I'm sure you can imagine how busy they are on evenings like this."

Rabecca's eyes were fixed upon him once again as he neared her. "Perhaps I can assist you." He held his hand out for Rabecca to greet her as he continued, "I am Rowan Rasland, what seems to be the trouble here?"

Her anger once again made the words that she spoke seem harsh. "This doorman is trying to insinuate that I am a minor trying to pass as an adult."

Rowan looked deep within her bright green eyes before next speaking. "You must excuse Norman, he is just trying to protect me." His gaze turned from Rabecca to Norman. "Let me see her license." Without argument the license was placed within his hand and Rowan's eyes quickly glanced over the written information before he stopped upon the photograph. The expression of sorrow melted as his dark eyes reflected the pure image on the card, and the longer he stared dismay appeared to replace the pain that once lingered within his expression.

Rowan's voice slightly trembled as he spoke to Norman, still focused upon the picture. "Norman, stamp Ms. Hollyard's hand."

Rowan gave Rabecca the license as pure shock crept over her face, and as he witnessed this expression of innocence a slight smile formed from his firm lips.

"I cannot afford for someone like yourself to come to my establishment and not be satisfied. Therefore I would like you to be my personal guest this evening."

The pink tint was still upon her face as Rabecca smiled quickly and turned her eyes from Rowan to her friends. "I would take you up on your offer, Mr. Rasland, but I can't just leave my friends behind." Rowan's eyes moved over Rachel, Porter, and then stopped on Brian who was closest to Rabecca's side, and as he studied Brian's features he could see the anger that he expressed through his eyes as he glared back.

Rowan once again turned his attention toward Rabecca and smiled, showing his white teeth. "The night is yours, my lady. Nothing that you can ask of me will truly make up for the grave mistake that has taken place this evening."

He looked at Rabecca as he signaled with his hand for Norman to stamp their hands for admittance. "Your friends are welcome as well."

Norman passed the three remaining licenses back as he reached for a small rubber stamp in his pocket. He then began to leave a pair of small, red, slanted eyes pressed to the right hand of each of the four. Norman then motioned behind him as he said, "All of you will have to enter through here and go to the window on the left for your alcohol bracelet."

Rowan moved closer to Rabecca as he placed his hand upon Norman's shoulder. "That will not be necessary. I assure all of you that your needs will be met without them." Norman opened the door while Rowan tried to hide another smile as he looked at Rabecca's face. "If you would allow me to escort you I am sure that I know the room here that you would most enjoy."

Rabecca took his left arm with a smile that she could not be rid of as Rowan led her through the door. The others followed close behind their steps and after Norman could not see them clearly he took the hand-held radio from under his coat and sent a message to all security to pass around to the other workers.

"Everyone listen carefully. Mr. Rasland has guests tonight that he has just met, and I want everyone to take very good care of them. This goes double for the woman that is on his arm right now. She has actually put a real smile on his face."

Rowan's path stopped in the center of the lobby of the club as his employees greeted him, trying to hide all signs that they knew briefly what had happened only seconds ago as they passed. Rabecca, Brian, Rachel, and Porter stood in amazement as their eyes glanced over the room, which was painted a pale white with antique mirrors, prints and paintings that adorned the walls. The walkways that led to different rooms were decorated with black velvet drapes that extended the length of the wall and pulled back with fiery red, tasseled cord that was only a few shades brighter than the thick carpet beneath their feet.

The lobby filled with echoes of different styles of music and voices of those who sat within Victorian style furniture that was scattered throughout the large room. Rowan turned so that he could face his guest, releasing Rabecca's arm so that he could have free movement.

"This is the Club Unknown. Each of the seven rooms here has a different theme, and needless to say each room has its own style of music and attracts different types of people. I tried to appeal to every class of person from the youngest generation to the generations of the past to present. The first room that was finished was my personal favorite because of how dark in nature it could be. I think you will like it a great deal, Ms. Hollyard."

Rowan began to walk toward the first room to the right as he continued. "You are all allowed entrance to any of the rooms that you wish, also anything that you want to eat or drink is on the house. Just tell your server or bartender that you are my guests. But I am sure that, thanks to Norman, this information has spread like a wild fire by now."

Rowan reached the edge of the corridor when he noticed that Porter and Rachel had already began walking from one corridor to another, trying to decide where to go first. Behind him Rabecca followed without concern, yet Brian stayed to her back keeping his anger-filled eyes on Rowan. He turned to face Brain and as their eyes locked together Rowan showed no emotion as he spoke to Rabecca. "Ms. Hollyard, would you care to join me for a drink in the Darkness?"

Before Rabecca could answer for herself, Brain moved between them and said, "I'm not so sure that I want my fiancée going with you alone, Rasland."

Rowan only smiled at the sight of Brian's first expression of his growing fury, which had made his body begin to tremble. Brian moved closer to Rowan in a way trying to intimidate him, yet before Brian could have a chance to speak another word out of rage a hand was upon his shoulder turning Brian's attention away from Rowan.

"Brian, what the hell is your problem?" Rabecca's words stunned Brian, causing him to forget his rage that was directed toward Rowan.

"First of all, Brian, I am not yours to control, you don't own me, and second you have never proposed with a ring so you cannot call me your fiancée. And judging by the way that you are acting right now, if you were to ask me to marry you more than likely I would laugh in your face at you even believing that there was still a chance after you have acted like a child, not just in front of me, but toward a true gentleman who is the only reason we are in this club!"

Rowan walked around the two of them so that he could place a kind hand on Rabecca's shoulder. She continued to stare at Brian's eyes as if she were trying to blind him by the arrogance that bred within his mind.

"Well said, however, do not be too hard on the young lad, for it is only human nature to want protection for someone whom you care for."

Brian stood speechless as Rabecca turned back to Rowan and said, "I think I would love to take you up on your offer, Mr. Rasland."

Rowan began to walk through the entrance to the room, and as he almost faded from sight he called back to Rabecca, "I will await you at the bar, just in case you need a moment alone with him."

Brian's eyes were turning more red with each passing second and were slowly filling with tears. Rabecca glanced to see Rowan disappear within the dark hall and then looked at the tear that fell from Brian's eye and said, "I don't need a moment alone with you. Tell Rachel to find me when she is ready to go, Brian." With those final words Rabecca left Brian to join Rowan within Darkness.

Rabecca's ears filled with the beat of the heavy and dark music as she walked through the curtains. Her eyes adjusted to the dim light to find the dance floor in the center of the room, filled with those dressed like herself, having no regard over what other people thought of them. From the center of the room Rabecca's eyes began to wander, taking in all of the details of this unfamiliar, yet alluring place.

The walls were covered by an artificial stone paneling, which gave the room an appearance similar to a medieval stone castle. Mounted to the walls were brass candle holders that embraced fake candles, giving off the flickering glow of a flame due to the bulbs within them. Dark, wooden tables and chairs surrounded the dance floor in a circular pattern, which ended either to her left with two tables in the shadowy corners, or the right with the bar.

A black light sign that read: *Darkness* hung on the back wall of the bar, casting an eerie, purple haze upon the bottles of liquor in front of it. Tall bar stools were empty in front of the bar, all except the middle where Rowan sat talking with the African-American bartender. Rabecca wove her way through the people and furnishings, slowly reaching Rowan; as she passed patrolling security they all smiled at her.

As she reached the bar Rowan turned and smiled. "That did not take long, please have a seat."

Rabecca smiled in return, yet under the smile a concerned, almost mournful, expression hid. The bartender dried a glass and, smiling at Rabecca as she glanced his way, he said, "You must be the vigorous young girl I've been hearing so much about. Hi, I'm Tony."

Rabecca smiled again and then turned her eyes to Rowan and said, "I don't know how to act with all this attention, Mr. Rasland. I've only been here for a few minutes and it seems everyone already knows all about me."

Rowan laughed quietly as his eyes became brighter each time Rabecca's face was gathered by his eyes. "Yes, Norman does have a way with letting everyone know everything that happens here. Especially when it concerns me. But with all formalities out of the way please call me Rowan."

Rabecca gave a sly expression, trying to still hide her true emotions and thoughts. "I can do that, but only on one condition, call me Rabecca."

Rowan closed his eyes as if he had heard a song sent to him by heaven and he bowed his head, signaling that she had her wish. "Well, Rabecca, you drive a very hard bargain and I do believe we can compromise on this. But I must know this: What would you like to drink?"

Rabecca's concern melted for a moment as signs of embarrassment showed upon her face. "I'm sorry, Rowan, but I forgot to mention that I don't drink. If it wasn't for all of this excitement that has happened within the past few minutes maybe I would have remembered when you asked me to join you."

Rowan could not contain himself from smiling again as he watched her slowly turn red from the embarrassment. "That is fine, my dear Rabecca." Rowan's eyes flashed to Tony as he said, "I'll have my usual Cabernet Sauvignon, and I think that a Shirley Temple would be perfect for Rabecca to start with, gracious sir."

Before Tony could finish pouring and mixing her drink Rabecca was wearing a blank expression as she went deeper within her own thoughts. Rowan could do nothing more than watch her as if he were studying each line that made up her face. Tony finished his work and placed the glasses before them, shattering their concentration.

Rabecca smiled politely as she thanked Tony, then her hand gently lifted the glass to her lips. The smile faded quickly as she began to stare at the cubes of ice floating in the vibrant red liquid.

"You are troubled by him." Rabecca jumped slightly at the sound of Rowan's voice. She took a deep breath and tried to answer, yet all she could find to give was a sigh. Rowan stood and took Rabecca's hand.

Her eyes looked at him with a childlike innocence, "Come with me, you have far too many things upon your mind to have a good time right now…"

Silence fell between them as the music filled the space between them and their thoughts. Rabecca held Rowan's hand tight as he moved around tables and through couples on the dance floor to one of the tables in the corner of the room that was hidden by shadows. Rowan pulled out Rabecca's chair, trying to be polite and respectful to her. He then took the seat across from her and folded his hands upon the table top.

"This is my normal table that I sit at each evening, we should not be disturbed here by those who are employed by me."

Rabecca's hand gently rubbed the glass, wiping the sweat away from its surface, and, though she tried hiding her emotions, each careless movement and look gave away the falseness of the impression she was attempting to give.

He looked upon her with kind eyes, and as worry began to fill Rabecca again Rowan smiled, trying to hide a guilty look. Her eyes glanced quickly into his and turned downward, avoiding the contact that felt too revealing. "I just don't understand him. Brian is somewhat of a nice guy, but I feel that he is expecting too much of me at this point in my life." Rabecca took a quick drink from the glass before her to prevent herself from continuing with that conversation. "I can't keep on talking to you about this, but even though I just met you I feel like I can talk to you about anything."

Her eyes lifted to meet Rowan's reassuring face as he pulled his chair closer to the table. "My dearest Rabecca, I cannot bear to see you waste this evening away with worry. It helps to talk about your problems with a non biased soul." With that invitation in hand Rabecca could not hesitate with her words, though she did try.

"I met Brian the same day that I met Porter and Rachel. I had just enrolled in college as a freshman and I did not know a soul there, not even my roommate. My first class was psychology and when I entered the lecture room I knew then how over my head college life was for me. I took a seat in the back of the room with a space between three other people and myself.

"Almost all of the students that were in front of me were talking in low voices until the professor came in and sat down before the class. He introduced himself and gave the first assignment, and that was to take the class time to interview three different people whom you did not know and decide if you could be friends with them and why. I chose the three closest to me, and they were Rachel, Brian and Porter.

"They were as scared and overwhelmed as I was. We talked the entire class and made plans afterward to have lunch later that day. Before I had time to completely realize everything that had happened I had found three good friends. Then one night when we were all at the movies Porter asked Rachel to marry him and she happily accepted his proposal. Brian, like always, followed Porter's lead, but he did not take it as far as being engaged. Instead we just started dating.

"That happened about three months ago, but recently Brian has been hinting about marriage, taking me to jewelry stores, and dress shops that specialize in wedding gowns. I've tried talking to him, but each time I start he gets a real mad look and then it changes to tears. I don't want to hurt Brian, because he is an okay guy. He just will not accept that I am not ready for the 'American Dream' like he is.

"I want to live my own life before someone else tries making a life for themselves and me."

Rabecca buried her face in her hands out of frustration caused by talking about Brian. Her eyes were clinched tight, trying to hold back the tears that were quickly forming. Rowan's hand brushed her cheek, trying to offer some comfort and understanding. His hand went under Rabecca's chin and urged her to look at him. Her head lifted and eyes opened, showing the red that had over taken the white.

One single tear streamed from each eye, but never fell from her face due to Rowan's gentle hand wiping them away. She turned her face away to dry her eyes and noticed Brian standing at the bar.

Rowan glanced to see what caused Rabecca to pause and quickly turned back to her. "I must ask you one question and you must be honest with me."

She sat silent with her red eyes focused upon Rowan, awaiting his words. "Do you love him?" His eyes were cold and serious as if at that moment he had turned to stone as he awaited her answer.

Rabecca's eyes and face went blank as she stumbled over different thoughts and answers, but as she started to answer she could not find the words to do so. Rowan's expression remained cold and frightening like a bust carved out of marble until he took Rabecca's hand in his and smiled.

"Forgive me. I know it was an unfair question, however you have already given me your answer. Rowan leaned on the table top trying to get as close as possible to Rabecca.

"You see, my dear, you are like me in so many aspects. You are a wild and free spirit, someone who cannot be tamed or controlled. If by some chance you are caught you can never be truly happy ever." Rowan's words touched Rabecca in such a way that she could not be touched by hand alone. At that moment though life and music continued all around them neither one cared to notice. Time had stood still for them so that this moment would never end. They began to feel as if they were one; as each second passed their heart beats and breathing came closer to being synchronized.

"There you are, Rabecca. We found Brian at the bar working on getting three sheets to the wind." Rachel's words stop short as she noticed the hands on the table creeping away from hers.

The moment was broken, left only to be a memory for each. Rowan did not have to look upon their faces to know that tension was building between Rabecca and her friends, and the silence that was between them now was only causing more discomfort for her.

Rowan quickly stood to greet them, trying to mellow the growing moods. "How very rude of me. You must forgive me, it seems that I was so taken with this spirited young lass when we first met I forgot to get properly introduced to each of you." He smiled politely, trying to hide the disappointment of their interruption.

Rachel stepped forward quickly to answer, however not before Rabecca could move between them. "Rowan, this is Porter and Rachel, and I'm sure that they do understand. Right?" Rabecca glared with warning at Rachel as if she could read her thoughts.

Porter stood slightly taller than Rowan, and as he looked ever so slightly downward he offered to shake Rowan's hand. "It's nice to meet you again, Rowan."

He took Porter's hand in his and met his grip with ease while continuing to smile. "That is some grip you have, Porter. You play football right?"

Porter grinned childishly and answered in a deeper, more ego-driven voice, "Yeah, I guess the grip gives it away."

Rabecca eased away from Rachel, still keeping a watchful eye upon her as Rowan stepped forward to attempt having a civil conversation. "Ahh, Rachel, believe it or not Rabecca and I were just speaking of you. In fact all of you." Rowan lifted his hand to Rachel, still trying to act polite, and as she backed away he folded his arm to his abdomen to bow.

"I bet you and Rabecca were talking about all of us, seeing how you are so taken with her and everything, Rowan."

The cruel, hopefully stinging words that flew from Rachel's lips caused Rowan's eyes to glance up at her, revealing that the polite manner had been melted by her words and replaced with a spark of anger unlike any that Rachel had ever experienced. Rowan quickly stood erect, causing one side of his face to be covered by thick, brown hair as his glare was upon her.

"Rachel, I think we need to have a nice, friendly chat alone." Rabecca grabbed Rachel's arm and led her to the edge of the dance floor with each moment revealing her true emotions. Rowan's eyes remained locked upon them as if he were a predator who had just found their prey until he heard Porter's cough beside him. He gave a small laugh, trying to cover up the annoyance that he was feeling as his attention turned to Porter.

"That is some woman that you have, Porter. But she can be a little too quick with the tongue from what I can see." Rowan took his seat, trying to resist the urge to look again at Rabecca and Rachel.

"Well, Rowan, I can say honestly that what you see is what you get with Rachel. There really isn't anything fake about her."

Porter took a seat beside Rowan and, as they sat there with silence between them, the urge to see the happenings became far too great for them both. Their heads turned and eyes were met with smiles walking toward them, smiles that gave the impression that all worries of the world had been lifted from the shoulders of the ones wearing them.

Rachel had no more than gotten near Rowan before she began to apologize. "I am so sorry, Rowan, I had no idea what had happened or what was really going on between you and Rabecca."

Rowan's eyes looked past Rachel to see Rabecca's angelic smile. Rabecca stopped beside Rachel and took notice of the devilish look within her eyes. Confusion grew on Porter's face as he began to inquire about what was being spoken of. Rachel looked at him and, without using words, he knew to wait until later.

"Rachel, I will accept your apology, however I would also like to ask you from now on to learn all of the facts before coming to your own conclusions." Rowan's words were slightly harsh, but all who were around the table knew that he spoke the truth, even Rachel.

Rabecca sighed with satisfaction before she asked, "So what do you two think about Rowan's club?"

Before anyone could answer Rabecca's question Tony interrupted with a hint of severity within his voice. "I am sorry to interrupt you and your guests, Mr. Rasland, but the gentleman at the bar is demanding another drink. I have already served him more than the limit because he said that he was with you. Also he said something to the effect of that he might as well drink your alcohol seeing as how you are stealing his future wife. But after I refused him he became very irate and is saying that he is about ready to come to you and have a show down."

Tony moved aside to allow Rowan a clear view of the bar. Brian was slouched upon the stool on the far end of the bar with his upper body being supported by his arms braced upon the top of the bar. Rowan watched his sloppy movements as he began turning his head left and right looking for Tony, until he turned completely around and leaned back against the bar.

Rowan did not pity Brian for his choices, instead he only sighed in dispirit before he responded. "Brian is one of my guests this evening. He is nothing more than a harmless drunk looking for excuses right now, Tony. His only weapons now are slurred words, which he will be lucky to remember in the morning. In my opinion as he is looking at us the his nerve is growing and he should have enough to confront me shortly. But as soon as he stands the blood will rush to his head and he will collapse."

By the time Rowan finished speaking everyone at the table was watching Brian watch them. It only took seconds for Brian to place one foot upon the floor and begin to stand. He stood there unsteadily like an old tree within large gusts of wind, and like an old tree with roots weak from centuries of standing he fell without effort to fight.

Rachel was the first to speak as she began to search for the keys to her car. "Well, people, I do believe that is our sign to leave."

In silence Rabecca, Porter and even Rowan moved to show support. Tony began to walk back to his bar but stopped and turned to speak with Rowan again. "I'm going to call Norman back here to help carry the boy to the car."

Rowan and Porter followed Tony and quickly picked Brian up by his arms and propped him upon the bar stool once again. Rebecca pulled Rowan away from the group so she could talk with him again in private.

"Rowan, I'm sorry about the way he has acted, and because he ruined the night before it really even got started." Rowan could not contain a kind smile as she reached for his hand.

"My dear, you need not apologize for the ignorance of others. I only regret that this ignorance will end our time together."

Rabecca could not find words for the growing sorrow that she could not explain. A sorrow that she did not want to explain, a sorrow that she ached for an end to. She could only look upon Rowan with eyes longing for something that she could not have because she knew not what it was, yet she knew that Rowan already had the answer, too.

"Hey, boss, we're ready to move him." Norman's voice caused Rabecca to jump and snap out of her thoughts.

Rowan nodded to Norman to continue as he sadly smiled at Rabecca. "I will escort you out."

With that being said between them they began the slow, sad march into the cool night air. The short walk was agony for Rowan, and though Rabecca had just met him she could sense the trial within his painful silence. Norman and Porter put Brian in the back seat of the car as Rachel unlocked the driver door. Rowan leaned to Rabecca's ear to whisper, but before he took the first breath to speak a voice called out from behind them.

"Rowan!" The voice was filled with anger and hatred, and though not very deep it still sounded intimidating to Rabecca and Rachel.

Rowan turned quickly, finding someone whom he knew all too well. He was tall and slender with oily, blond hair that reached the collar of his olive green military vest, which showed many signs of wear, including large dirt stains. Razor stubble covered his face that had lines etched into it deep, showing his age was near forty.

"Good evening, Jon, I take it that you are here for the normal weekly harassment that you seem to enjoy putting me through."

Rowan's tolerance was wearing thin for this person and the very tone within his voice told the tale. Jon came closer to Rowan and Rabecca and as he did so Rabecca moved behind Rowan to be out of this odd man's grasp.

"You have everyone else fooled, Rowan, but not me! I know what you are and I will stop you, by the Almighty I swear this!"

His voice was shaky and smelled of an odor similar to death. Rowan did not respond to Jon's comment but did notice that Norman had stepped to his right side.

"Norman, please escort Jon back to his van and try to explain to him better about trespassing laws. Perhaps you will have better luck than what I have had."

Norman did what was requested of him without any hesitation or question, yet as Norman grabbed him by the arm and led him away everyone's ears were filled with Jon's fading words.

"Don't let him fool you! He is not what he appears!"

Rachel quickly got in the car and unlocked the passenger side for Porter, leaving only Rowan and Rabecca outside alone.

"You must forgive me for that man, Rabecca; to him I am the most vile creature on this planet. But usually when you are insane I guess you must choose a target for your frustrations."

Rabecca smiled and took Rowan's hand again and held it tight as she spoke. "Don't be too hard on him. After all, we are all a little insane, we have to be to survive."

Rowan laughed and, for a second, forgot about goodbyes until Rabecca continued. "I don't want to go, Rowan, but I have no choice."

The engine of the car started and the tail lights caused a red glow upon the ground. Her hand began to pull away when Rowan said, "Wait," and his hand released hers and moved for his back pocket. Rowan quickly placed a small white card in her hand. "This card has the club number, office number, my home number, and the limousine number. Meet me for dinner tomorrow night."

Rabecca tightened her hand around the card before placing it in the small black purse about her shoulder. "I don't know…I am staying over thirty miles away from here."

Rowan's eyes became bright as he flashed another smile at Rabecca. "I would swim the seven seas to look within your eyes once again, for no distance is too far for a prize so sweet."

Rabecca's pale makeup could not hide the bright red that her skin had turned upon hearing Rowan's words. "I'll think about it," and with one last smile and a quick kiss blown to him Rabecca was within the car. Rowan watched as the vehicle began to pull away and though he longed for more time with her he knew that she would call.

Norman met Rowan walking back to the club entrance and smiled as he saw the new life upon his face.

"So, boss, is this one more than just a dinner date?" Norman's voice held the excitement of a hopeful teenager anticipating his first date.

"Norman, my dear boy, Rabecca is much more than you could ever imagine. Call the car around, the sun is soon to rise and I need to rest for the evening to come."

Chapter Two

December 16, 1998
Dear Diary,

I know it's early in the morning and only a few hours since my last entry but I could not wait to tell you about what happened at the club. I guess you can say that I met a knight in dark armor. His name is Rowan Rasland.

Like usual with Brian, Rachel, and Porter the night started out dull, but for once it did not stay that way! Like normal those three decided to dress conservative instead of walking on the wild side like me, but for once dressing "gothic" paid off.

The doorman wasn't going to let me in but the owner, you guessed it, Rowan, came to my rescue. He let all of us in for free and let everything we wanted be on the house!

But also like normal Brian began trying to show off, trying to impress me, but only made me start realizing more about myself and what I really want. Well, that is with the help of Rowan. I feel like I have known him for years, if not forever, and I can tell that he feels the same way. He knows what kind of a person I am and what I feel and I know that he will not let another soul know.

I would have loved to spend more time with him, but Brian got drunk, and we both know what happens when Brian starts drinking. So we loaded him up and here we are, back in the house of boredom.

I know that I have left out a lot of details, but it's late and I have to get some sleep. But before I go let me tell you why I need sleep.

Rowan gave me his card with numbers to the club, his office, home and limo! Yes, you heard me, Rowan owns a limo! But that is beside the point. The point is Rowan wants me to have dinner with him tonight!

I never gave him a definite answer. But as I have always been told, playing hard to get never hurts.

Rabecca

The night sky faded quickly as dawn broke over the horizon, causing the moon to lower for its slumber. The sun warmed the air slightly as its rays caused little rainbows upon the frost from the night prior. Rabecca lay within her warm bed, peaceful, with a small smile on her face as she dreamed of Rowan. This was the first time in months she had been able to sleep without nightmares of her possible future invading her subconscious thoughts.

She could have slept there for time unknown without worry if there were no disturbances, yet at that very moment footsteps were coming closer to the white painted door of her room. Rachel stopped in front of the guest bedroom of her mother's house and lit the first cigarette of the morning before knocking quietly first and then louder until Rebecca's eyes sprang open.

"I'm awake already, Rachel, damn!" The door knob turned and Rachel bounced in with a smile. With a chipper voice Rachel said, "How did you know that it was me?"

Rabecca sat up with her hair tangled and eyes still looking very tired and took Rachel's cigarette from her hand. She inhaled the smoke deep and answered with a rough voice.

"Only you can be this annoying and wake someone when they don't have classes because they are on Christmas vacation."

Rachel began to bounce on the bed, trying to act and sound like a young child. "I know, but you love me anyway. Come on and get dressed so I can take everyone out for brunch at Tee's."

Rabecca glared at Rachel with a look that showed clearly that she was not amused as she continued to smoke the cigarette. She stood, leaving the cigarette hanging from her lips as she stretched and asked with a groaning voice, "What is a Tee's?"

Rachel jumped up off the bed after a final bounce and reached in her pocket for another cigarette. "Tee's is the best little restaurant for good ol' home cookin' without having to cook it yourself around here, and besides, everyone in town stops there almost every day."

Rabecca walked to the door and closed it and stared at her face where her makeup had rubbed together as she slept. Her bear toes dug at the light tan carpet as she enjoyed the cool fibers between them. After one last puff she put the cigarette out and turned to go into the bathroom near the closet.

The water flowed into the sink as Rebecca reached for the wash cloth that hung above the toilet. Rachel leaned against the door frame, watching as she washed her face and dried it with the matching towel.

"You know I'm surprised that you haven't asked about Brian yet this morning." Rabecca turned, facing Rachel as she squeezed through the small gap between Rachel and the door. Still walking with an unsteady step, Rabecca went to her bed and dragged the old faded blue suitcase from under the bed frame, lifting it to rest upon the mattress.

"Does he feel bad, Rachel?" Rabecca's voice held no concern within it as she began to unbutton the purple flannel top of her pajamas.

"Of course he feels bad! He had four double shots, which is about seven shots over his limit." Rachel sat back on the bed with the cigarette still smoking as Rabecca completely undressed before her.

"Good. I hope that Brian feels as bad as he acted last night." Rabecca's cream-colored body shivered slightly in the cold as her dark brown nipples began to harden, which caught Rachel's eye and caused her to secretly lust.

"Rabecca, I know that you are upset with him, but he doesn't even remember much of last night." Rachel tried to keep her eyes from wandering over the bear flesh of Rebecca but could not stop until Rabecca's jeans slipped up to her waist and were buttoned shut.

"I don't care if Brian remembers much of last night! It's not an excuse for what he's done." Rabecca pulled a brush from a cosmetic bag attached to the lid of the suitcase and looked at Rachel. Rachel's eyes and head quickly turned downward with embarrassment at being caught studying Rabecca's breasts, and as the brush began the first stroke through the masses of black locks of hair She smiled secretly to herself.

"I don't know, Rabecca, he is your man. So what are you going to wear today?"

Rabecca had finished putting on a crushed black velvet shirt over her body that had flowing sleeves that covered her hands when they were at her sides. "I was thinking about something like this."

Rachel looked up to find Rabecca standing in front of her, posing with her arms extended outward with the cuffs of the sleeves hanging just above her stomach.

"Nice. But don't you think it's a little too cold for that shirt? After all everyone can see how perky certain parts of you are."

Rabecca looked down and saw how the cloth molded to her body, which allowed every curve of her upper body to be seen. She smiled as she looked at Rachel again. "I thought it would be fitting punishment for Brian to see exactly what he is coming so very close to driving away, and not be able to touch them one last time."

Rachel stood and walked to the bedroom door. "I'm going to stay out of this one, Rabecca, even though I do think you should at least sit down and talk to Brian about everything."

Rabecca sat upon the bed and began to put on her socks and shoes. "I thought you were going to stay out of this one."

Rachel opened the door and walked out, but right before she shut the door her head came around the corner to be seen once more. "I am staying out of this one, Rabecca, and if you are really this unhappy with him I'll tell Porter to sit in the back seat with him so that you can sit beside me up front during the ride there." Rachel shut the door quickly with those final words before Rabecca had the chance to say anything else in contradiction.

Rabecca was once again left to dwell within her own thoughts as she tied the last shoe and reached for her purse upon the night stand. Her hand unzipped the top, carefully reaching inside for the antique silver cigarette case and lighter that her aunt had given her as a gift before she died. As she pulled the case from the depths of the purse a small white card fell out and landed on the floor between her feet. A smile grew on her face as she picked it up and read the name Rowan Rasland at the top. She could still hear his voice and see his smile in her mind as she had the night before.

The silence of her thoughts was broken by a car horn being sounded to tell her that everyone was ready and waiting. Rabecca's thoughts remained on Rowan as she took a cigarette from the case and lit it before blindly walking through the house and through the front door.

The car was already started as she sat in the passenger seat beside Rachel and as the car began to move Porter said, "Good morning, Rabecca, and how are you doing so far?"

Rabecca looked behind her and smiled. "Not that bad, but I could be doing better if someone wouldn't have gotten me up so early this morning."

Rachel grinned, looking almost evil as she took her eyes off of the road for a moment. "Well, I'm sorry, guys, but Tee's is only serving breakfast for another two hours and I don't want any of us to miss out on great country cooking. Besides I've been craving anything from there for weeks now."

Brian looked as if he were a member of the walking dead within his pale skin and dark circles under his eyes. "I don't even want to think about food!"

Porter and Rachel waited to see if Rabecca was going to comment and after a moment of silence and feeling the tension running between them in the car Porter quickly answered. "My friend, what do you expect when you start drinking like a fish?"

All went silent again as Brian began to wallow within his misery. Rachel turned the stereo on, trying to ease the mounting feeling of discomfort. Music pounded through the speakers, yet the sounds were not heard for everyone was within their own world of thought about the situation that had began only a short night before.

The trip to the small white building that was a house at one point in time was short; however, the agony of the discord was enough to make everyone feel as if it took lifetimes to end the quick journey.

A small white and aqua sign sat in front of the converted building near the road that read: *Tee's. The place where home cooking is king and the hospitality makes you feel like one of the family.* A parking lot had been built in the rear of the restaurant to make up for the lack of parking in the front and upon the building's sides.

After Rachel slowly prowled through the isles of the parking lot she finally found a free space in which she did not hesitate to pull the vehicle into. "Okay, so they're a little busy. But I promise that it will be worth it after you try one bite of their food."

Before Rachel turned off the engine Rabecca opened the car door and began walking to the door. She did not care if cross words were being said about her, and as she neared the green door that entered into Tee's she did glance back once to see if there was anyone attempting to quicken their pace to catch up. The door knob turned and Rabecca walked through, into the strange surroundings. Tables of different shapes and sizes were scattered throughout the restaurant, most of which were taken with the regular patrons.

The wait staff only consisted of two women, one of which was close to her sixties with a gray frost-colored hair and lines carved deep within her face from years of a hard, long life. The second was in her forties with shoulder-length blonde hair and a pleasant smile, though her thin face was beginning to show her age well. Both of them wore forest green aprons with *Tee's* printed across the front in white letters, and as they joked and laughed with customers they had known for years it became clear to Rabecca that they were all like family though they probably never saw each other much beyond these walls.

Rabecca could hear the voices of her friends drawing closer behind her so she quickly moved for a round table that sat within the back corner of the restaurant. Though it sat six she pulled out the seat that allowed her back to be at the corner so that she would have plenty of space between Brian and herself. She took a menu with haste so that she could appear to be busy as they entered to join her.

Rabecca's eyes fixed upon the menu and then took notice of how homemade they looked. They were flimsy because of the thin paper and store-bought lamination sheets. Each one bore a large paper clip on the left that held the specials of the day on a small square of white paper.

Brian was the first to sit down across from her and try to make conversation. "You sure were in a hurry to get in here. Are you that hungry, dear?"

Rabecca sat there with her eyes glued upon the menu, acting as if she had not heard his words. Rachel and Porter sat on each of side Brian leaving two empty chairs beside Rabecca.

No one could say anything before the blonde waitress came by and knelt beside Rachel. "It seems like it has been forever since I last seen you girl." A smile parted her lips, exposing her gleaming white teeth. Rachel leaned over and put an arm around, her pulling her close. "I've missed you, too, Ms. Tracy." For a second it seemed to Rachel like she had stepped back through time when Tracy had taken care of her when her mother was at work.

"So are you going to have your usual, doll." Rachel looked at Tracy with a big smile and the answer was made known to her. "That's what I thought, and what about your friends?"

Porter was not slow with his answer, however it sounded like mumbling in Rabecca's ears as if someone was speaking from across the room. Yet as Brian began to answer his voice interrupted her thoughts once again. "I don't know, Rachel, I really don't feel like I can handle eating anything right now."

Rachel took the menu from in front of Brian and hit him upon the head with it. "Of course you don't feel like eating anything right now. But if you don't then you will just feel worse later on today." Rachel smiled again at Tracy as she put the menu back in the center of the table. "Just give him the same thing as I am getting, Ms. Tracy."

Tracy smiled again as she made note of Brian's order and then directed her attention to Rabecca and said, "And what for you?"

"Just coffee for now please." Tracy stood and started to walk away and then turned around with an embarrassed look on her face. "Where is my mind today? What would everyone else like to drink?"

Rachel laughed under her breath and before anyone else had the chance to tell Tracy what they wanted Rachel spoke. "Coffee. We are all big coffee drinkers now that we are in college, but we'll need a lot of cream." And with a final scribble upon her ticket book Tracy was gone.

Echoes of conversation filled the small restaurant as the four remained silent. Porter and Rachel sat there uncomfortably as Rabecca stared into space and Brian sat rubbing his eyes, trying to lessen the throbbing of his head. He finally looked up and noticed the way Rabecca was dressed and smiled. "You look really good today, Rabecca. I hope you didn't go through all this trouble just for me."

Rabecca looked him in the eyes and glared as if he insulted her beyond every conceivable way of using words. "Don't worry, Brian, I didn't wear this for you. Believe me it would be the last thing I would wear for you right now." Her eyes locked upon him as if they could burn through his body and destroy the very unseen fabric of his soul.

"I'm sorry, Rabecca. I don't really remember what I did last night but Porter has told me some of it, and I acted like a spoiled little brat." Rabecca's eyes did not leave his for a moment as she forced herself to continue looking at him, though doing so disgusted her.

"Believe me, Brian, when I say that you are not even beginning to touch the surface of how I think of you right now." Rabecca's words were cut short as Tracy returned to the table with a tray upon her right arm loaded with coffee and cream. "Here we go, guys. If you need anything else just catch me and let me know."

Once again there was silence between them all as they each took their time preparing the coffee the way they each preferred it. Afterward they each sat trying to enjoy the one thing that could possibly go right without question. Rabecca reached within her purse for the cigarette case, trying to wake herself up better than what she was. The flame kissed the tip of the cigarette and as the smoke rolled from the red hot tobacco toward Brain it caused the few sips of coffee that he had to settle hard upon his stomach.

Brian's head lowered and his eyes closed as his stomach began to churn and another deep breath caused smoke to fill his lungs again. "I'm not feeling so good," and with that, the effort of speaking those few words caused his stomach to feel as if it were a volcano ready to erupt at any second. Brian sprang to his feet and, with his hand covering his mouth, he made a mad dash for the sign on his left that said restroom with a large black arrow pointing downward.

Rabecca looked at Porter and Rachel and coldly said, "Now wasn't that predictable?"

They both sat there dumbfounded by the cold, emotionless sound of her words, unsure what to say or do next. Porter took one last drink before standing. "I think I'm going to make sure he is okay."

Before he walked away Rabecca said, "Good. He obviously needs someone to hold his hand and I'm sure as hell not going to do it anymore."

Porter did not acknowledge Rabecca's words as he walked to the restroom. Rachel looked at Rabecca with an angry yet questioning expression on her face.

"What is wrong with you, Rabecca?" Rabecca watched Porter walk to the opening to the hallway where the restroom doors were and then looked at Rachel to answer.

"I can't help it, Rachel. I thought I was going to be okay with him today, but each time I look at him or think about last night I keep getting more and more angry at him."

Rachel closed her eyes and shook her head in a disapproving way before saying, "But all of that is in the past, Rabecca. You can't hold it against him forever for acting a little protective. In fact, you should be proud to see that he does have some sort of a backbone!"

Rabecca was becoming more annoyed with Rachel with each word that passed through her lips, and it became more evident as she put out her cigarette in the glass ash tray near her and reached within the case for another.

"Proud of him! Yeah, Rachel, I'm really proud of Brian for acting all nice and sweet as long as other people are around. Then while we are alone trying to pressure me into various sexual acts that he reads about or sees over the Internet! And it gets even better when he tries to say that it will be okay because I am going to marry him!"

Tears began to swell within her eyes as past memories were flooding her mind as if to haunt her for one last time. Rachel sat shocked at what Rabecca had just told her and the look within Rachel's eyes showed that she was searching for something to say.

"Rabecca, I never knew. I mean you already told me about the marriage thing last night, but how could he try…I mean." Rachel could not finish as Rabecca took the paper napkin that was wrapped around her flatware and dried her eyes.

"It doesn't matter anymore! I'm finished keeping his dirty little secrets so that he looks spotless and clean while I look like the bad guy to everyone else!"

Rachel was still unable to believe what her ears had allowed her to hear, and the shock was enough to make her act as if she had forgotten about it already. "Perhaps you and Brian need to visit one of the campus counselors when we go back. Maybe they could help you guys."

The napkin lowered from Rabecca's eyes as disbelief set in upon her face at what Rachel had said.

"Didn't you hear me! Brian is trying to force me into doing things that I don't want to do! He is trying to control me, change me into what he thinks I should be for him! And all you can say is perhaps we need to see a counselor when it is Brian who is the sick one! I don't need friends like this!"

Rabecca slid her chair out hard and carelessly so that it hit the wall with a loud thud. She slung her purse over one shoulder and walked around the table to leave. As Rabecca came close to Rachel she quickly grabbed her arm before she could pass.

"Rabecca, wait. I'm sorry, I…" Before Rachel could finish Rabecca interrupted her.

"I know, Rachel. I'm sorry, too. I'm sorry that I ever trusted any of you." Rabecca pulled her arm loose from Rachel's grasp and began to walk away. She turned once thinking of what she had said and thought of apologizing until she saw Brian and Porter returning from the restroom. Without another second of thought she turned back and walked through the stream of people coming in the door. The sudden rush of cold December air caused Rabecca to shiver as she left the comforts of the warm, aromatic restaurant.

Her mind swam with thoughts of where she could go to escape the turmoil of her own thoughts, but she knew they would follow her no matter where she hid. Her eyes glanced over the landscape trying to find someplace to go when she noticed a small park across the main road. Rabecca tossed the half burnt cigarette from her hand and began to run to the street's edge. Few cars were on either lane of the road and almost all of them were turning into the entrance of Tee's. She knew that someone would be following her path quickly, therefore she wasted no time crossing the two-lane street as the wind blew in her face, causing her hair to be caught, trailing her and becoming tangled within itself.

Rabecca slowed only after reaching the edge of the park beside the small entrance that led to the parking lot. The ground was hard and cold beneath her feet as she looked for the best place to sit so she would not be so easily noticed from the roadside or the entrance of Tee's. Two large trees grew close beside each other near the fence of the park and separated it from the cold and wild hibernating woodland behind it. A small merry-go-round with blue hand bars was at the edge of the park near the larger of the two trees.

Rabecca walked slowly to the merry-go-round listening to the brown grass crunch with each step until her foot sank within the sand that surrounded it. Her mind wandered to her childhood when she did not worry about life and when her mother took her to the park.

Rabecca's life was so carefree then and as she longed for it once more tears began to fall in waves from her eyes. She wished to live for the moment once again, leaving the rest of her life to be figured out after that moment was over and the next was already before her. As Rabecca sobbed she did not look nor listen for sounds of anyone else approaching, and as Brian touched her face Rabecca jumped backward and looked up with red eyes and a wet face.

"Don't be so jumpy, it's just me." Rabecca backed as far away as she could as Brain knelt on one knee. "I really am sorry about last night, and I know you are very mad at me but I don't know what to do so that I can make it up to you."

Rabecca sniffed as she looked at Brian with her red eyes and dried her face with the sleeve of her shirt. "Do you really want me to tell you what you can do for me! Forget about me, leave me alone and don't ever bother me again."

Brian looked at Rabecca with pain in his eyes as he asked, "What do you mean, Rabecca?"

"I told Rachel your dirty little secret, Brian. I told her about how you try to control me, trying to push me into marriage, and most of all trying to get me to do those things like the pictures and movies you are always forcing me to look at."

Brian's eyes changed within that moment from being filled with pain to anger as he sprang up off of his knee. Brian's face began to turn red with anger and as he spoke his voice became gradually louder. "How could you do this to me?! You promised me that you would never tell a soul as long as you lived!"

Rabecca reached within her purse with more tears building within her eyes as she drug out another cigarette.

"That's right, Brian, you're not the sparkling clean picture of innocence that you once were in their eyes. They know the truth about you, Brian. They know that you are nothing more than a controlling pervert now." Rebecca's voice cracked a little as she finished her words. She watched as Brain's body began to fill with fear at the thought that someone else knew his true secret. Rabecca put the cigarette to her lips and inhaled the smoke deep within her lungs and watched the smoke escape her mouth little by little as she finished speaking her mind.

"Don't worry, Brian. You're more than likely safe. Rachel and Porter won't tell anyone else and more than likely they won't ask you about it. Instead they will always be talking about you behind your back, wondering what sick desire that you are wanting someone to fulfill for you next."

Brian's emotions began to run rampant as he searched for something to say to Rabecca, yet as he tried he began to cry, which quickly turned into a wail. Brian turned and ran blindly toward Tee's with the arctic-like air burning his tear-filled eyes and face. Though deep within Rabecca's heart she felt bad for telling Brian what she had done, she still smiled slightly because she had at least won the last argument that they would probably ever have.

Rabecca slid forward enough so that her feet could easily rest upon the ground once more. Slowly she pushed herself from left to right with thoughts of her childhood and Brian mingled together until she came to realize the new truth about her life. With a shaky, excited, yet unsure voice Rabecca said to herself, "I'm free."

That thought remained in her head as she quickly pushed herself to the left and lay back upon the cold steel as her eyes watched the gray sky. For one brief moment in time Rabecca felt like she once did as a child, being carefree and knowing all was going to be okay. But as all moments do, it faded and worries of Rachel trying to talk to her again, and attempting to fix all of the problems within her life rushed back to mind.

Rabecca sat up expecting someone to be standing above her judging her actions, yet the only image that filled her eyes was the hand-forged steel gates of a small but well-maintained cemetery.

There were three headstones within the spear point boundary; one looked worn and was crumbling with age but the two others were still somewhat legible. Rabecca stood and walked to the gates as if some unknown force was pulling her to do so, and as she pulled on the rust-covered gate it screeched and popped as it opened. One by one Rabecca walked by each headstone, studying each interesting design until she came to the first name that was female, Kyra Rasland. Beside this headstone was another that looked almost identical with its Celtic knot work around the edges that bore the name Rowan Rasland.

Rabecca's eyes widened as she looked below the name at the birth date of December 11, 1925. Her mind raced with ideas of Rowan's age after she noticed there was not a death date chiseled upon the stone.

Softly to herself Rabecca said, "No, this can't be my Rowan, if it was he would be seventy-three years old and he doesn't look a day over twenty-five."

Rabecca turned to leave when the thought of where she was to go entered her mind once more. She stood in discord as she thought about going back to Tee's so that she would at least have a ride to a place where she could make arrangements to go somewhere else, but she did not want to deal with anyone with a biased opinion.

She stood at the gates silently debating on what options she had available, and as she gazed across the park grounds she noticed Rachel's car pulling across the street to the park entrance. Within seconds Rachel, Porter and Brian would be at her side trying to lure her back and forcing an apology out of her for saying what she knew to be true.

Rabecca made her decision as she hurried to duck behind the largest headstone that was worn by weather and was in the far corner of the small cemetery. The air whipped the branches of the bear trees causing all sounds to be drowned out until she heard Brian's voice.

"She was right here on the merry-go-round just a minute ago when she told me that she was going to destroy me in any way possible starting with the both of you."

Rabecca was enraged at the lies he had just told Rachel and Porter. Though her first instinct was to leap from behind the stone that masked her presence and crush all that he was trying to do she did not, for deep within her soul she knew that Rachel would never believe her. She could hear footsteps near, yet she could not tell if they were coming closer or going farther away.

Rabecca looked around the edge of the headstone carefully so that she would not be seen and found Brian within Rachel's embrace acting as if he had just felt the worst heartache that he could ever feel. Rachel rubbed his back trying to console him, while speaking to him so softly that Rabecca almost couldn't hear what she was saying.

"Don't worry, Brian. Rabecca probably didn't mean a single word of what she said. And even if she did you should know that we would never believe something so horrible about you."

Brian took his head off of Rachel's shoulder and as he did so Porter put his hand upon Brian's shoulder reassuringly. "Of course we wouldn't believe it, Brian. After all you were brought up in a nice, upstanding environment and we know that you understand the difference between right and wrong."

Rabecca's eyes started to fill with tears, but she fought it off because if they did not have trust in her and anything that she said then they were never truly friends to begin with. Rabecca pulled her head back away from the corner and could feel her heart slowly breaking as she realized that, though she was now basically free, she was also alone, thought of as an outcast by those who she believed to care about her.

Rachel said, "Lets go, guys, Rabecca is a big girl and can take care of herself. We'll wait for her at my mother's house, she doesn't have anywhere else to go, so eventually she'll show up."

Rabecca's heart sank as she heard their footsteps slowly fade away until she heard the car doors open and then shut. The engine started and Rabecca fought the urge to run after them for she had never truly been alone before. Nonetheless she stayed crouched behind the stone until she was sure that they were far from sight. She stood and walked to the gates where she remained motionless, thinking of where she would wander within this small town that was quickly becoming her worst nightmare.

Her pride was the main enemy she had, for it would not allow her to seek help from anyone unless she had no other choice but to do so. As if she were marching from her own funeral Rabecca walked through the gateway and shut it, taking one last look at the cemetery almost like if she were pondering if death would be better right now than life, until her eyes laid rest upon the grave stone that read Rowan Rasland.

A smile grew across her face as hope began to raise her spirits. Her hands went numb as she walked across the street trying to think of what she could tell him other than the truth. Rabecca's mind drew a blank as she reached the front door of Tee's and entered the building again.

The aroma of food filled her nose and made her mouth water as she walked over to the cash register. Conversation had become louder since she was first there due to more people arriving as each minute passed. Rabecca awaited at the glass-topped counter that held the various homemade desserts until a voice drew her attention from the case.

"May I help you." The voice was deep, but kind as was the bearded face that the words came from. Fine lines became more visible as he smiled and rubbed his partially bald head. Rabecca tried to smile to be polite but could not keep it long because she was shivering so much.

"Where is your pay phone?" Her voice was unsteady as she asked. His eyes sparkled with light as he looked closer at Rabecca's face and notice the still-drying tear lines.

"I'm sorry, miss, we don't have a pay phone here, and the nearest one is about three miles down the road." Distress filled Rabecca's eyes as she began to think she had made a mistake, but before she could think of what to do next his voice stopped her.

"Do you mind me asking what's the matter?" Rabecca's defenses were down and before she could think about what she was saying she had told this perfect stranger about how her boyfriend was a sleaze, and instead of trusting her word the one true friend she thought she had turned her back, leaving without knowing where she was at.

Rabecca stopped for a breath and then realized what she had done, causing her to become slightly embarrassed. His smile made her feel as if this happened every day.

"I understand. My daughter and her boyfriend seem to constantly be disagreeing about one thing or another, and then I'm called in for the rescue when she wants to leave. Step around the counter and use the store phone. If you need to wait here for someone to come and pick you up then feel free to. I'll get you a cup of coffee to warm up with."

Rabecca smiled and was able to truly mean this one as she stepped around the counter and thanked him; then with a flash it seemed as if he were a ghost as he disappeared within the back of the kitchen. Rabecca nervously opened her purse and pulled out the card with Rowan's numbers upon it, trying to decide which number to call first.

With an unsteady finger Rabecca dialed the first number and pressed the cold, black plastic of the receiver against her ear as it began to ring.

"Thank you for calling the office of Rowan Rasland. How may I assist you today?"

Rabecca paused at the sound of the cheerful voice on the other end of the line before clearing her throat to speak. "I need to speak with Rowan please." Her heart was pounding harder with each passing thought of speaking with Rowan, and as the voice began to answer she took a deep breath to prepare for speaking to him.

"I'm sorry but Mr. Rasland is not here right now. If you would like you can leave a message but it may be tomorrow before he can get back with you."

Rabecca's heart sank back into despair and she found herself in a state where words could not describe her emotion, let alone could she find the words to answer with ease. "No, that's okay. I'll try later."

She quickly hung up the phone and looked at the card once again, hoping that the next number would prove to be more useful. The thought of calling him at home entered her mind, but it seemed too much like asking for help to Rabecca, yet after a brief pause to think she decided that Rowan would not have given her his home number unless he wanted her to call. With that thought in mind Rabecca pushed aside all fears and dialed before she had time to second guess herself.

The phone had not completed the second ring before it was answered. "Rasland residence, this is Norman, what can I do for you?"

Rabecca's voice started to freeze, but trying to remain calm she forced herself to speak. "Hi, Norman, this is Rabecca. I need to speak with Rowan please." Her eyes closed now that she could not hold back her anxiety any longer. She took shaky breaths that echoed through the phone and though Norman was already speaking he could hear this well over his own voice.

"Sorry, Ms. Hollyard, Rowan's out on business. What do you need?" Rabecca fell completely silent as the world around her disappeared, while what hope she had found seemed to melt away as Norman's words continued to echo within her mind, causing her to feel like she was now without anyone within this cold grave called reality.

Rabecca's first reaction was to cry out into the abyss that surrounded her, yet with all of the will power that she had left she restrained from doing so. She felt as if her eyes could explode from the amount of tears that would flow if they were allowed to come, but she knew that the moment for crying had long since passed and now she must depend upon herself.

"I'm so sorry, Norman. I shouldn't have called. Good-bye." The phone had already begun to leave her ear when he screamed into the phone in hopes that Rabecca could still hear his voice, "Ms. Hollyard, wait!" Her hand stopped and though Rabecca did not want to listen anymore due to the thought of embarrassment because of her situation, she still put the receiver against her ear once again.

Rabecca remained silent, hoping that Norman would not notice that she was still listening, but the echo of her breathing was enough to inform Norman otherwise.

"Rabecca, I know you're still there, and I have a feeling that something is wrong. Mr. Rasland gave me direct orders to have you picked up if you called before he returned. Where are you at?"

Rabecca thought of hanging up the phone and calling Rachel. Also she thought of running far away and trying to forget all of her troubles. Yet as she looked at each option, only the one upon the phone now was the one that held a small glimmer of hope.

"I'm at a small country restaurant called Tee's." Rabecca almost choked upon her own words, for in a way she had admitted defeat yet claimed victory within her darkest moment.

"I know where that is. Just sit tight, Ms. Hollyard, the limo will be there as soon as possible." Rabecca could not disagree, even though she did wish to refuse. But before the chance was given Norman hung up the phone in haste, leaving Rabecca to listen to the dull sound of the dial tone.

She could have called Norman back and told him to forget about it, or she could have just left. However, the thought of seeing Rowan again did intrigue her no matter how much gloom surrounded her life.

Rabecca sat at a small table for two near the front door, beside a window to give herself a better vantage point to seek her approaching ride. Her eyes wandered to the window where she daydreamed of a better place with a different life. One in which she could do anything and go anywhere, living how she wanted with little if not any regard to what other people said she should do with the life she was given. Like a child with more freedom she would live on a whim. Go wherever the wind may take her like a falling leaf if it was her wish. She dreamed of visiting lands that were unknown to her. Places where she had only read about, which fired her imagination and desires that were secretly locked away within her own mind so that they were safe from anyone's judgment.

Rabecca had passed many long hours, that would have been filled with boredom, in this way and sometimes she had just slipped into it such as now when she meant to be doing or watching for something, or even someone. All noise around her had faded away and did not mean anything to her within the world she was in now, for no amount of chaotic conversation could disturb her thoughts. Then as easily as Rabecca had slipped away to her own world she was pulled back by a small tap upon her shoulder.

"Ms. Hollyard, the limo is waiting for you outside." Her eyes cut away from the window to find a short, large man dressed in a black suit, with light gray hair and a mustache to match, standing beside her. Rabecca stood to follow this man who, without doubt, was the driver of Rowan's limo, and after she checked to ensure that her purse was still upon her shoulder they began to walk out.

Each door that she came to was held open with respect by the driver until Rabecca found herself in the back of Rowan's large black limo. Her eyes stared in wonder as she looked over the fully-stocked mini bar, custom stereo, television systems and the soft black material that covered the interior. A large black tinted window separated her from the driver and as the limo began to move the window lowered.

The driver gazed back at her through the rearview mirror as Rabecca let out a deep sigh of relief. "The name is Clifford. I just want you to know that Mr. Rasland instructed me to make sure that all of your needs and wishes are met. So if you need anything, Ms. Hollyard, please let me know." Rabecca smiled at him reassuringly as he put all of his attention on the road and began to raise the window.

"Wait," Rabecca cried out in a quick voice, causing Clifford's eyes to glance into the rearview mirror again and the window to lower.

"Please don't call me Ms. Hollyard. I am in no position to be addressed so formally. Just call me Rabecca, and you can leave the window down so I don't get lonely or lost back here."

Clifford smiled as he put his attention back on the road before he responded. "That's no problem, Rabecca, if you would like we will talk about anything that you want."

Rabecca sat quietly, thinking to herself what to bring up as conversation when a question came to her. "Clifford, how did you know that I was the right person?"

The limo came to rest at a red light, giving Clifford the chance to reach beside him and slide a large piece of paper into the back that caused Rabecca to reach almost to the window's edge to take hold of it.

"Mr. Rasland gave this to Norman last night after you two met. Norman said that Mr. Rasland spent hours last night working on it."

Rabecca turned over the paper only to find a hand-drawn picture of her face, which captured almost every detail, as if she were looking into a mirror. He had initialed the work on the lower right corner with two large Rs. Just by looking over each line Rabecca could tell the careful, almost loving strokes that Rowan had used within this representation of her. She knew not the words to comment and was glad that Rowan was not there expecting good or harsh words about his work, for all she could do was look at it and smile.

"Norman said word for word to me that Mr. Rasland was quite taken with you, Rabecca. So much in fact that you were all he talked about last night when I drove him home."

Rabecca put the picture aside as she began to blush slightly. Whenever she thought about Rowan all of her troubles seemed to melt away, leaving only a feeling of blissfulness and a questioning of *why her*.

"Clifford, what is Rowan really like?"

The light turned green and once again the limo began moving to its destination. Clifford was thinking carefully about how to answer and when he started to answer his eyes were looking at Rabecca through the mirror, again finding that she had moved forward as far as she could.

"Mr. Rasland has always been kind, especially to those who need help. A good example is me. You see I have only been his driver for about a year now, and before that I drove commercial vehicles. One day when I was coming home after dropping off a load, a car full of young, dumb kids cut me off and then slammed on their brakes. I swerved, trying to miss them, but I still clipped the back bumper and caused them to lose control and crash into a guard rail. Out of the four people in the car only the driver was wearing a seat belt and only she survived. Shortly after that I lost my job and my wife, who left me with what I believed to be nothing. I went on a huge drinking binge and one night I stumbled across Mr. Rasland's club. I drank there until the idea of suicide came to me. I had thought about it before, but never had the nerve to do it until then. I was on my way out from the club when Mr. Rasland approached and threw me in his office. And after I woke up the next morning or night, whichever it was, he offered me a job and a place to live. Mr. Rasland showed me that I had more to live for than what I had thought. The only thing I have ever found odd about him is the fact that he always looks so sad and yet he is able to cause almost anyone to look at themselves in a new light. But ever since last night he seems to have found a new spark of life himself, almost as if the sadness has been lifted off of his face and a smile was made just for him to replace it. To be honest about it, Rabecca, I think that it has a lot to do with you. There is something about you very special and Mr. Rasland can see it."

Rabecca lay back upon the soft seat, overwhelmed not only by Clifford's brief life story but by what he had told her about Rowan. The limo stopped at a large set of gates that sat side by side, fending all away from the cobblestone drive that met the road. On the driver side a steel box sat upon a pole mounted firmly into the ground.

Clifford pulled a plastic card from his suit coat, slid it through a magnetic strip reader, which caused a small green light to glow, and the gates began to open inward. The limo then pulled forward, traveling upward over a hill. As the long black car began to top the hill Clifford turned his head to look back at Rabecca.

"Not that many people get the chance to see Mr. Rasland's home, and speaking from a personal first timer's experience, you may want to brace yourself for a shock."

Chapter Three

Clifford opened the door and allowed sunlight to spill into the car. Rabecca squinted her eyes as she stepped out and took her first up-close look at Rowan's home.

It sat in the center of a large area of fenced land. Trees had been specially placed for an added touch of beauty when the spring awoke them from deep winter sleep. The mansion was only one level and was constructed of hand-placed gray stone. The exterior walls seemed like they could tell tales from ages ago when man was still young in this world because of the aged stone.

The roof was composed of three gables with the one in the center being the largest. On a casual glance the home almost resembled the architecture of an old-world gothic church. Especially with the large, circular stained glass window, which made the shape of a Celtic cross.

The front door laid directly beneath the largest gable that extended outward to cover the entire front porch. Large stone pillars supported the massive weight of the roof.

Statues of gargoyles, large and small, lined the sides of each window. It looked as if they truly guarded the home from attacks of spirits and physical beings alike.

Rabecca was consumed with awe as she stood in disbelief about the site before her eyes. She was not sure if what was before her was ancient or new. But there was a presence of age that flowed off of each fragment of the beautiful art work before her. Excitement filled her more with every second her eyes remained focused upon it. Rabecca felt as if nothing could have torn her eyes away from absorbing each minor detail, until a familiar voice sounded from beside her.

"If you're this impressed with the house on the outside you should love the inside."

The sudden voice caused Rabecca to jerk her focus from the mansion to her side where she found Norman. He was dressed casual in a shirt and jeans instead of the suit that he wore for appearances at the club.

Rabecca tried to sigh under her breath so Norman and Clifford could not hear. But as she did so Rabecca noticed for the first time since she had left the comforts of the limousine how chilled her body had become. Norman remained polite as he looked her over once. He noticed how convulsive-like her shivering had become since she set foot into the open air.

"Clifford, why don't you pull the car around to the garage while I take Ms. Hollyard in. She needs something warm to drink, seeing how under-dressed for the weather she is." Clifford quickly agreed and returned to the driver seat. The long, black car followed the cobblestone driveway around to the side of the house where it disappeared from their sight.

Norman opened the front door and, with one last glance at the marvel before her, Rabecca followed him into the warm recesses of the large manor.

The door closed, which left Rabecca to stand for a moment so that her eyes could adjust to the low intensity of the light compared to that of the world beyond the walls. When her eyes did adjust to the light Rabecca noticed a resemblance in Rowan's home decor compared to that of the Club Unknown.

A deep red rug with black tassels led from the front door to the large Great Room used to entertain guests. Dark blue fabric covered the cushions of each furniture piece. Each chair, table and sofa looked to be hand manufactured with curved cabriolet legs with ball and claw feet. Tables in equally placed pairs lined the walls with dark finishes. Each table had a marble top that held lamps that gave a dim light. But this light could not compare to the light given by the fireplace.

Along the ceiling and floor ran a delicate, carved molding that matched the hardwood floor in color only. It aided in giving a certain grandeur to the room itself.

Norman walked the path that the rug made with little regard to the lavish environment that surrounded him. But he did pause to wait for Rabecca to catch up to his step. She was engulfed with the surroundings that seemed like a scene from one of her greatest dreams—or even her darkest nightmares. It depended on whom or what influenced them. Her eyes were flooded with each detail of the room. This included three doors, one on each wall.

Norman opened the detailed wooden door that was almost parallel with the front door. There he awaited her to step over the threshold to a new room. As she approached he said, "After you."

Rabecca stepped over the threshold with a little hesitation. She found herself in the dark of the unknown room. Norman stepped close behind her and turned a light dimmer switch by the door frame. It caused a fine crystal chandelier that hung over the long rectangular table to glow with a dim light that slowly became brighter.

The carpet was like a cream satin that took the impression of a footstep easily. The dining room smelled fresh. It was as if it had never been used. Though it was well decorated with the table centerpiece and wall tapestry of ancient mythological animals, the room felt empty.

Norman did not offer an explanation of the room. Just as casual as before he walked around the edge of the line of chairs about the table and through a doorway on the left. The doorway had white curtains drawn back that exposed the narrow hall that led to the kitchen.

A cool air arose off the black and white tile floor and counter top. Both resembled a large checker board because of the tile. Most of the appliances had been built into the wall or counter top. The exception was the large stainless steel refrigerator that sat to the left, parallel from the counter top range top and sink. A coffee maker sat close to the corner of the wall and near the oven as a fresh pot of coffee brewed.

Clifford sat at a small table made to accommodate four.

"It's about time you two made it. I was beginning to think about sending out a search party to find out if you were lost."

Norman looked strangely at Clifford before he opened one of the cabinet doors that lined the top of the wall above the sink. His hand reached in and retrieved a set of three crystal coffee cups. He placed a cup in front of Clifford and one at each side of him. Norman then pulled out a seat for Rabecca to use. She could tell that they still wanted to shower her with politeness. She fixed her eyes upon a large bay window beside the back entrance. The window allowed a great view over the open space of the land. The view ended at the dense forest, which looked as if it stretched out into infinity. Scattered amongst trees, horses ran wild as they had done long before their domestication.

Her view was blocked as Norman's arm went in front of her face to fill the cup. The coffee was followed by antique ceramic containers that held cream and sugar placed in the center for everyone to use.

Norman sat across from Rabecca and smiled as he noticed that she still seemed to be nervous about being there. Norman awaited his turn in preparing his coffee as he allowed Rabecca and Clifford to do so before him. His hand stirred the dark black liquid as he watched it turn into a light brown. Only then did he begin to question her.

"Ms. Hollyard, you look like something is bothering you. Do you mind if I ask what it is?"

Rabecca looked deep within his eyes. Though she could see kindness she would not allow her guard to fall again. When she answered they could tell that it was colder than the winter breeze outside.

"Life. To be more exact—my life, and that is something I really don't want to talk about right now."

Norman drank deep from the cup as he tried to avoid the cold sound of her voice. After he had swallowed the last gulp he had taken Norman said, "I'm sorry if I offended you."

Rabecca looked down toward her coffee. Just then she realized how harsh her own words sounded.

"No, I'm sorry. It's just that so much has happened today. I've found out how many friends I really do have. I don't have a right to treat either of you like this. Right now, besides Rowan, I don't know how many other people I think I can trust other than you two. But you have to stop calling me Ms. Hollyard. It makes me feel like I have done something great to earn your deepest respects."

Clifford slouched over and rested his arms on the table edge. "To be completely honest you have." Rabecca looked at them both, confused, as Clifford continued.

"I haven't been working for Mr. Rasland as long as Norman has. But from what I have been told, and what I have seen personally, last night was the first time I have ever seen him happy. I mean, last night when he got into the back of the car he was whistling. It was like he had something new to live for."

Norman looked at Clifford. He knew it to be a warning not to take the conversation any further. When he realized that Rabecca had noticed, Norman stopped and smiled.

"It isn't polite to talk about someone when they are not here to defend themselves."

Clifford drank his coffee to avoid saying more on the topic. Silence had fallen between them, followed by a feeling of unease.

Rabecca waited to see if either of them were willing to say anything else.

When she thought the tension had grown to be too much she spoke.

"I take it both of you live with Rowan here."

Clifford looked at Norman to see if he was going to answer. As he did so it seemed to lighten the atmosphere.

"Yep, Clifford and I live in the north wing. Mr. Rasland keeps the south wing for himself and his private collections."

Rabecca nodded her head with a curious look on her face still. "Okay I've already heard Clifford's story of how he came to be associated with Rowan. But now I'm curious as how your life became intermingled with his."

Norman laughed as his eyes stared off into the distance and his mind's eye looked back on his past.

"It is really a long story. But I'll try to make it short. I was born into a dysfunctional family. My father was a drug addict and my mother wasn't much better. She would do anything to get money to support her habits and his. And when I say anything I do mean anything. I barely scraped by in high school because I fell into the wrong crowd. Eventually I was made a part of a gang at the age of eighteen. I ran with them for a while, getting myself in trouble with the law until I had a big wake-up call. I was following this guy in the downtown city streets. A place where even the rats were afraid to show themselves. I was planning on mugging him. He was walking slow and as I sped up to catch him he turned a corner that led to a dead-end alley. I thought that he was going to be an easy victim, especially since I thought he made a wrong turn. I went around the same corner expecting him to be somewhere within the shadows. I looked everywhere in the darkness but he wasn't there. As I turned around to leave he was there behind me, watching each movement that I made. When something like that happens it throws you for a loop and you don't know what to say. I thought about running past him but it was like he could read my thoughts. As I thought it, he looked at me with cold eyes and shook his head no. He walked up to me and looked deep within my eyes. Still to this day I cannot forget what he said to me, which was: *You have not been following me. I've been leading you here since you first noticed me. In life sometimes the predator is the prey and they never know it until they are backed into a corner with no place to run. With no place to hide. You could be so much more if only you had the chance to develop yourself. Come with me and let us talk. I have an offer that you cannot possibly refuse.* After that night I moved in here. Mr. Rasland gave me the chance to further my education if I wanted and a job as well. The rest you know. You've been to the club. That has been ten long years ago. And each morning that I wake up

I am thankful that I met him. Who knows, by now if I did not meet Mr. Rasland I could be dead or in prison. Could be both by now."

Rabecca smiled at Norman's tale of kindness and said, "It sounds like the beginning of a movie. A young troubled boy meeting a fine, distinguished man…" Her words cut short as she started to think of the headstone that she had seen. She then remembered Norman's age in the short tale of his life. "Wait a minute. If you were eighteen, that means Rowan would have been around fifteen! That's impossible. Right?"

Norman and Clifford looked quickly at each other with a shocked expression mixed with fear. Norman stood quickly and looked at his gold wrist watch and said, "Time does fly when you're in the middle of a good conversation. But you have to excuse me. I have some things that I have to do before I get ready for work and open up the club."

Clifford followed Norman in standing and said, "I know what you mean. I need to prepare the car for this evening when Mr. Rasland wants to go out."

Clifford quickly walked out of the kitchen and left Rabecca and Norman alone. He finished the cup of coffee with one drink and looked at Rabecca. "I'm sorry we both have to run off like this. But if you want to go back the way we came and go through the Great Room, take the door on your left and after that the first door on the right. There you will find the entertainment area. There are dozens of DVDs and compact discs. If there's nothing to your liking there is always pay per view. Also if you would like you can look around the house. Just don't go into the south wing. Mr. Rasland is very protective of his collections and privacy."

Norman walked away before Rabecca had the opportunity to ask another question, even though she wanted to pressure an answer out of him.

She was left alone in good faith that she would stay away from Rowan's wing. Rabecca continued to sit there as she sipped her warm coffee and thought to herself.

Something is not right with his story. I wonder what they are trying to hide from me? Or protect me from? Or maybe I am very attracted to an eighty-year-old man who doesn't look a day over twenty five? …Yeah right. And I'm going to wake up any minute now and be filthy rich and traveling the world on a whim!

Rabecca stood and walked through the dining room back toward the formal Great Room. There she stood and overlooked everything one last time before she turned to the door on the left and opened it. There were no signs of life as she looked and listened. All she heard was the crackling of the fire that was so near her. She closed the door behind her and caused an echoing thud. It caused her to shiver due to the cold, empty sound of being alone in a large open home. She opened the first door on the right as Norman had said. She reached around the wall and felt for a light switch before she walked in.

With a click the overhead light came on to show the luxuries within the room. Against the far wall a big screen television sat with shelves on both sides filled with movies. A pool table sat closest to her with a rack of different pool sticks near a large stereo system. The stereo was held within a shelf with speakers mounted upon the walls and ceiling. A large sofa was placed in front of the television.

Rabecca sat upon the sofa and sank into the soft cushions. She reached for the remote control on the coffee table before her. Mindlessly she flipped through channels, not paying attention to what was on the screen. Her own thoughts overwhelmed her perception of what was around her. The screens of color slowed until they stopped. Rabecca was then deep within her thoughts.

Things around here are getting too strange for me not to have answers. I do like Rowan a lot. And I'm pretty sure that he feels the same way. I'm his guest. Though I don't want to overstep my boundaries I do believe that I deserve some explanations. And unless I'm mistaken they're somewhere behind the forbidden door.

The television screen went black. Rabecca stood and felt her purse to ensure it still hung from her shoulder before she left the room. She walked softly, though she was the only person in the house. As Rabeeca reached the Great Room her eyes were filled with a sight so beautiful that tears almost fell from her eyes.

The sun had started to set in the West, as it always has in her life. But she could not see it within the natural colors that she had always seen. The sun hung at an angle with the stained glass. The rays were changed into the colors of the glass. The image that the window formed had been thrown onto the floor before her.

The violet circle was split by the crucifix, which shown in a red that was intensified by the rug that laid upon the floor. The room was flooded by the color and more light than when she first entered the house. Her eyes wanted to wander and explore each fiber that made up this room in the new light. However, desire still burned like an inferno within her mind—the desire to learn the secrets—Rowan's secrets that the door across the room guarded.

Everything is so elaborate here. Even the simple kitchen seems to have a certain presence. It is so familiar to me and comfortable. Like being with

47

Rowan. But why would he hide something from me, or is he? It could be Norman being overprotective again.

With a final look at the sunlight painting on the floor she allowed it to fade from her mind. Just like it would soon do as the sun disappeared for the evening. Rabecca neared the door. With each step closer to the door her breath became shakier as she became more nervous. She reached for the door knob with an unsteady hand and turned it gently. It gave a loud squeak and caused her to gasp quickly before she released her grip.

With a low voice Rabecca began to talk to herself in an attempt to calm her nerves. "What are you getting nervous about? It's just a door, not a portal to another dimension. Just open the door and walk in. It's not like anyone else is here."

Rabecca took a deep breath and reached for the door. The knob turned quickly and caused it to screech loud until the knob stopped. She pulled on the door, but it would not move. As she realized what had caused the door not to open she reached into her purse. "Locked. It really doesn't shock me. I'm glad that I learned other things besides how to sell girl scout cookies."

Rabecca knelt in front of the door knob and peered into the brass key hole. She pulled her hand out of her purse and held a bobby pin and a small nail file. With a patient hand Rabecca picked the lock one tumbler at a time. She continued until she was able to turn the lock with the file.

Rabecca stood with a smile of satisfaction on her face and opened the door. One more screech echoed from the knob as she did so. A cold breeze rushed from the dark corridor and caused Rabecca to shiver. She reached around on both sides of the walls. Slowly she felt the cold stone as she searched for a light switch. Farther and farther her search took her into the hall. She hoped that her hand would stumble across the small controller of modern light. Rabecca was about to give up. Thoughts of turning around already filled her mind. Then at last her hand found what she so desperately searched for.

The click that came from the light switch echoed from off the walls farther into what appeared to be an abyss. Slowly light began to grow down the hall. Black steel chandeliers were held in the air by thick chains. Unlike the room from the club, gas candles danced above her head, causing her own shadow to dance.

"Okay, there is no reason to be nervous. It's just a house. A spooky part of the house. But nonetheless this is Rowan's home. He's just into old style architecture or history, or something. It's not like Frankenstein's monster is here waiting for me to be his bride."

Rebecca tried to find comfort within her own words. But there was little to be found within this cold, lifeless part of the house. Fear grew little by little as she continued to stare down the hall that was beginning to look more like a dark tunnel of her imagination. She thought of turning around again and completely forgetting about the exploration of the wing. But pride and curiosity still pushed her onward. The hard, stone floor echoed with each step. This caused Rebecca to become more frightened with each step that passed in front of the last.

She came to the first door on her left. Rebecca ached to be somewhere with a warmer atmosphere. Her hand reached for the knob as she hoped that this room was not like the hall that she stood in. Her eyes closed as fear caused her to expect the door to have a beast waiting for her on the other side. But as she turned the knob the door creaked and remained shut. She let go of the door knob, relieved, yet frustrated at being stopped once again.

"Great, another locked door. There has to be one that is as easy as turning the knob and opening it around here."

Rebecca went from door to door and checked to see if each was locked as well. With each door she found bolted tightly her determination grew until she reached the last door. Rebecca had become weary and was tired of finding only crushed hope, even though she could have easily picked each lock; however, Rebecca knew that she was going to have a hard enough time re-locking the hallway door after she was finished. She reached for the knob to the last door and turned, expecting disappointment. But as she pushed the door she found that it moved easily. It also opened without sound, as if this door was used often.

Dim light came through the large window on the left. It only allowed Rebecca's eyes to see dark shapes that filled the room. Her hand moved to the wall as she searched for another light switch. She found one quickly, which caused each table lamp and floor lamp to come alive, revealing all that was in the room.

The room was furnished simply with a large wood desk that showed signs of age in the middle of the room. Beside the window frame, large bookcases sat behind the desk filled with many volumes of leather-bound books. A set of small delicate chairs sat in front of the desk with tables on each side. Two floor lamps were in the corners closest to Rebecca. As she walked around the large table that separated the room her eyes were drawn to the objects that rested upon it.

Maps of various countries laid spread open. They looked like if they were touched they would crumble into dust. A large sword laid partially wrapped within a plaid cloth that looked worn and faded by time. Rabecca dared not touch anything upon the table for fear of damaging something. But fighting the urge to do so was difficult. She then moved to the desk to look at the small desktop lamp. Her eyes then moved to the large leather-bound book. It was marked with a black ribbon that so gracefully parted the pages. At the top of the book sat a small jar of ink. A metal-tipped quill pin with a long white plume sat in a wooden stand near the ink.

Rabecca rubbed her hand along the edge of the book feeling the time-worn-and-cracked cool leather cover. Each dark brown stitch that held the leather in place looked frayed. She lifted the pages until they were open where the ribbon parted and began to read.

December 16, 1998
2:45 A.M.
The veil of sorrow has parted, showing me a small ray of light. Her name should be that of a goddess from the old times forgotten; yet for one so beautiful the name is so simple. A new life has been set before me. A life that until only hours ago I thought was lost from me until the end of all days.

"Well if this was not a sight that I thought I would never see." Rabecca jumped at the sound of his voice because it sounded as if it had came from out of nowhere. She turned nervously and found Rowan only feet from her, smiling.

"I didn't mean to invade your privacy, Rowan. Please don't be upset with me. I've already had a really bad day."

Rowan moved close behind her and closed the book. He then placed a comforting hand on her shoulder. "My dear, I know that Norman probably warned you about coming into the south wing. But the one thing I have failed to teach him is that there is an exception for almost every rule. There is no need for you to worry. When I said that no wish of yours, that I can fulfill, will ever be able to make up for the mistake that was made last evening, I did truly mean it. Therefore, if you wished to be here then so be it."

Rabecca turned with a smile of relief as Rowan watched the tension melt away from her entire body.

"Why don't you take a seat and we will discuss what happened between you and Brian this morning." The smile disappeared and the color drained from her face. She slowly sat in the large rolling chair behind Rowan's desk.

"How did you know? I know that I didn't say anything to Clifford or Norman." Rowan leaned against the desk, partially sitting while he stood and looked at her again with a smile.

"It is not important how I know. What is important is that I do know. In time perhaps I can explain everything. Until then just understand that there is no need for you being worried or afraid. You are safer with me in my home than with anyone else or anywhere else in the world."

Rabecca looked into his eyes as if she searched for something so obvious yet couldn't be seen.

"I'm not afraid. If I was before I came here I cannot remember, because as soon as I got here, knowing that this was your home, it went away. But I have to know how you knew. Or who told you."

Rowan knelt down as Rabecca sat so that he could be closer to her. He looked at her and the smile faded. It left only a concerned expression that surrounded eyes so full of caring. To look at them would cause the coldest of hearts to thaw within their gaze.

"Rest assured that no one told me of anything that happened today. If you would prefer for now you can think of it as a lucky guess. You cannot begin reading a book from the middle and expect to understand everything that has happened before those pages. But you do have my word that I will tell you everything, in time. For now, though, forget about that and open yourself to me. Tell me what happened so that you can relax this evening. Tell me so that at for least one night he, nor anyone else, can cause you pain or worry."

Rabecca's eyes filled with pain. Then they filled with tears as she thought about the events that happened only a short time ago. She could not speak as all of the intense pressure that had built broke through the gates of her mind. All of the frustration was released in the form of tears that streamed downward along her face. Rowan, with his cool touch, gently wiped away her tears until she leaned forward and fell into his awaiting arms.

He held her close as she buried her face into his shoulder and hair. She sobbed until exhaustion within her eyes stopped her tears from flowing. Rabecca pulled away gently, just enough to look at Rowan's face. His heart melted as he gazed upon the innocence in her eyes. Rabecca moved closer to Rowan's face with desire. She ached for his lips to be pressed to hers as if one. Rowan put his hand on the back of her neck to lower her head. As he pressed his lips to her forehead Rabecca's eyes closed, savoring the kindest touch she had ever felt.

"Not yet, my dear Rabecca, not yet. I will not, cannot take advantage of you in this time of emotional distress. To do so would break every moral fiber that is left in my body. And it could cause you to think of my words as only that, words. You mean far too much to me to have that happen."

Rabecca pulled her head back. She leaned back into the chair and kept her eyes on Rowan as she did so. Rowan remained knelt down before her as she re-accounted all that had happened since she had been awakened. He listened patiently until she told him what she said to Rachel about Brian. Rowan stood enraged and turned his back on Rabecca as she continued. When she had finished Rowan walked the floor in silent contemplation over Brian's true self.

Rowan finally stopped and looked at Rabecca as she watched and awaited his words. She rolled the chair back as fright filled her. Rabecca looked upon his face and saw an expression that she never thought Rowan could have gotten. He did not look like the same kind person who Rabecca had come to know. In fact, though she knew it was Rowan, he looked nothing like himself.

His eyes had became darker and yet more radiant. Lines appeared deep and cut jagged around his mouth. Rabecca was not sure if it was the lights or her imagination but it looked like he had also turned pale. Like his heart had slowed or completely stopped beating. As Rowan spoke his voice sounded as if it was mingled with a low, menacing growl.

"He deserves to die for what he has done to you. Slowly tormenting you with a perverted mind. Trying to have you bend beneath his will. Then denying that he has such obsessions."

Rabecca's eyes had completely filled with fear caused by his words. But not with fear of Rowan. Instead it was fear of what he may have been willing to do.

"Don't say that, Rowan! You can't! I don't care what happens to Brian. But I do care what happens to you. If you care for me as much as you say then promise me that you won't do anything drastic."

Rowan turned his face from Rabecca in shame. He then realized that anger had taken over his reason. When he thought of what he had said to her guilt overwhelmed him. Rowan could not bear to face her knowing what he had said, knowing that he allowed Rabecca to see a side of himself that he did not even like to think of. He stood there silent in disbelief at what he had done. With all of his will, Rowan tried to fight off the emotion that he so hated at times. Then he noticed that a soft hand was pressed against his face. Rowan allowed his head to follow the motion until he looked down at Rabecca's innocent eyes. She stretched her neck upward and gently put her lips to his. All anger was gone as this moment of passion grew stronger, until they stopped and held each other close.

"Promise me. If you do care, if you do love then promise me that you will not go after him. Everything that happened between Brian and me is in the past because we do not have a future. We never did. I just don't want our future to be brought to an end before it even gets a chance to really begin."

Rowan heard Rabecca's words and held her tighter than he ever held anyone before. He knew now that she had realized how strong the love he held for her was. Rowan had no choice but to promise her. Once he did he knew that it was a promise he could never break.

"I swear upon my life and my honor. I swear upon the love that I have found—the greatest treasure in the world—that I will not harm him unless he causes you pain once again. I can forget what is in the past now; however, if the past repeats itself then I am not sure if I can control myself again. And I cannot say if he will survive to regret it. As long as you, my treasure, can accept that then we will not have this discussion again."

Rabecca smiled unlike any smile before. Though Rowan could not see it he knew that she was content with the conditions of his promise.

"I can live with that, my sweet angel. I truly can as long as I never have to leave your side again."

Rowan's embrace loosened and as he did so Rabecca looked at his face again. She found that it had returned to the kind face that she had remembered. Yet it was still different. He looked at her with worry in his eyes and a questioning that she could not explain.

"You cannot say that yet. I wish that you could stay with me and never have to leave me ever. But you cannot say that you will until I tell you of my darker side of life. I do not know how you will react once I tell you. Though I would usually take my time when it comes to this matter I know our time is short. I want you to be able to leave with your friends if you wish."

Rabecca smiled, though she did not know what Rowan spoke of. But she remained understanding.

"There is nothing in the world that you could tell me that would make me want to leave you. Just tell me and get it off of your chest."

Rowan's gaze was locked upon her eyes. He wished that what she said was true. Though he did trust Rabecca with all of his heart something made him hesitate.

"No, Rabecca. I cannot tell you yet. Let us have dinner first. I at least wish to remember this evening as being perfect before it has the chance of being destroyed. Besides, you haven't eaten all day and you must be famished. After dinner I promise I will tell you; for better or for worse I will tell you."

Rabecca continued to smile a giddy schoolgirl smile. She slid her arms away from Rowan and took his hand within her own.

"I don't know how you are doing that. But I'm kind of anxious to find out. You're right, though, I am starving, so I'm ready anytime you are, my love."

Hand in hand they turned out the lights and left the room. As the door shut behind them they both knew that a new chapter of their lives had been opened from the moment they had first met. As they walked down the cold, dark hall Rabecca secretly wondered what could be so hideous to hide, while Rowan secretly worried if the truth would drive her away forever.

Chapter Four

"We've been here all day and we haven't seen or heard anything from Rabecca. I hate to say it but even after we had such a bad fight I'm still getting very worried about her."

Brian, Rachel, and Porter sat upon the guest room bed where Rabecca had been only the night before. Silence fell between them. It seemed as if they had all found a world within their minds to make time seem as if it passed quickly. Yet, their patience had been tried until the point of breaking. Brian and Porter hoped for a phone call, or even a knock at the front door. Rachel was immersed within turmoil of her own moral beliefs and the common courtesy of not revealing personal secrets of another. However, there is a time and place where almost every rule must be broken.

"Okay, guys, I think we are left with only one option now. Perhaps if we're lucky her diary may have some answers. Or even clues to tell us where we should go from here."

Brian stood so that he could face Rachel with ease and said, "Rabecca has a diary? She's never told me about this."

"Of course not! Almost every girl has a diary...You know, someone who is always willing to listen and can remember everything that she wants to remember. It's so that later on down the road of life it can be looked back on."

Brian's heart pounded harder as he thought of what could be written within its pages. "Where does she usually keep it?"

Rachel stood and pulled Porter up with her as she did so. "Well, at the dorm she usually hides it under her mattress."

Without any hesitation Brian raised the mattress. There he found the flower-print covered book. Before anyone else could come near the diary he reached down, grasping it firmly, and brought it close to his side. The mattress dropped and bounced with a small thud. The sound springs rattling lingered for a few moments before it faded. With haste Brian thumbed through the pages until he came to the last entry. His eyes scanned over it carefully until he finished the last page. He then tossed the book upon the bed. It laid open where the last entry ended. Porter looked at Brian as the full effect of Rabecca's crushing words destroyed his heart. Rachel picked up the small book. Her eyes read over the words that were written earlier that morning.

Rachel's eyes widened as she finished the entry and dropped the diary back onto the bed. "We've got to go to the Club Unknown now! Hopefully if we are lucky we haven't missed our chance to catch up with her."

The smell of exotic foods filled the air. The aroma caused those who awaited their meals to dream of what the delicacies were going to taste like while their mouths watered with anticipation. Casual and business conversations almost covered the light piano music that played from the speakers mounted within the ceilings. Oriental servers rushed from table to table to wait on each person's individual needs. Two wooden dragons acted as pillars to an archway that was separated by curtains from the rest of the restaurant. Beyond the watchful eyes of these large guardians the atmosphere was more calm. Only a few guests were scattered about the room. Here everything was about taking the time needed to do things proper.

A small table for two sat near the large oil painting on the back wall. It held tropical fish depicted beautifully with each well-placed brush stroke. A bottle of wine sat in the center of the table, chilling as the two who talked in a worried bliss awaited their meal.

"Okay, Rowan, I'm not going to ask you how you know so much about me. But I am curious about what else you know...I guess things that you haven't said to me yet." Rabecca sat with eyes filled with more love than what most people could conceive as Rowan answered her.

"I am not sure if I should tell you. Much of your past, my dear, is filled with painful memories. I do not wish to drag them up to the surface." Rowan carefully took the wine and poured a small glass. He watched its deep red color swirl.

"Oh come on, Rowan…I can handle anything you have to say. How many times do I have to tell you that nothing is going to ruin this night, or what we have?"

Rowan sipped his wine and enjoyed the well-developed flavor. He looked into Rebecca's eyes and felt the warm sensation of their newly combined love.

"As you wish, my dearest. As you wish. Your father was an alcoholic who drank himself to death early in life. It left you only with your mother and a few other relatives. These other relatives did not want to have anything to do with your mother. They blamed her for his death. Also because they did not want anything to do with her they did not want anything to do with you as well. Your mother lived until you were ten. Though she loved you with all of her heart it was not enough to save her after the car wreck. Once again it involved someone who was drunk. You were taken into state custody. You were then passed from foster family to foster family until you were eleven. Your father's mother then decided to take guardianship of you. She gave you a home without love. She paid for you to attend a Christian academy. But she did this only because she refused to have someone under her roof who did not know and fear God. She did not want you to be like your mother: a child of nature, a pagan as they are called today so commonly.

"You stayed very true to your studies, knowing that it would be the only way you could escape the rule of your grandmother. But what time you were not working on your studies you spent at a local teenage gathering place. There you met who you thought was your first love. You did everything you could trying to make him love you. This included shoplifting cigarettes. When you were almost caught you then realized that he did not care. You knew that you were just looking for someone to accept you for who you are. From there you turned to God, seeking answers and acceptance in which you did not find. Then you turned to yourself, for you knew that you were alone. You graduated and had a scholarship offered to you. Needless to say you very happily accepted. Shortly thereafter you met Rachel, Brian, and Porter. The rest you have already told me."

Rebecca looked at Rowan in dismay. She wondered if there was anyone other than him who could know everything about her. All without her having to speak a single word. She wanted to say something to him. Yet all she managed was a smile and to take his hand. Rowan took another drink of wine before he finished his small display.

"One more thing, my love. I am by no means an angel sent here to answer you prayers. I am sure that I am the furthest thing from an angel, or a devil, that you will ever find."

Rabecca pulled his hand close to her face and kissed it softly. "By biblical terms and standards I don't believe that you are an angel . I know that you are not from heaven. I don't know how I know but I do. But I already know of some of your good deeds in offering chances at a new life. You don't have to explain them to me. I do know that I can say from the bottom of my heart that no matter what you have done before you will always be an angel to me. Everyone makes mistakes in their lives. As long as we learn from them then they really don't matter all that much."

Rowan closed his eyes. It showed that her words had touched something that he did not care to remember.

"Rabecca, you speak wise words for your youth. However, there are exceptions for every rule. Sometimes you must take a chance in making the same mistakes in order to be happy. But we should leave this conversation now. Our dinner is being brought out. We will continue with this afterward. I just hope that my history does not repeat itself once again."

The car screeched to a halt in front of the club. The sound caused all who awaited entrance to stare in wonder as three rushed individuals got out of the car and ran to the door. They stopped at Norman who had just let two people into the club. They panted and tried to regain their breath while Norman said, "I'm sorry, kids, Mr. Rasland's invitation was only good for last night. So if you want to get in you're going to have to go to the end of the line and wait like everyone else."

Rachel was the first to step forward as she swallowed deeply, trying to cure her parched throat. "Where's Rabecca?"

Norman looked at her as if she were crazy and said, "How should I know? I'm not her father! Hell, you are all her friends, you should know better than I do!"

Brian had caught his breath. He walked up to Norman so that he could look him dead in the eyes. "Damn it, we've read her diary! We know that my fiancée is somewhere having dinner with your boss! If you don't tell me where she is, I swear I'll—"

"You'll swear what? I could break you in half right now without a second thought. Or without even breaking a sweat! But I'm not going to. Just to clear things up, from what I have heard you're not Rabecca's fiancé! Now if I were you I would leave before I have a change of heart."

Porter grabbed Brian's shoulder and pulled him away from Norman. "Come on, man! It's not worth going to jail or the hospital. Not yet."

Porter and Rachel led Brain back into the car. They expected him to turn and attempt an attack at any moment. After he was in the car they joined him. The car pulled away from the club's entrance. Norman kept a watchful eye upon them. He watched until he felt that it was safe to continue with his work as the potential patrons began to complain.

The car moved into an isle and parked. Patiently they watched and waited for any signs of Rabecca or Rowan. Brian still ranted under his breath while Rachel and Porter made themselves comfortable. They expected a very long wait. They all kept their interests upon the building as they looked for some sign of hope; however, as they kept their eyes locked no one noticed the figure that crept ever so slowly closer.

A loud knock on the passenger window startled them. It caused them to jump as they turned their heads toward the direction of the pounding. Porter sighed and looked back at Rachel and Brain. "It's just that crazy old guy from the other night. I think we should at least hear what he has to say if nothing else."

Porter rolled down the window. Jon knelt down to make his words more easily heard.

"Are you with him or against him?"

The three looked puzzled at Jon, then at each other before Rachel asked, "Against who? The doorman?"

Jon pounded the top of the car out of frustration. "No, Rowan Rasland! Are you with him or against him?"

Brian heard the name and it caused the fire of fury to be ignited. His thoughts turned to that of Rabecca being somewhere alone with Rowan. "We're against the dirty son of a bitch, and in my opinion I wish he was dead!"

A smile grew across Jon's rough face that exposed his yellow teeth, some of which looked as if they were rotting away with each day that passed. "Good, good! Follow me to my van. There is something we need to talk about before we go after that vial creature spawned in the bowels of hell."

He turned and scampered away like someone or something watched his every move. Rachel looked at Brian with spiteful eyes as if she tried to burn a hole through him for involving them into a situation that they knew nothing about. Before anything could be said to him Brian opened his door and followed Jon's footsteps.

Rachel looked at Porter and said, "Do you think we should follow him or what?"

Porter shrugged his shoulders, opened his door and stepped foot out. He then waited for Rachel to join him before he started to follow. The three arrived at the back of the rusted, once-blue van just as Jon threw open the doors. He started to dig like a mole through various papers and trash that laid upon the floor. A stench rolled out from the van. When it filled their noses it reminded them of the smell of a garbage dump on the hottest summer day of the year. They held their breath until Jon spun around with a grin. He slammed the double doors shut while he held something within his hand.

"Finally I have someone who will listen to me! This has to be a gift from God!"

Brian backed away from Jon as he thought that following him was a mistake.

"No, no, don't go! I'm the only person who can tell you the truth about the one who calls himself Rowan Rasland."

Rachel stepped a little closer as she asked, "What do you mean the truth about the one called Rowan Rasland?"

"No one can tell what he is. That is, how he survives. I first met Rowan years ago when I was a small boy living in Heritage Landing with my parents. They did not get along all too well. One day my mother had taken enough of my father's mental, verbal and physical abuse. She went to a lawyer for a divorce. She took me with her because she was afraid that if I was the only one home then my father would start treating me like he did her. That lawyer's name was Samuel Rasland. He showed no signs of being any different than you or I, but as my mother told him the complete story of what was going on in our home he seemed to change. He became a darker person. Samuel hid it well from Mom. But I could see that something was not right about him. He had all of the papers drawn up and before I knew it they were divorced. I was left living with my mother in Heritage Landing far away from my father.

"Months went by and I grew more accustomed to having only a few visitations with my father. Then on March 11, 1976, God I can't believe I can still remember that date, I was on the bus heading for my father's apartment.

I expected everything to be the same. I would stay there for a few hours and leave. But when I got there his door was open. I went through the apartment until I got to the bedroom. There I found my father's lifeless body in Samuel's arms. Samuel lifted his head from my father's neck and blood ran down his face. My father's throat was ripped out. I tried to run but when I turned around he was there waiting for me. I can still remember his cold touch as he took me by the neck and lifted me off of the ground, choking me. I can still hear the demonic sound of his voice as he told me to go and never speak a word of what I had seen. Then as quickly as it all happened it was over. I ran out to the street pay phone on the corner and called the police. They found me there on that corner and went to investigate what they thought I supposedly saw. But there was nobody there. Not even the lifeless body of my father. My father became a missing person who no one cared enough about to look for. I didn't think anymore about it until this damn club opened up and made headline news in the papers last year. He gave an interview to promote the club under the name of Rowan Rasland. Beside the article they printed a picture of him standing in front of the club."

By the time Jon had finished with his story, Brian, Rachel and Porter stood far away from him. No one had the nerve to say anything except for Brian who asked, "Are you trying to have us to believe that Rowan is some kind of vampire or something?"

Jon threw his arms in the air and shouted. "Yes, dear God, yes! Finally someone who I don't have to explain it to! Finally someone who will help me rid the world of this thing. This creature!"

Rachel had found that more of her nerve was being lost the longer she stayed there and listened to his ranting. Yet there was still something that made her stay. A fascination with the unknown had overwhelmed her, though common sense told her to flee.

"You cannot just go around wanting to kill someone because they have the same last name as someone from your childhood. I mean, sure, he may be related to this Samuel but Rowan can't be the same person. Personally I can't just take your word on this. You also seem to be a little too psycho for my liking."

Rachel turned to leave with Brian and Porter who followed as Jon stood there dumbfounded for a moment. Then he remembered the papers in his hand. He ran up to the three and screamed to the top of his lungs. "Wait! I have proof, I have proof!"

Brian, who was on edge because of Rabecca, turned to face him. But before anything could be said or done Jon forced the thin, aged papers into his hand. Rachel and Porter looked over Brian's shoulder as he straightened the two separate pieces and glanced over them. The date on the first clipping read *March 12, 1976.* Their eyes continued downward where the headline read: *Respected lawyer, Samuel Rasland, accused of murder and disappearance of client's ex-husband.* The second was dated a year ago to the very day of December 16, 1997. It read: *The Club Unknown, shrouded in mystery, now brought into the light.*

Porter looked at Jon and said, "These don't prove anything, you freak! Damn, I knew we shouldn't have followed you out here!"

Jon began to laugh uncontrollably before he said, "Unfold them and compare the pictures before you jump to conclusions, my boy!"

Brian unfolded the clippings once again. He looked down in disgust as the last bit of his patience was being worn ever so thin. Then his eyes widened in disbelief. "I can't believe it! It's Rowan."

Rachel started to disagree in anger until she, too, looked closely. All she could manage to mumble was, "Oh my God!"

Jon danced foolishly in a circle while he sounded as if he chanted. "They see! Their eyes have been opened! They see!"

Brian reached for Jon and grabbed him by the shoulders, then he shook him angrily. "Stop that! We didn't come here looking for Rowan! We came here looking for my fiancée who happens to be with him!"

The craziness melted from Jon as he heard Brian's words. For the first time since they all had started speaking he sounded sane and serious. "She's with him? Your fiancée is in more danger right now than what she or you could ever possibly imagine. Take this cell phone, my number is programmed into it. Go, try to find her. I'll stay here and call if he or they show up. You do the same if you find them.

The two who felt as if they were of one presence sat comfortably after their large meal was over. Rowan finished his wine as Rabecca lit a cigarette and inhaled the gray smoke deeply.

"You know, I feel kind of bad leaving Clifford in the car while we were in here eating this delicious meal. Do you think we should bring something out for him?"

Rowan smiled as he savored the smell of her cigarette before he swallowed the last bit of wine. "No, my dear, you don't know Clifford all that well. If my estimates are correct then he has already called from the limo and had something brought to him. It should be on my tab."

Rowan stood and helped Rabecca out of her seat. He acted as if it were a natural part of his life and took her in his arms. Softly he whispered in her ear, "For better or for worse the evening must continue on."

Rabecca remained quiet as Rowan escorted her beyond the dragon pillars and outside. The limousine waited in front of the restaurant doors with its engine already started. Clifford stayed within the driver's seat as Rowan opened the door for Rabecca. The large window that separated the front seat from the back lowered as Rowan stepped in and shut the door. Calmly Rowan looked at Clifford and said, "Take us to the family cemetery."

Clifford drove as Rowan raised the window so that he could be alone with Rabecca. She looked at Rowan confused and asked, "Why are we going to your family cemetery at night?"

Rowan looked like he dreaded what was to soon come. It could be heard in his voice clearly. "My dear, almost all of my secrets in some way either begin or end there in that cemetery."

Unease fell between them with the silence of the trip. Rabecca could not stop herself from looking at Rowan, who forced himself to look her way. A new pain had filled his heart. Yet unlike the pain she had seen in the past upon Rowan's face there was more than the pain of being alone here. Fear had encased him in silence. As she watched the one man who she knew feared nothing until now, it caused her to ache with desire. She wanted to take Rowan into her arms like he had done for her before. Rabecca fought the urge to embrace him. Somehow she knew that he hated to show signs of weakness. But her eyes still showed signs of sympathy. They both remained within their own worlds of thought until the limousine slowed to a stop in a parking lot. Rowan opened the door without speaking or making the slightest sound. He stepped out and offered his hand to Rabecca to follow him to the gates.

The cemetery had changed from the one she had known during the light of day. Night had brought with it a fog that rolled along the cemetery grounds. It also spilled across the once peaceful looking park. Rowan walked hand in hand with Rabecca slowly. Rabecca knew that it was like a death march for someone who walked to their own execution.

As they reached the gates Rowan released her hand and reached to pull the steel gate open. Yet before he could get it completely open Rabecca put her hand on his shoulder. The touch caused him to look at her for the first time since they left the restaurant. "Rowan, you don't have to do this. I don't care what your secret is. Keep it to yourself if talking about it is going to be so difficult."

Rowan finished opening the gates before he turned and placed his hand on her face softly.

"Rabecca, I wish that I could keep this from you. I wish that I did not have to worry about losing you because of this. However, if you are truly wanting to be with me then I must tell you. If only to possibly keep you from discovering what I am from another source and then leaving. As much as it will hurt me if you leave, I would rather have it come from my mouth than another. That way I will be able to remember that I told you. That way I can at least say it was your choice to leave. Not fear caused by the dark side of me that you knew not of."

Rowan walked through the gates gracefully as if he were a spirit who had risen from one of the many graves. Rabecca followed close behind Rowan until he turned to face her.

"I am sorry that I had to bring you out here. I have to apologize because I know that you have been afraid of graveyards at night since you were a small child. If it is any comfort whatsoever only two of the three graves here are truthful. They are the ones of Kyra Rasland and Samuel Rasland. Though Samuel does not rest there."

Rabecca's discomfort turned into confusion after she heard Rowan's words. Her eyes looked over the headstones as she tried to understand what he meant. "They look real enough to me."

Rowan's eyes closed as he prepared for everything to be told without regard of how Rabecca would react. He then spoke with a heavy, old accent rolled within his words.

"My real name is Rowan O'Rafferty, as it is known today, from the clan of O'Rafferty. I was born on the year of our Lord, August 1, 1471 in Ireland. Each one of these headstones excluding one has been a life that I have lived before."

Rabecca backed away from Rowan a few steps as she said, "I'm not sure if I believe in reincarnation."

"My love, if only it was as simple as reincarnation then I would never mention it; however, I am afraid it deals with much more than that. I died in the year 1498 when I was twenty-seven and I continued to live on. I have survived from day to day and year to year for the past five hundred twenty-seven years. Do not fear me, Rabecca, for I am not any different than when you did not know this. I eat, I drink the same as you. The only difference between us is I must drink blood to survive. Otherwise I will become weaker with each passing week. I am sorry that I cannot put it in easier terms. But when you live with this every day for five hundred and twenty-seven years sometimes being blunt is better than trying to hide it."

Rabecca was speechless as she watched Rowan come closer. He raised a hand to wipe away a tear that fell from her eye. But before he could touch her she jumped backward. His hand lowered as he moved back in an attempt to make Rabecca feel more comfortable.

"This is not the way I wanted it to be, Rabecca. I did not bring you here to feed from you. Or to bring you into the darkness I call a life. I brought you here so that you would know the truth. So you would realize that the world that you live in is a false reality. Reality is that my kind has been here since before recorded time. We are hunted and sometimes killed because we are feared for being different. I am not a monster, a mindless beast with the only thought in my head being to kill. I can love. I can cry. I can bleed. I can die. But not as easily as a human can...I have left a book with Clifford for you to read. I already knew that you would back away from my touch as soon as you learned the truth behind who and what I am. He will take you wherever you wish. All that I ask is that you take the book and read it before you make your choice. If you love me now—or should I say, before this moment—then please give me this one chance. Go now. But realize that you, Rabecca Hollyard, hold my heart that you thawed from its icy cage. If you do decide to leave it and me then know that no matter where you are or what you do I will love you until the end of my days and beyond."

Rabecca backed away slowly as fear gripped her mind. She turned and started to walk away with haste in her step. Her own thoughts then interrupted and chased away the senseless fear.

What am I doing? So what if he is different! If I run from him just because he is different, or believes everything that he has said to be true, then I am no better than those who would try to kill him for being this way.

Rabecca ran quickly to Rowan who stood looking down at a grave mournfully. He turned to the sound of footsteps that came toward him quickly. Before he could have seen her face clearly he had been caught within Rabecca's arms. She passionately kissed him as she tried to make him forget all of his worries. Rowan's tense body relaxed slightly at her touch. As she pulled away to look at his face she noticed his eyes had become tear filled at the expression of her lasting love.

"Don't worry, my dear, sweet Rowan. Nothing has changed in my heart. I will read your book and then decide what I want. Just like you have asked me to do. But I do have some things to work out for myself before I can truly make up my mind without doubt. No matter what I choose you have not lost me. I would tell Clifford to come back for you, but I know that you want to stay here for a while. Besides, if what you have told me is true then I'm sure that you can make it home before I get to wherever I am going. I shall see you soon, my angel within the darkness."

Rabecca turned and ran back to the limo like a child who was eager to go out for ice cream. She quickly opened the door and jumped into the back. The door slammed behind her before she knocked on the partition that Clifford sat in front of.

The window lowered and Clifford looked at her with a smile. "Well I'm glad to see that Mr. Rasland's secret did not scare you away."

Rabecca laughed, still a bit nervous, as she said, "It started to but it dawned on me that he was the same Rowan that I am falling in love with and…"

She paused and then exclaimed, "Wait a minute, you know what he is!"

Clifford laughed as he reached to his side. He lifted a large leather book and handed it to Rabecca. "Of course I know. I didn't believe it at first, but after being around for a while and seeing things. Hearing stories that he sometimes tells it becomes very clear how old Mr. Rasland is. Sometimes you can hear it in his voice or in the type of speech that he uses."

Rabecca held the book tight in her hands and could smell the musk scent of age upon it. "So Rowan did take Norman off of the streets when he was eighteen."

Clifford smiled again and said, "Yep. That's the reason why Norman wanted to cut the conversation short today in the kitchen. Norman does everything that he can to protect Mr. Rasland because he is the closest thing to a father that he has ever had."

Rabecca continued to look at the book in her hands and wondered what it held. "Clifford, I need to go some place where I can get a cup of coffee. Some place where I can stay as long as it takes to read this thing."

Clifford started the engine and turned on the headlights. "Don't worry, I know the perfect place to go. It's not too far from here."

The limo had left as Rowan stood and watched it move farther away from him. Tears ran from his face as he looked back at the headstone. He read the name softly to himself as he had done many times before; yet this time it was not because of sadness.

"Kyra, my love from so long ago but not long forgotten. She looks so much like you. But she is nowhere near what you were. Her passion and will is far greater than what you ever had. I will always love you. But I cannot live within the past anymore. I will not forget you ever. Nor will I stop loving you; however, Rabecca has showed me that I cannot live in the past. I now have so much to live and fight for. I will still visit your grave and tend it. Sometimes I know I will still long for you. But my future is calling me to live instead of longing for something I can never have. Farewell, I hope you are as happy as I."

Chapter Five

The limo stopped in front of a small building with a neon red rose in the front window. Clifford opened his door and quickly walked around to open Rabecca's door. But before he finished his job Clifford was met by her as she stepped out of the limo and smiled at him.

She shut the door with book in hand and said, "Thank you, Clifford. You can leave if you want to because I don't know how long I will be here."

Clifford reached in his pocket and pulled out a plastic card and handed it to her. "I am afraid I cannot leave until you are ready, Rabecca. I received my instructions earlier today before I picked up the book tonight and put it in the limo. The card is one of Mr. Rasland's credit cards. It was with the instructions. I am also to tell you that you can use the card freely. I am to take you anywhere that you need or wish to go."

Rabecca hugged Clifford and said, "Thank you, Clifford, and just in case you are wondering I have pretty much made up my mind. But I have to read this first because of a promise I made to Rowan."

As she let go of him she noticed the employees within the small restaurant were at the windows. She could tell that they wondered what was going on outside the store. Rabecca went to the door and pulled it open. As she walked into the restaurant the first thing she noticed was the sign about the grill that read: *Welcome to the Java Rose*. Rabecca sat in a far booth in a corner that felt the most private. She laid the book in front of her. She stared at the cover that had become dark and had started to crack in places due to age and weathering.

A waitress drew Rabecca's attention away from the book who said, "Welcome to the Java Rose. What can I get for you tonight?"

Rabecca smiled and answered, "Just a cup of coffee and some cream. Do you mind if I stay here for a while and read this?"

The waitress laughed and said, "Honey, I can tell you're not from around here. We won't be getting busy for another seven hours. So you just stay as long as you want. None of us mind a bit."

She took off quickly and returned with coffee, a spoon, and cream and sat it on the table. As she started to leave again Rabecca's eyes followed her. She noticed details of the small restaurant.

There was a bar area in front of the grill with vinyl covers on the stools that were colored red and green. A juke box sat in a corner near the front door. It was made of glass like most of the front of the building. The wait staff and cook sat in the back as they spoke softly. They all smoked cigarettes as they took advantage of the free coffee and other drinks the restaurant sold.

Rabecca's eyes drifted back to the book as her mind drifted within her own thoughts. For a moment she released her thoughts to fix her coffee, only to be pulled back into them again afterward.

Is what Rowan told me true? I've always thought that vampires, the undead, were just something real in the movies. But Rowan is nothing like Dracula. He's not like any other vampire that I have seen portrayed by Hollywood actors. And he's not like any vampire that I have ever read about. But it does make a lot of sense, and no sense at all at the same time. It would explain the headstone with his name on it. It didn't have a death date. I have to read this book! What am I doing here just thinking about everything?

Rabecca felt the edge of the book before she opened the cover. She found that the first page was blank. Her heart raced as her mind filled with ideas of what she was soon to read. Her eyes studied the blank parchment that was yellowed from age, and crinkles and folds that had attempted to be straightened and flattened over time. It left only signs of its battle scars caused by the ongoing fight with time.

Rabecca lightly rubbed her hand over the page as if she expected dust to come off with her touch because of the stale smell of the pages. She started to turn the page but stopped herself. The corner of the brittle page crumbled within her thumb and index finger.

"Damn! I've got to be more careful or else this thing is going to fall apart. Or turn into dust before I can read what is written after this page."

Rabecca held her breath as she turned the page. She tried to be as gentle as a spring breeze that blew at night. The page flipped over. As it landed and remained whole Rabecca let the breath out deeply. She pulled her hand back.

It shook slightly as she did so. Then her eyes caught glimpse of the extravagant hand writing that could only be done with quill and ink of days passed. At that moment Rabecca's heart skipped a beat. She realized that what Rowan had told her was true and not a delusion.

The
Book
of
Rowan

To whomever may be reading this:

You hold within your hands a true tale of epic portions. However, seeing as how eyes other than mine are glancing over these pages then I have given this volume to you, though this is very unlikely. Or my enemies have gotten the upper hand in my age-old battle for survival. No matter which of these options is true it does not worry me. If I have allowed you to view this then there must be a good reason for me to do so. If I have perished at the hands of my enemies then at least I know that someone, somewhere will know the truth about me and my kind. Nonetheless, I must try to protect my family, if there are any left. Therefore, if you attempt to search throughout history for any signs of my legacy then I warn you now that all efforts are in vein.

Rowan

August 1, 1471

I am born only sixteen short years after the Wars of the Roses had begun. It was a time of great turmoil in England; it was due to the houses of York and Lancaster and their ongoing fight to quench their thirsts for power. However, due to fate I was not forced to suffer through this unjust time in England, for I was born to my beautiful homeland of Ireland. My childhood was not a truly notable experience. I spent my young life in solitude from other children by orders of my parents. Like most children I would have disobeyed my parents if I had the opportunity to do so. Yet my parents were counting on me to do exactly that from birth. That is why Margrette became my caretaker from the first breath that I took.

She was young and so full of life when I was a child. Her only wish was that I could always be happy. To ensure this, Margrette would do anything within her power to ensure that I was worry free. Margrette was not of my blood; but even till this day I wish she were my true mother instead of just being my mother in thoughts only.

As I grew so much older than two and three I realized how little interaction my parents had with me. I would hound Margrette about their location day and night. I can still hear her answer ringing in my ears and echoing throughout my mind.

"My dear angelic Rowan, your parents are highly respected members in this land. They arrive home every night late. Immediately they go to bed. Then as soon as the sun begins to peak over the horizon they rush off. All this is to ensure that you will have a better place to live in when you get older."

I can clearly remember how puzzled I was at first by that answer she had given me so many times in so many different ways. Then one dreadfully stormy evening in 1481 as I neared my tenth year of life I was awoken by the monstrous thunder that echoed within the manor. Normally I would have called out for Margrette when I was so full of fright. But something caused me to hold my tongue; it was as if some unknown phantom had covered my mouth and was urging me to venture forth for the warm comforts of my bed.

I peeled back the coverings that warmed me. As my feet found placement on the cold stone flooring my mind screamed for me to stop, hide and to call out for my Margrette so that she could come comfort the dread that filled my body to the point of aching. Though I did not wish to leave my room, I could not find the power to fight the force drawing me away—away from the confides in which I felt safe in. With each step that drew me closer to my chamber door I found myself shaking more dreadfully than before. Whether it was out of fear or the cold, damp air I cannot recall if I ever knew.

The iron-hinged door opened as I used all of my strength to move its solid mass. As it opened wider the hinge let forth a mournful wail as if the movement caused the door great suffering. Dim candlelight was my only escort from my chamber and through the corridors of my family home. I began to search the halls for the cause of my unease. But as I look back now upon that night I realize that I was not so much searching as much as blindly being led by fate to force my eyes open for a brief moment.

As I neared the great hall I noticed the faded glow of a fire. The closer I got the brighter the light became, until I found myself peering around the corner into the chamber where I found Margrette sitting calmly. My parents walked around her slowly as if they were stalking prey.

"Margrette, my innocent young flower. You have served us well these past ten years," said my father with a hollow voice.

"Thank you, my lord." Margrette looked as if she tried to hide tears that were trying to form in her eyes.

My mother stopped behind Margrette and began to gently play with her hair. "But there comes a time in everyone's life when innocence is lost. It is up to the person whether their loss will come with purpose or the lack there of."

"Yes, Margrette, my loving wife took the words from my own thoughts. Now comes your choice; shall your innocence be lost later without meaning? Or would you choose to sacrifice it now and gain from your loss instead of a lifetime of regret?"

My father unsheathed a dagger that he wore at his side; he placed it upon

Margrette's lap. Without a word spoken further Margrette took the dagger and placed it against her wrist. Slowly her flesh opened so that her blood could come forth and greet the night air.

Though I was only a young lad, I still remember how the scent of Margrette's warm stream of crimson flooded the room. The scent filled my nose with each breath, inviting me to come and savor the harsh truth of my existence.

I did not understand what took place, or why a fire had sparked within me as I witnessed these events. It wounded me to watch Margrette's river of life flow from her body. But what came next was to instill fear within my soul for many sleepless nights to come.

She lifted her wrist; before a single drop could fall from her flesh my father lapped at the blood like a dog driven mad from an unnatural thirst. My stomach turned and my heart pounded at the sight. I tried to force a scream from my throat. But I was unable to make fear release its icy grip from my neck. My body froze, causing me to become weak in the knees. My mother then took the dagger from Margrette and carved a deep canal within her own wrist.

My young eyes noticed the difference in my mother's blood; it began to pool thick as mud from the moor and as black as a shadow.

As Margrette's body tensed in a moment filled with pleasure my mother forced her wrist to Margrette's mouth; it filled with the nightmarish blood. The entire act took less than a few minutes and then it was over. All three broke the bonds that held them together. Then they began collecting themselves. I ran with tears that streamed down my face while I hoped and wished that this nightmare would end. My sobs filled the halls as my cold feet and numb mind took me back to my bed chamber. I closed the door quickly and dived into my bed; quickly I covered myself completely with only my sobs to comfort me.

Thunder continued to crash about me. It drove all sounds of the world around me out from my mind. My world had become a silent realm in which no one could save me from. As I hid there, filled with my fear and disbelief, I never heard a soul enter my bed chamber; yet still something deep within the pit of my emotion-filled body told me I was no longer alone. My body shook from knowing that they were there. Though I knew I was not hidden I hoped that they could not find me.

A hand slowly pulled the covers from my head. As my eyes were exposed to the light of the dim candle I found the monsters from my nightmare that I so loved had surrounded me. My eyes first locked on Margrette. Out of a moment of pure reaction I found my arms wrapped around her and my face buried deep into her breast.

Her hand ever so lightly stroked my head as she said, "Rowan, it's okay, you were only having a bad dream. Nothing more."

I pushed myself away from her and began to look at them all in a state of terror. "I saw it, Margrette! I saw it all as I am seeing you now. I saw you and Mother cut your wrist as Father…"

I could not finish my words before I began to push myself farther from them. Father began to laugh loudly. His voice echoed like a demon that laughed at the tortured souls in the bowels of hell.

Margrette held both of her wrists in plain view for me to examine. "Rowan, no one cut anything. If I had just cut myself there would be blood or some sign of a wound. Come here, my little one. Everything is as it should be."

I was not put at ease by her words. Still being a child, though, I could not stop this sight from making me feel better.

She held me tight for a few moments before kissing me upon the forehead. Margrette then laid me back down into bed before they left the room.

As the door shut to leave me in the dark, I sprung forth. I ran to the door to listen to what was being said. Their voices were muffled by the great wooden door; however, I could still hear them well enough to hear my father's deep voice.

"You handled that well. Now remember you still have responsibilities to my son. However, things have changed now. You shall remain in his life for another four years before you must fade away into the shadows. We cannot afford for him to learn of his blood lines this young in life. Later things shall be different and then we can all be together."

I did not understand what my father had meant with his words; however, after that night I remained silent about what I had seen and heard. Margrette had changed somehow. But being young I could not decipher what it was. That is beside the fact that she did not venture forth into the day much with me so that I could play with her. Nonetheless, I still loved her and cherished every day I spent with her. Secretly I dreaded the day that would soon come— the day when my sweet Margrette would leave my life forever.

August 1, 1485

Ivan the Great had founded Russia by the time of my fourteenth birthday. Much like the Tartars, the day I thought would never come had arrived. Margrette had allowed me more and more independence. She let me leave her supervision to enjoy the day and to explore the many rooms in the manor. Sometimes I would spend all day wandering around the manor halls trying to get lost as if I tried to escape something that would never leave my side.

It had been a particularly long day as I searched throughout the library. Doing so caused me to come as near to the dungeon as I was allowed; however, hunger caused me to turn back and search out Margrette. Usually she would be found within the kitchen as she prepared some sort of meal for us to enjoy together during the day. Within the back of my mind I thought about what my father had said to Margrette during what seemed to me lifetimes ago. I never thought that this day would be any different than days that had passed, yet my young life was destined for change on this fated day.

As I neared the kitchen I noticed that I did not hear any sounds echoing from its doorway, nor did I hear the sound of songs that Margrette sung or hummed when she did something alone. An eerie sense of loneliness filled the halls. I searched for her until I came to her chamber door, which stood open. Nothing remained of Margrette's. Nothing except for a hair ribbon of sky blue that I knew her to wear wrapped around a parchment. Scared of what I would find I reached for the parchment and slid the ribbon loose. Slowly I unrolled the jagged edged parchment and began to read the words that crushed my heart on this sad day.

Rowan, my little one,

Forgive me for leaving like this. I have tried to tell you before this day. But I could never stand to break your heart like it has been now.

I know that you do not believe it now, but it is easier for this to have taken place in this way, even though we never had a chance to say farewell. Stay true to your studies. They will serve you later in life.

Remember, little one, this will not be forever. We shall see each other again one day. Until that day comes know that I will always be thinking of you.

I have made arrangements with your father to send messages to me from time to time. Take care, my young Rowan, and be sure to write often.

Until we next meet,

Margrette

I threw the ribbon and parchment upon what was once Margrette's bed. Without thought I ran to the front gates as I cried more heavily with each step that passed. When I passed through the gates I searched frantically for her until my young legs could not carry me any farther. I fell onto my knees with outstretched arms. I turned my face to the midday sky and howled her name as if I were a wounded beast. There I stayed and cried until my wail sounded as if it spawned from a banshee's throat instead of my own. I cried until I found no more tears that I could shed, until my eyes were so sore that I thought some of those tears could have been blood drops.

I picked myself up from the patch of earth that had caught my tears and walked back toward my home; I had to have looked like someone, or something, that had just clawed its way free from its own grave. I felt as if I could no longer continue to live, for the one person who was my mother, my caretaker, and my only friend had left me alone. I had no one else to turn to except for a hall of books and scrolls that only spoke to me when I forced my eyes to glare at their pages. As I re-entered the now hollow halls of what I called home I realized just how alone I was. I wandered aimlessly for what must have been hours. I wandered until I came to rest at the great table that was within my father's library. A single book laid before me open. I stared at it and hoped that it would provide me with some answer to my dilemma. The fall of night had begun in which I showed little regard. In fact, I showed no sign of visible life until a candle lit before me and I found my father glaring down upon my sad face.

"How long wilt thou forget me, O Lord? forever? How long wilt thou hide thy face from me? How long shall I take counsel in my soul having sorrow in my heart daily? How long shall mine enemy be exalted over me? Consider and hear me, O Lord my God: lighten my eyes, lest I sleep the sleep of death; Lest mine enemy say I have prevailed against him; and those that trouble me rejoice when I am moved. But I have trusted in thy mercy; my heart shall rejoice in thy salvation. I will sing unto the Lord because he hath dealt bountifully with me."

His strong hand came to rest upon my small shoulder as he tried to comfort me the best he knew how.

"I know she's gone, son. But there is one thing that we must learn from life—that is everything does change with time. This book before you is filled with wisdom. Perhaps you can learn from its teachings. If nothing else you can at least learn a few life lessons from its pages if you listen well."

This moment was my first introduction to any kind of religion with what was known as the Gutenberg Bible. Though this book was only Psalter, it still was enough for my mind to become fired with thoughts and questions that I could not conceive the answers to. This book caused changes within my once mundane existence. I began to pray for everyone I cared for, for those whom I did not know of. I tried not to ask for anything for myself. That is, except that I would someday see Margrette again safe and sound.

I now knew that I was no longer alone, at least in spirit. This helped to pass the long hours in the day while my parents were gone. When they returned we would speak of what I had learned that day. This would often turn to long, detailed conversations centered around theology.

Over the months that passed I learned much about myself and of my parents' thoughts. It did bring us closer than what we ever were. A limited trust started to grow between us; therefore, it led to an agreement for me to expand my knowledge. With no complaints from either side my father made arrangements for the head of the church in town to pick me up in the early morning. This was to be done before mass so I could use their library and return just before the sun completely fell for its rest. This chance opened my eyes to many new viewpoints, due to many new works that I considered masterpieces. But most importantly this agreement led to me meeting my second friend ever, Father McDonnell.

He taught me the most beautiful language that I had ever heard in my young life: Latin. Father McDonnell never tired of constantly honing my skills at this master's language; nor did he tire of what seemed to be relentless questioning about God or the tales told within the hand-scribed pages of books, all of which spoke of his many different wonders and miracles.

Years began to pass by me like leaves that were blown by in the wind. My relationship with Father McDonnell and God had grown stronger. As I approached closer to my manhood, I watched Father McDonnell grow older and older. It led me to question why it appeared as if my parents never seemed to change with time that passed him and I by. I was still filled with questions. These questions led to many enjoyable conversations with Father McDonnell. One of which involved my questioning of my parents' lack of aging.

His voice sounded so noble, as if God had singled him out to speak his word. "Rowan, I know it seems as if they have not aged. But you must understand that you are around them constantly. In your eyes they appear the same. This is as it will always be, even when they are old like me."

I could not put what I truly meant into words; therefore, I acted as if I accepted his answer. Little did he, or I, know what was soon to come.

April 18, 1489

I am eighteen. It was only four years before that Henry Tudor had united the houses of Lancaster and York to overthrow King Richard III. This unification marked the long, awaited end of the Wars of the Roses. Yet with one end of senseless death came another with the Malleus Maleficarum. It read to me as a detailed set of instructions to identify witches so that their tortured souls could be sent to hell. I had learned with the years of study with Father McDonnell that people were afraid of what they do not understand. Due to this fear justification was found for all actions that were taken. Justification could even be found within the eyes of God.

I had tried to bury myself deeper with God's word so that I may forget what I was suffering through with each day that passed. I felt nothing but the pain of complete exhaustion during the hours of day, followed by the pain of an undying hunger during the hours of night. I prayed each day for the suffering to be lifted from me so that I could be set free from this torture-filled illness. I attempted to view this plague as a test set before me, a test to find my limits of faith, and this kept my will strong.

And so time passed with agony for me until the long, fated night when the dark secret of my existence was made known.

I arrived home as I had for years at this point. The sun had begun to fall, the time when I exchanged one type of suffering for another. As I made my usual trip throughout the halls to the library I noticed things were not as they should have been. Torches had already been lit and placed to light my way. It seemed as if this journey was pre-planned before my arrival. The door stood open to the library and candles were placed upon the table. There I would sit for hours while I looked over the different texts that I had borrowed from the church earlier in the day. Though I found this to be quite odd, I reasoned that it had to have been my parents. They must have arrived back from their duties of society early, I thought. Without a second thought I went about my routine of placing books and scrolls upon the table. Carefully I would organize those which I wished to look at first.

The iron hinge of the door screeched, which drew my attention away from my chore. This was only because my parents rarely disturbed me while I read at night. I turned and expected to find Mother or Father behind me, awaiting to inquire how my day had went.

Yet there she looked upon me with loving eyes, a look that I had remembered she gave from my childhood. For a brief moment I was a child again. I rushed toward her with arms open wide to embrace her as tears filled my eyes. As I held her tight I cared not of how or why Margrette was back, I only cared that she was with me now.

She stroked my hair like she did when I was only a young boy. It caused me to grip her tighter as I tried to hold back a flood of joy-filled tears; however, many did slip by. "Rowan, my sweet little one, how you have grown since I last laid eyes upon you."

Perhaps if she never spoke a word, or chose her words wiser, I would not have thought or cared about anything. However, the word "grown" echoed within my mind. It caused my thoughts to become more rapid. I forced myself to recall what Margrette had looked like on the very last day we were together. I closed my eyes tight as I tried to remember every detail through the haze that had entered my memories with the time past. Slowly I forced myself to recall the details of certain features, such as wrinkles or gray hair. I found that I could not recall any of these features. I pushed myself from Margrette's arms and looked upon her with eyes of disbelief.

"Margrette? No, this cannot be so...I refuse to accept that this is you. Perhaps a relative or a dream. I must have fallen into a slumber while looking over the texts I brought home."

I tried to find comfort within my own words. I attempted to convince myself that my logic was correct as I continued to watch Margrette. She walked to the table and glanced over the various materials I had returned with and smiled. "You did remain true to your studies. I knew you would. You were always an obedient boy."

I placed my head within my hands and tried to drive away this haunting image from my sight. As I turned my head upward I found that she was no longer in front of me. Instead she stood to my side.

"I know that you do not trust your eyes and ears right now. But if this were a dream would you feel this?"

With speed I had never seen before, Margrette's hand darted toward my arm. She had pinched it with such strength that it could only be described as a snake bite. As the pain shot threw my arm Margrette jumped backward with a coy, childish smile on her face. "Catch me if you can."

With only a moment of hesitation on my behalf Margrette was gone within a blur. I tried to follow close behind. It was like trying to catch a wild deer that bounded through the forest to avoid being sighted for a kill. I paid no attention to corridors and halls that she led me down. Then she passed through one door I knew all too well from my childhood fears. At first I thought that I was mistaken about her descent downward into the dark recesses of the dungeon. Then I heard Margrette's echoed voice from the depths, as if inviting me to continue the hunt.

I pushed all adolescent fears from my mind to track Margrette's laughter. With each step that led me farther down, light seemed to retreat from the unholy place. A stench unlike anything I had ever smelled before filled my nose to welcome me to my worst nightmares. Only my imagination could have given me ideas of what would be found at the bottom of this unknown hell.

My foot made the last step to the bottom. My eyes allowed me to find only darkness; my ears found only silence. My nose found the stench had grown so strong that it stole my breath and left me to gasp for a single mouthful of pure air. A spark had given life to a single flame. That flame chased the shadows that filled this room to their respectful corners. It also revealed Margrette and my father. They stood amongst a pile of decayed corpses that oozed foul fluids into the ground beneath my feet. When my mind made the connection between the stench and what I had viewed I could not refrain from vomiting. I had fallen onto my knees and soiled myself with a mixture of earth, those foul fluids, and my own vomit.

"Why have you led me here to this ungodly place?"

All that could be heard was the thunderous sound of my father's laughter before he spoke to me. "What a strange choice of words to use on the night you learn of you birth right, Son."

I heard his words, yet could not focus on comprehension of them. My thoughts were clouded with the rot and filth that surrounded me there. I wanted to flee from this horror, yet even the strength needed to stand had left my body. It left me motionless as one of the uncountable lost souls that rested in that pile. I found that I could not move. The hands of my father lifted me off of the ground like an infant. He then braced me against the damp wall.

"Rowan, you will grow accustomed to this in time. Your mother and I have lived like this for centuries."

I felt the color drain from my face. I stared at his bearded face, unable to force my eyes to meet his. "What are you?" I tasted the decay in my mouth as I took a breath to utter those simple words.

"No, Son. It is not what am I. It is what are we. You are blood of my blood and flesh of my flesh; therefore, you and I share the same fate. But I can see that the dungeon is not the proper place to continue this. Margrette, help your brother up the stairs."

I can remember so very clearly how I wished to fight back, to resist even their touch upon any part of my body, clothed or not. Margrette carried me up the stone staircase without any signs of strain physically. As we crossed the threshold of the dungeon door I felt the decayed air leaving my body with each breath.

I started to regain my thoughts immediately. My first thought was for God to rid me of the demonic undergoings about me. The journey ended within the library. Once there I was placed to rest within my favorite chair. I raised my eyes and found that they both stood before me. They looked as if I was expected to question why.

The silence was broken by father. With each spoken word he moved closer to me.

"Perhaps leading you to the dungeon was too much. This is to be an introduction for your beginning, so you can understand what you are to become this night. You see, I—we—are unlike anyone else that you know in this world. We are beyond the laws of nature and beyond the laws of man. Law was written by man and we are so much more than mortal. As for God, well there is no other creature in this world as powerful as he. At least so I am told. Yet he cannot even let us know death. The exception is the look within our prey's eyes just before the last drop of their blood spills onto our tongue."

His words only caused my mind to attempt coming to a realization of the answer to this riddle. My mind raced as I met his eyes. I found that the eyes of an animal glared back at me. There was no concern of these words causing the seed of fear to be planted within my soul.

Margrette moved forward and knelt beside. She tried to take my hand within hers while she spoke. "This is your destiny. Just as mine now involves taking care of you forever." My eyes jolted from Father to Margrette as I questioned her statement. She then smiled in a slightly lustful way.

"That's right. Margrette has been far much more than your caretaker, lad. It has, and will always be, tradition. When a vampire child is born, a young girl or boy is chosen to raise it until a certain age. Then the caretaker is made family so that someone older will always watch after the natural born, also providing any service the natural born requests."

With those words I understood what was intended to be. The thought of Margrette being taken into my bed as my wife discussed me. It also shattered the image of how I viewed her.

I looked back at Father as I refused to hide the disgusted look upon my face. "You are telling me that I am betrothed within the eyes of Satan?"

Margrette moved away from me as Father continued to speak.

"I see that trying to make you understand using only words is going to be hopeless. Bring in the child!"

Mother walked in from the next room with a disdain look upon her face. She held a small newborn child within her arms. The poor thing did not have a clue what kind of monsters were at its side. Ever so gently the sleeping babe was laid upon the table. Father, who looked and smiled, then reached for his dagger. With a quick movement of his hand the innocent life that laid upon the table screamed in pain. Its small leg had been cleaved open, all so that blood could be allowed to pour freely and stain the soft skin.

"There, now let us leave so that nature can take its course. Enjoy this moment, Rowan. It will be the sweetest blood you will ever taste."

They left me with only the child's screams. They filled my ears as if they were begging to have me take the pain away. I stood to rush toward the child. The scent of the warm, fresh blood filled my nose; the scent caused my pain to be known to me as an unbearable hunger of blood. I looked down at the child who had suffered needlessly, and I was torn. I thought of devouring the infant's source of life to end my own suffering. Then I thought of the immense pain that this new life had been put through. There was no just cause for it then, or now. I knew that a choice had to be made; either save or take this life. I took off my shirt and wrapped the infant's wound as I attempted to stop the blood that flowed the best that I could. I tried to muffle the child's screams as I said a quiet prayer.

"O, Lord, my heavenly father. Help me save this child even if I cannot save myself."

Run, that was the only thought within my mind. I can remember hoping that I would not be caught; however, I knew that I could not be stopped. The child had to survive. Perhaps God was on my side that night. I found as I began to flee the manor of my nightmares the child had been comforted within my arms, the arms of something born unholy.

Yet, as evil as I knew I was, we were granted safe passage through those shadowy halls. I stooped only after we were met by the cool air of night. We had escaped. I was then left with the question of where I was to go. There was only one answer to be found: Father McDonnell.

I traveled long hours on foot that night. Through the cold I tracked as I expected my nightmares to follow close behind me. My worst fear then was being captured and drug back to that fortress of hell. Only when I caught view of the church did my mind ease. I entered and found Father McDonnell knelt in prayer. He was unaware that I had returned to escape those horrors with such a young life that had suffered due to my existence.

"Father…help!" The were the only words I found the breath to slightly mutter from my exhausted body. They caused Father McDonnell to gasp. He gasped out of being startled at first. Then as he turned quickly he saw the horror caused to the babe I cradled in my arms.

On that fateful night I made the mistake that has haunted me, due to my peers, even until this day. I am sure I will face it more in the decades to come.

I explained all that had taken place. All who resided at the church began to work on the wound; it was made sure that the wound was properly cleaned and dressed. It took a few moments from what I can remember before my words were truly comprehended by all. Then the questions began while crucifixes were drawn from under robes and shirts alike.

"Did you taste any blood?" I could tell then that there was a new concern. They questioned what had walked through the holy corridors on this occasion.

Before I could answer I found that I was backed within a corner. A wooden crucifix was placed firmly upon my forehead.

"It is fine, my son. You haven't been tainted by the evil you parents have willingly attempted to expose you to. Do not worry. We have means of purifying the souls of those who have been tainted. Tonight you shall stay here where you can pray for strength. By morning all should have changed."

If I would have thought more clearly at that moment I would have resisted. Yet before I could have accepted Father McDonnell's offer I was led to a chamber. I was instructed not to mention what had happened ever again. The door was shut firmly and bolted from the outside. There I was left in the small quarters furnished simply with a rope-framed bed and hay-stuffed mattress. The only window was large enough for the smallest of children to possibly squeeze through. I knew that I was expected to do as I was told by the father. Yet, as I stood there aimlessly, I stared out the narrow-slitted window. I saw the torch flames that gathered in the bleakness of the night. My thoughts gathered as well. I watched them as they marched off in the distance toward the manor I had called home for eighteen years.

I did begin to pray with the wails of the infant that faded within the halls. Yet I did not pray for strength for myself, nor for the torch bearers. Instead I prayed for forgiveness for myself. The only thought that filled my mind was honor thy father and thy mother.

1498

I am unsure of the month exactly. Yet I am sure that nine years had passed since the night of horror had begun. The infant survived by some miracle. He lived there with Father McDonnell and myself at the church. I was forced to stay there. Though I had not mentioned my origins since that night, I can still remember hearing whispers when it was believed that I could not hear. The hunger had become almost intolerable a year earlier. It caused me to refuse food almost all together, except on rare occasions. The pain caused by the light of day had also intensified. It left me to be a recluse in the hours of day, however, active long after most were asleep at night.

Father McDonnell and I had long since grown apart during this time. He would not confirm, nor deny that he led the townspeople in what was so happily referred to as the cleansing. These were the people who thought I should join my parents in their fate.

I would have done so, happily enough, yet I knew that it was Father McDonnell who kept the wolves at bay. He implied that if I were truly a threat then God would not have allowed me to reside in his house. Yet sometime during those nine years I had lost the faith I once was so proud to have found.

I longed for escape of some kind, whether it be death or the chance to leave the land of my birth. I would have volunteered to sail with explorers such as Christopher Columbus, John Cabot, or even Vasco da Gama. But at the time I thought that I would surely be needed there. Father McDonnell had been becoming more elderly with each day that passed. Therefore I wondered secretly how long I would be allowed to live after his last breath was taken. A day…perhaps a week was the longest, I thought. Yet I knew I would be hunted due to the dark blood that coursed through my veins.

October 27, 1498

The bitter cold of an Irish winter had already filled the air to the best of my memory. I can remember that I prepared for my last days as well. Father McDonnell had fallen very ill. It was rumored that he would not survive to see many more sunrises.

I believe it was the fifteenth, or perhaps late enough to be considered the morning of the sixteenth; Nonetheless, I am positive that it was one of the two. I was in silent contemplation of my last request. All that I wanted to ask was that it was a quick and merciful death. I then heard the first screams of the attack. The sounds resembled that of a flock of sheep being slaughtered by a pack of starved wolves. At first I was certain that my time had come. I knelt in prayer for a last time. I hoped that even though I was lost the mercy given to all by God would be given unto me as well.

Another scream and a thud drew my eyes open and to my chamber door. The screams had stopped as I took notice of the blood that seeped under my door. It called to me in its most alluring way. I could hear the unspoken promise of the life-giving power if I would only partake in it. I remember that I stood, trying to keep a firm grasp upon the hunger, though it tried to overwhelm me as I moved to open the door.

His name was Michael. Nine years before I had saved his life when I brought him here; however, I wondered why the death of this child was allowed to happen. He and I struggled so hard to escape and survive the darkness of my family. I heard the slight gurgle of breath that expelled from his lungs. As I rolled him over from his back to front I saw the final breath as it caused the remaining blood to bubble. He had bled out through the torn flesh of his neck.

Poor Michael's eyes still were frozen with terror. I can never forget that I witnessed their final glazing-over with death. I wanted so badly to cry out to God. Ask why. To beg God to let me take his place. Yet I could not rid myself of the blood's call. Nor the sweet stench that empowers blood with more life. The stench I have come to know simply as fear. I do not know if I could have resisted if it were not for an unknown voice.

"If you want it then take it. But by now the blood has already started to cool and more importantly clot."

As my eyes raised, my body had been overcome by the dark lust. I found what would have been a well-dressed, brown-haired boy of around the age of nineteen. Still-drying blood was caked onto his face. His white silken shirt that flared at the cuffs had been heavily stained with blood.

"You've suffered long enough, Rowan. It can all end tonight with a simple part of your nature being fulfilled."

I was far past the point of answering or understanding. I can only look back upon it all and attempt to decipher what happened.

"Come, come now, Lucious. You should know that the poor boy is far too gone as of now. That is unless you wish to communicate through growls and snorts."

Another one had appeared dressed in the same manor. This included the blood that covered him from head to toe.

"William, hold your tongue. You know he could come to remember this one night. Audrius is awaiting his presence…Grab him, but be careful. He is capable of anything right now."

I remember being led through the halls of the living chambers. Even now I wish there was a way I could have stopped myself from remembering the scene.

Bodies of those I once considered friends were scattered everywhere. Blood covered everything. Books, walls, doors, crucifixes, nothing was too sanctified for them not to desecrate in some fashion.

They took me beyond the church walls as if to gloat. The village that surrounded the church had been slaughtered as well. All of the homes were engulfed within flames.

Out of the flames, or at least that is what it seemed like then, emerged a dark figure. That figure drug a battered Father McDonnell at his side. I collapsed, unable to fight the hunger at that point. I could not hear the voice of my new captors, nor were they any concern of mine at that moment. All I can remember feeling is the constant, driving passion of the lust. I could not move without pain. Yet I could not stop my mouth from covering Father McDonnell's throat as it gushed forth blood. His limp body had been thrown to me like a scrap of food tossed to a starving dog.

October 31, 1498

I had woken in a large bed within a still larger room. It would have held six of my bed chambers at the church. The coverings and pillows were all satin. Though they were very persistent, as they invited me stay, I could not recall how I had arrived. Nor was I able to recall why I was no longer at the church. Yet I did not question how or why, for not even my family's manor held so much decor of wealth.

A single candle had been lit prior to my awakening. But I did not know who else was there. I lay there motionless as I awaited to see if someone or something would stir me from what was thought to be only a dream. But after nothing was heard or sensed I decided to peel myself from the cold comfortable bed of satin, if only to enjoy such a vivid dream for a short time. Then as I removed the layers of cover away from my body I caught the first glimpse of my cloths. They were the same simple cloths I had no choice but to grow accustomed to wearing. To be exact they were the same set that I had wore days earlier. But now they were stained with a mixture of earth, sweat, and blood.

I remember that my nose filled with the scent of the dead blood. It carried the odor of decay that caused my memory to slowly trickle back to the death of my old friend.

"Correct…you killed him."

Instantly I started to search the room with my eyes as I slowly stood. It was a very clear and well-spoken voice that sounded as if it came from my bedside. Yet, as I finished the search, I found that I was still alone.

"No…I did not mean to…I would not have if…" I spoke aloud in my defense but was cut short by the disembodied voice.

"Yes, you did mean to, Rowan. I was there. And there was no mistaking that you meant to regardless of the situation. But that is of no matter. You see, he was already dead. They all are. It may take forty years or so for them to realize it. But they are all dead. Therefore why not have their death hold a greater meaning if it means our survival?"

A new rage had filled my body. It gave me sensations of hatred that I still cannot describe accurately as I screamed. "Show yourself to me, coward! You dare to say such things yet you lack the convictions to face me like a man!"

"I have been here the entire time. You just chose not to see me. There is no need to scream. It just shows how weak your emotions make you."

I saw him before me then. He stood covered with a black cloak with the hood down. His brown curly locks were allowed to spill across his shoulders. Before another word could be spoken between us I lashed out. I had every intention of thrusting my fist through his skull.

Everything seemed to move slower as his hand opened. He caught my fist before it ever made contact with its target. I can still clearly remember that I heard the snap of the bones in my hand; however, by the time this occurred the pain only meant more rage for me to direct toward he who I viewed as a foe.

"Impressively strong for your young age. However, I am not here to fight you, which, if I may add, you seem to have a passion for. I am here to train and mold you into the path your parents wished you to travel."

I still do not know why, but somehow his words penetrated the sense of blinding anger. For the first time in my life I had found myself unable to find the drive to fight. Part of me did want to collapse and grieve over the loss of my family; even thought they were monsters in their own right, they were still my family. I managed to push away the tears and sorrow into a dark corner of my mind. The strange one before me released the grasp he had on my fist. In a way he admitted defeat in that moment.

I allowed my hand to fall to the side. That is when I first noticed what I had unwittingly become. The pain which I thought should have been unbearable was no more than a dull ache. I felt the bones realign themselves as the process of mending together had begun. A process that should have taken weeks, if not months, happened in minutes, all without the risk of the injured hand becoming lame and useless to me in the future.

Motionless and silent I stood during the moments that followed. I began to sense my body. I searched for some signs of what life normally would provide. A heart that should have been racing from such a conflict was only found faintly beating. I remember that it was as if concentration upon it being found was all that caused it to continue the appointed task; however, it was beyond normality of human existence by far. A breath that should have been taken deep and labored from exertion had never been taken. Even as I awaited, it was not taken. Then what had been my worst nightmare was confirmed through personal experience. My parents, whom I secretly hoped were touched by insanity, had been completely honest about the blood line I had sprung from.

"I am known here as Audrius, leader of this family of adopted pure bloods. You have already met Lucious and William, though I do not believe you remember too much of them yet. Tonight begins your lessons of how a civilized blood drinker should act in a world currently controlled by the mundane existence of life and death. Come and let us get you cleaned and dressed in a more proper attire for the last and current controller of a pure, dark blood line.

January 1499

At this time, two long months, I continued to live with Lucious, William, and Audrius. It seemed much longer than what it truly was. The entire time they schooled me in refined behavior of a nobleman. Yet Audrius had attempted to press another lesson upon me: a lesson that Lucious and William both followed without question. Was it out of fear, or true faithful belief in the emotional lessons of Audrius? I shall never know that truth now.

The nature of taking the life of others to continue my survival had become natural, like how a bird learns to fly. Though I did not enjoy killing, I aimed my thirst at those who caused grief and misery for their own pleasure. This habit offended no one. Usually there was no one who cared in common society about such a person mysteriously disappearing. Yet my emotional practices had angered the trio. More than once I received a lecture from Audrius. It was always about how emotion was a mere human tool to cope with the hardship of life, how all like us should learn to repress that same emotion. So that we would never be weakened. So we could be perfection, a model for all of our kind to follow.

We were not to feel happy, sad, longing, love, loneliness. We were to be nothing more than shadows of life. Never were we to interfere with human life. The only interaction that was allowed was if we brought a life to an end. I learned to suppress what I truly felt when around them. While this was done I also found that my mind could be locked safely away. It prevented my mentor from learning my secrets.

I had also come to enjoy the finer things that the world around me had to offer. Yet deep in my mind I longed for something that a filled coin purse could not find for me.

It was shortly after the news about the merchant Amerigo Vespucci exploring a new world was made known that I, too, found a new world to explore; however, mine was not discovered by sailing untold miles.

Her name was Elania. A name that I wished to write in the heavens. Yet I should have know that she would have been condemned for my affections.

She was by far not of noble blood. But her face could have passed for more than noble. In fact, adorned in the proper silks and jewels she could have easily passed as the daughter of a Roman senator in ages passed.

Elania was born to a family of simple bakers, and she was trained in that skill since a small child. They all cared little for chasing after dreams of becoming rich, or even a higher ranked class in society. Her entire family was rooted very well. They knew where their place in the world was, though she was the only one who remained unwed. They also believed that a noble would dare not lower themselves to leave their carriage to see what goods were available. That is what their servants were for.

I first caught glimpse of her in an act of kindness that was very rare for the times that we lived in.

I still remember so clearly the flour that clung to the sides of her smiling face and strands of loose hair. She quickly passed out rolls and breads of every type to the entire society of the city who called the streets their home. Then as quickly as she had brought the breads they disappeared.

She turned to walk back into the bakery and was met by an older man with hair and a face etched by a life of hard labor. I later came to know him as Jonathan, father of Elania. At that time of our first meeting I was compelled to leave the shadows from where I watched to enter the bakery's door.

Without trying I entered as quiet as a ghost. I had quickly become caught up in the aroma of the warm bread that filled the shop. This scent was the first pleasant scent I can remember since I was changed. It was a welcome change from the rotted garbage and refuse that filled the poor areas, the areas in which I hunted for the misery bringers that suited my pallet.

A gasp and the soft sound of a roll that landed upon the floor drew my attention. I found that it was the angel who had caught my eye in the moments before.

"I am sorry…I heard no one enter." Her eyes glanced over me from head to toe. She noted the fashion of my dress before she suddenly dashed for the back as she called out. "Papa! A noble in the shop!"

I was almost embarrassed when I remembered my choice of clothing. I had known that this place was deemed not proper for anyone of stature to be seen in. Though I could have disappeared instantly before they returned, I stood firmly. I heard two sets of footsteps that approached.

"Elania, this is impossible. You know nobles are too arrogant to lower themselves." His words stopped when he found that I awaited their return.

"Sir, I apologize." Before he could continue I stopped him with a raised hand. I then asked of the types of bread he made there.

Instantly, as if he had been well rehearsed for just such a day, he snapped to, speaking of the intricacy of each type of bread.

From what I can remember he gave the speech well. But I heard little of what he said. My eyes had locked on Elania as she smiled. Nervously she played with a lock of loose hair that had fallen away from the cord that held the rest pulled together.

"Which would you like?" I looked at him and tried to hide that I was unaware of his descriptions as I answered. "I will take them."

His eyes narrowed as he stroked his thin, white mustache. "Which ones?"

I untied the purse from my side and handed coin and all to him. "All of them."

He then poured some of the coins into his hand. His eyes widened as he looked back at me. "But, sir, this is far too much gold for a shop full of my simple breads."

"Spend it as you see fit. Perhaps by a dress for your daughter. Maybe a ring as well."

I turned and started for the door when he stopped me. "Do you have a carriage or wagon to carry them for you?"

"I am not bringing them with me. Pass them amongst those who are tired and starving. Young and old first."

"Yes, sir. But please honor us by joining us for a humble dinner for your generosity."

I smiled as I looked back at Elania. "Tonight I regret to say I have prior engagements; however, tomorrow would be more suitable."

"Tomorrow it is then. Wait, sir! Your name, I've been in such disbelief I forgot to ask."

"Rowan." I walked out the door and into the darkness to stalk the night for my prey before the first rays of morning light.

1506

For seven long years I had hidden my relationship with Elania from Audrius. During this time I had also kept hidden the secret of why Elania never saw me during the hours of light. She had suspected that I was hiding something from her; however, she would never push seeking an answer too far.

Most evenings when I visited Jonathan and Elania we would discuss what had taken place in the world outside of all of our grasp. It was caused by either monitory status or in my case a series of keepers.

Sometimes, when possible, if the events of the world happened to come too near to us I could not resist taking them to see. In March of 1500 I had heard of the African slave trade. There were many stories of how much different these people were for us. Yet when we saw entire families being ripped apart as they were bought, sold, and traded as live stock we all agreed that it was unjust. We all refused to take part in such things.

Yet on the night of September 17, as I neared the bakery with a watch from Jonathan made by Peter Henlein in Germany, I had different plans than a normal night spent with Elania.

Audrius had spent more time with Lucious and William instead of questioning my whereabouts and actions of each night. I felt confident at that time. I believed that I could leave them with no repercussions. I planned to do just that. I also planned on taking Elania to be my wife if Jonathan allowed it to be so.

According to the German time piece it was 9:03 when I arrived at the door of the bakery. All seemed normal by appearance. The light of flame flickered from within. Yet the nose of an animal and blood drinker alike could smell the scent of charred human flesh and death that faded. I instantly thought of Elania, that she was in grave danger.

I do not remember how I came to be within the small, wooden building. Nor do I care even now if I may have exposed part of my nature to some passers by on the street. The scent was stronger within the doorway as it filled my nose. The sight of blood filled my eyes. It covered the floor, walls, bread, even the ceiling.

Poor Jonathan's mangled body lay on the floor. There was too little blood within his body for it to have pooled around him. He had died with a horror-stricken face. The look had frozen with his dying breath. The expression looked as if even now the monsters still shredded his flesh savagely. At his side where a hand should have been there was only a bloody stump.

The sight of the blackened, still smoking skin of his hand tossed in the fireplace will continue to plague me. It only adds to the countless terrors I have witnessed.

I knew who was responsible for the events that had taken place there. Though I was severely angered by what had happened to Jonathan, whom I considered to be a friend, my thoughts still hovered over what had happened to Elania.

I tried to ease my worries after a quick search of the rest of the building. I found the scent of a French perfume that I had purchased for her months ago. The scent was older than that of the death. It did offer a little comfort. I knew that I had to confront Audrius, Lucious, and William. But I still hoped that Elania had somehow escaped the slaughter.

People and city walls became nothing more than a blur. I broke all rules known to me about allowing the true nature to be seen. The only exception was to those who were going to be your prey. Rules did not matter. Nor do they now. Who can govern something that they have no true control over? The only thing that concerned me was assurance that Elania was not in the clutches of those like myself.

Minutes after I had left Jonathan's cold corpse I arrived in the wealthier side of the city. I found the house that we all occupied had been left with the front door open. The scent of fresh blood filled the air. The smell rolled from the doorway. This caused my worst fears to flood my mind.

Cautiously I walked and expected to find Elania dead or dying, all while those three demons watched and took pleasure in her slow, painful death. Yet the first one that I saw was a servant boy who would do odd jobs. His mother tended to the house cleaning. She lay only mere footsteps away. The clothing that covered her breast was torn open. It exposed the gaping hole between them and the mauled bleeding wounds where her dark nipples should have been.

The more I searched the more horror I found. It all trailed to the room I occupied during hours of day only. A gray-haired black man that Audrius had bought from the slavers and had given the position of being a butler was next. Each limb had been torn from his body, then stacked neatly upon a table. They looked as if they were part of a vial sculpture that could please only the sickest of minds.

At my door sat a plate of human flesh. It was carved into thin slices with blood pooled around them. I knew that there were only three servants that worked and lived there. They were all dead. These bodies had not been mutilated in this manner. Panic swept over me. The door that was before me opened before I could rush in. Audrius stood before me with a wicked grin.

"Ah, Rowan, my sweet boy. You are just in time to take part in our moving party. We were all hoping that you would not miss it. Though the invitation you found was irresistible I am sure."

"What have you done, Audrius?" I snarled as I barged in. Within the room I found what I hoped would never be.

Lucious sat upon my bed where Elania was firmly tied down. He played with a lock of her hair. William casually looked up from her skinned and filleted leg with blood smeared upon his face. He had been licking away the blood that still pumped from her body.

How I wanted to rush to her. To take away the pain away. To tell her that everything was going to be fine. I did try, yet I could not match the strength of Audrius who held my arm as if I were a helpless child.

"This is what I have been trying to teach you! Your emotions have made you weak! Look at you. You're trying to fight me over this. Yes, with each beat of her heart she is stepping closer to death. But what does it matter? She was destined to die in time. So I decided that this was now the time."

With all of my speed, strength, and anger I struck at him. I knew that it was in vein then, but I still tried. Where my hand should have made contact it met only air. I once again turned to Elania. Audrius held her pale throat in his hand.

"You can end this all. Take her life. Show me that you do not care about her well being. If not, your fate will be the same as hers."

"Let her go, Audrius! I swear in God's name if you let her die I will…"

"Will what? Kill me? I'm sure to you it seems to be a noble concept. A fitting way to perish for you. But you lack the power. Now that you have made your choice you lack your life to do so as well."

If only I could have moved quicker, or perhaps even have rushed him, I could have stopped Audrius. Yet, as I had moved to save Elania he moved his hand. The room filled with the snapping of her breaking neck.

I do not believe that anyone could ever hurt me worse than with that one action. I was knocked off of my feet long before I ever reached Audrius. When my vision stopped swirling Lucious and William stood guard over me. Audrius then moved over me as well. He shook his head with disappointment.

"William, Lucious, I will await you outside. Kill this sorry excuse for pure blood and make it quick."

Audrius disappeared through the door as William and Lucious flung me from the floor. I was then almost standing in the wall in which I crashed.

William and Lucious began to close in on me as if I were a rabbit pinned beneath a bush.

"Should it be quick? Or slow and painful, William?" They were both prepared to spring for an attack at any moment.

"I do not care. Audrius should have let this happen the first time we all witnessed how pathetic he was, trying to live a mortal's life."

My eyes locked on Elania's lifeless body. That moment all of the pain and anger welled up within my heart. Within the seconds it took for them to begin their attack, all of my emotions had overwhelmed me; therefore, I cannot be exact about what happened next.

I remember that everything I did was in a pure, vengeful rage. I can remember the snarls. As well as the sounds of Lucious and William who tried to fight for their lives.

I came around to my normal self, not knowing how long had past since my black out; however, when I did, I found myself arising from over Lucious. His body lay on the opposite side of the room from his head. I knew not to worry about William. This was due to his head resting below Lucious' feet.

My body felt heavy. It was as if some part of me was growing rapidly. Slowly and cumbersomely I staggered to Elania. I knew that it was far too late. But I hoped that there was still a chance for her continued life. Her soft skin had grown cold even to my frigid hands. As I leaned to kiss her farewell I could have wept. I meant a prayer that I said, a prayer so that I could have taken her place. Yet when my lips moved from hers I saw the blood that smeared across hers. This caused me to quickly grab the looking glass that I kept at the bedside. My mouth and throat were covered in the thick, black blood, as was my shirt that was once a pasty white.

I then checked the remains of the two best students of Audrius where I found the faint mark upon what remained of their necks. I knew then that it was possible for me to die. But more importantly at the time I realized Audrius could join me in death.

A great feeling of sorrow engulfed me; though I could have been happy dying at Elania's side, I could not allow her innocence to have been taken by a heartless murder. I thought that Audrius was going to pay for his crimes against her. I thought that he would pay for all others who he slaughtered upon a whim as well.

The heavy feeling died within me as I went through the hell house. I recounted for all that had happened to each poor soul who resided with us monsters. This fueled both my anger and determination. The front door still stood open. It was to be taken as an invitation for anyone to come and witness the museum of evil. But the people of society who still gathered within this street paid no attention to the door. Nor did they notice me covered in blood. Or even Audrius who awaited across the street. He attempted to seduce what appeared to be a high-priced harlot.

"Audrius!" I screamed at the top of my lungs. I cared little about to whom I made my presence known. The people who were busy with their own lives on the street stopped in their tracks. They looked as if the lone sound of my voice cut through their souls. He turned to face me. We were then main attractions of a freak show no one knew lived so very close.

"My dear boy, it looks as if I underestimated you. Surely one who can kill his own kind without a shred of mercy shown is worthy of my continuing leadership and teachings."

Never before had the sight of one person disgusted me so much. Yet each emotion I felt at that time pushed me harder to continue my path of vengeance.

"This ends tonight, Audrius. I have lost everyone who meant anything to me. I have nothing else you can take from me except for my life. But know that I will use my final moments before death's embrace to ensure that I will take you with me."

Audrius looked as if he were going to laugh at what he thought was an empty threat by me. He may have told me so, but before a sound could pass through his throat and over his lips I was beside him. My fist struck his ribs. I hoped the force from that single blow would splinter his bones through the other side of his body and rip through his flesh.

Looking back upon this moment now I know that the watchers on the street had to be in disbelief, perhaps even fear, as, to their eyes, I disappeared and then reappeared by the man who I was threatened by only mere seconds before.

Audrius took the blow, though. It by far did not accomplish what I intended for it to do. The sudden change in his eyes told me he had not been struck in ages, let alone felt pain from a blow. Striking him felt so good, like it removed some of my sorrow, which urged me to continue.

I drew back for another hit when, out of a moment of desperation, I am guessing, Audrius grabbed the harlot by the arm. With all of his strength he threw her into me. Though I was willing to sacrifice anything I could to kill that demon, Audrius, I was not going to take her life to do so. The few seconds that it took for me to reposition myself for another offensive move against him was all the time he needed to prepare for me. I moved into his quickly-planned trap.

No sooner than I had passed up his distraction I found myself in immense pain. Audrius lifted me from the ground with one hand that impaled thorough my breast bone. Over and over again he struck me in the face until I lost consciousness.

I found myself in complete darkness. No floors for my feet to rest upon, nor walls for me to be blocked by. I thought that this could have been death. This was because I had not dreamed since October of 1498.

"Rowan." The thunderous voice sounded from behind me. I had not heard it in years; however, I knew all too well who it belonged to. Not questioning how it could be, I turned to face him, trying to hide my childlike fear.

"Son, your mother and I, and even Margrette are disappointed in you. Denying your natural-born heritage. Then running to a man who follows a god that we all could have seen fall into mythology."

Another voice echoed from the darkness as my mother stepped into view. "Yes, but at least now he has no choice but to answer the call of the blood. But poor Margrette. You broke her heart."

Then as if this moment had been pre-planned Margrette spun me around only inches away from her face.

"You killed us! Then you dared to leave me for that common mortal girl! I was the one who chased away your nightmares as a child. Not she! I kissed away your tears when you were crying! I loved you and was meant for you.

Yet you chose someone who would grow old and die before your very eyes over me!"

From all sides in unison they chanted, "You killed us! You killed us!"

I felt my mind sinking into the depths of insanity. I had begun to laugh and cry at the same time. Surely I believed this was my eternal punishment. This was my hell.

Then a fourth voice sprang from the nothingness that drowned out all others including my insane crying laughter. "Enough!"

I watched as the three who I did love, yet were the monsters from my original nightmare, faded back. They disappeared from where they had come. Tears continued to pour from my eyes as their words still echoed within my head. I did not see him approach; however, as soon as I found myself pulled close to him I knew who it was.

"There, there, my boy... You're fine. They can only haunt you if you allow them to do so."

I pushed myself away from him. All was confirmed though I knew not how it could be. "Father McDonnell? But how? You look so young and full of life. Am I dead?"

"No, my boy. You are no more dead than what you were mere moments ago before you arrived here."

I looked around once more to see if my surroundings had changed. Still I found only the darkness. "Where are we?"

"I am not sure exactly. But I believe that we are partially between a dream world and the crossing point of the dead."

Dead. The word wounded me to the core as I stared upon his face. I remember how I saw him upon my last somewhat mortal night.

"Father, I am sorry. I did not mean to kill you...I could not fight it anymore. I tried but..."

"Shh.... I know, Rowan; however, one way or another I was going to die on that night. It was all part of God's plan. Just as what you have done is part of it as well."

"But, Father, I cannot believe in that anymore. Look at me. I kill almost every night just to survive. That breaks God's law every time I awaken and cannot resist the thirst."

With a long sigh and a pat upon my shoulder he answered. "This is true. I cannot deny it. No man or spirit can tell you how to live your life. Or what to believe in. Yet this is true of everyone, human or not, in this world. But we are here to tell you something very important. Something to help you understand."

My expression was of complete bewilderment as I looked at him. "We? You mean my family tormenting me about my actions was to enlighten me in some way?"

"No, that part was a dream I believe." Her voice came from my side as if she had been there the entire time.

"Elania?" I turned and found her awaiting with open arms without a mark upon her body. I could not help myself. I held her and breathed deep her scent as if she were still very much alive.

"I tried to save you. I was not strong enough. I tried. I wanted us to have a life together" Tears once again filled my eyes. But not the tears of madness. I never wanted to let her go.

Yet she did push me away and wipe away my tears. "I know you tried. I know you really did love me. I would have married you. Even if you did tell me about yourself and warned me of Audrius, William and Lucious. But it is too late for that now."

Father McDonnell put his hands on both of us. He then looked me eye to eye like when I was a child. It had always been this way. It was to let me know this was a serious moment. "You see, my boy, this is what makes you different from your parents. It also makes you different from the other three. You still care. You still allow yourself to feel even though it can hurt worse now than it ever could before."

Elania smiled and still looked at me lovingly. "You don't have to be like them. Though their blood courses through your body. You do not have to act like them. Or even be the way they expected you to be."

"Exactly," Father McDonnell interrupted. "You still can be your own person. No one can take that from you."

I asked them seriously. "Is this part of God's plan? Does God have faith in me to do this?"

Father McDonnell answered quickly. "What does it matter? We have faith in you. Even though we were so different in life, you were, and still are, a good person.

My eyes fell back onto Elania in a longing way, "I know I will never see you again. I know there will never be another soul who could love me knowing that I am a monster."

Gently she kissed me as if to say goodbye. "You are not a monster. A true monster is one who does not care about anything or anyone except for themselves. There will be another who will come into your life in the future.

It will happen when you least expect it. She will love you more than I can tell you. She will know and will not care. You'll see. Remember our words. Remember we will always have faith in you, even during the darkest of times. But now you must go."

I tried to argue. I wanted to stay with Elania. Yet before I even had the time to wish them farewell they faded into the darkness. I was left alone once again.

I awoke to the sun's rays bathing my face. It caused me to scramble to my feet as I tried to find some way to shade myself out of fear. Yet when my senses came to me I found that the sun caused a discomfort to my eyes. But it did not char my flesh as Audrius had taught me to believe on my first night of being a blood drinker.

My wounds that I had suffered from Audrius had healed. The only sign of my injury was the hole within my shirt. My blood that had stained was indistinguishable from the blood that remained from my brawl with William and Lucious. The street that I should have awoken on was no more. I found myself in the middle of the wilderness with no knowledge of how I arrived there.

There were no signs of Audrius as well. No scents or tracks to offer an explanation of why or how I arrived. I searched over my body and found that everything was in place. This included my coin purse that was still firmly tied to my belt; however, when I felt of it I found it to be feather light. Quickly I opened it and found only a note that awaited my eyes.

Rowan,

Your lessons shall continue for however long it takes for you to learn. You will be by my side and follow my word; to you it should be law. I am the one who made you what you are; therefore, I leave you with exactly what I found you with. Nothing. In time you will learn that my way is the path of truth. The way you must live. I will always be in the shadows watching.

Your Mentor,

Audrius

August 13, 1784

Two hundred seventy-eight years have passed since I lost everything because of love. I have searched for Audrius but I never find him, as if he were nothing more than a nightmare that manifested itself in reality for a brief moment of my life.

I choose not to record these years in detail here, though they are recorded in my mind. I do not record them because I am not a soul like my friend Shakespeare. He would have taken the opportunity to create tales out of the construction of St. Peter's Basilica, of the Canbrai, Luther's Reformation, or the Thirty-Year War. Nor am I a soul like Bach who could have put these events into musical notes. Music that could stir the souls of men, women, and children alike.

I have decided to record the most personal events that have and will take place. This is so that if someone does get the upper hand against me the story of Audrius will be known. Hopefully he will be stopped if he has not already.

I now find myself in the American Colonies. Independence has recently been declared within this still harsh wilderness. Though I have viewed the most beautiful cities within the world, I find a certain comfort in watching this new world and country slowly develop before my eyes.

Yet there is still sadness here. I watch land being bought and sold by those who claim to have been here first. They show little to no regard of the native peoples who were here long before the first colony.

Their very way of life was one of peace and harmony with their surroundings. Even now they try to cling to these ways that I do not truly understand. Still I find it beautiful because there are great mysteries to be learned from them.

I did try once to learn; however, the one who held the most mystery, a holy man if you will, looked upon me and instantly knew that I was not like him or his people. I was not feared, or threatened. Yet I was expected to tell them how to save their way of life. They somehow knew they were fighting a losing battle against the foreign settlers.

I wish that I had that knowledge to share. I knew that they would have been the one group of people who would not have feared the truth about me.

I have wandered from the topic. I find myself doing this more often now. Recently I have been watching a small town grow to life from the wilderness. It is called Heritage in the area known as Tennessee. There seems to be a breath of hope within these people. There is even a possibility of this town surviving the tests of time to prosper into a large city. Possibly a city as large as London, or Paris. Only time will tell.

October 2, 1784

The anniversary of my changing into what I am is drawing closer. Even if I were not paying close attention to the days going past in my wilderness that I have grown fond of I could still feel this time approaching. Yet I am being drawn to Heritage as trade has started to become a major influence here.

However, part of me fears the idea of becoming happy. I fear that I will find Audrius has been hiding amongst my own shadow, that he has been awaiting a chance to accomplish his goal yet again.

A scream drew me away from my inner thoughts before I could finish. It is much later now than what it was before. It could even be early morning of the third. But that is not important.

The scream was female. Though I have adopted a nature of all events of the wild that take place for survival in a natural coarse of life, the scream of the poor terror-stricken female was not of the wild.

As I neared where the scream originated I found it was farther from town than where I resided. She was not alone but being chased by a predator of the wild. Her predators were from civilization.

"The harder you run, girlie, the harder this is gonna be on ya." The shout had come from behind her. They were trying to chase her farther from the town. It was clear that they were trying to cover their actions.

I moved quicker than a deer startled by a sudden noise. I wove in and out of trees until I had gotten ahead of the girl. Motionless I stood down wind of them all. Slowly I got a picture in my mind from their scents of how many there were.

The girl was actually a woman. The sweet scent of lavender mixed with sweat gave this away. Her pursuers were a total of four men. Their scents almost covered hers, which was a stench of sweat mixed with the foul smell of cheap alcohol and lust. I knew at that moment clearly what was being planned. It did not matter if their motives were unknown to me.

The wind changed directions. It left me with only the fading scents. As I awaited another sense to pick up upon where they were I was suddenly jolted as the woman ran into me. She landed upon her back from the force of her momentum halted suddenly.

I could hear her thoughts clearly: *Please no...oh, God, please no...*

The pure emotion of horror that poured from her trembling body filled me with both rage and sympathy. It caused me to feel more alive than what I had felt in ages. I knelt down beside her almost giving into the urge to pull her close, to attempt making her believe that everything would be all right. My unnatural sight allowed me to see the tears that streamed down her face. Then she screamed as loud as her lungs would allow her to do.

Her voice echoed off of the assortment of large deciduous and evergreen trees. It aided her pursuers in their perverted version of a fox hunt.

"She's over here!" Another shout came from the distance as the sound of their footsteps became far too loud for them not to be only seconds away.

Quickly I covered her mouth and whispered to where she could only hear. "Still yourself and remain silent. I will not allow any harm to come to you."

They had arrived. They searched in the darkness with no light. All hoped to find what was an easy target even for refugees of civilized life. Frozen they stood. They knew that they had heard the scream come from within this area; I could tell that an almost long forgotten animal sense had emerged. It told them the hunters had just became the hunted. The silence of the woodland and their unexplainable feeling caused them to lose their incentive to continue onward. It also caused them to argue amongst themselves.

It would have been so easy for me to have taken them all one by one. It would have given me pleasure knowing that they could never harm anyone again. But I wanted their rage and desire to resurface. I wanted them to fight me.

"Enough! You have all crossed into my domain without invitation. I claim the girl you seek as my own. If you stay here longer it will be a direct challenge to my claim, which you will pay for in blood."

Laughter was their answer to my lone voice threatening them, laughter caused by fear and disbelief. The laughter was enough of an answer for me to hold true to my words.

The first two fell quick, never knowing what had killed them or where it came from. A click followed by a spontaneous flash illuminated the nocturnal forest. It filled the air with the smell of spent black powder from a musket.

The hot lead pierced my flesh and passed through my body. It tore organs as quickly as my unnatural body could heal. The pain was unlike anything I had ever experienced before. It was the first time I had ever been shot; however, it caused the full force of the thirst to over take me.

It happened like when I was still somewhat human so many years ago. All sounds faded though I could see their lips move with screams. Yet I had no interest in listening to their curses or screams. I heard their hearts beat full of anxiety. It was the sweetest music that I had heard in so long. I nearly forgot what it was like to take the life of a mortal, a mortal whom I had caught in the act of causing harm to an innocent.

The first of the last two bled out quickly. Though it was enough to meet my needs I could not resist the second as he began to run. He had allowed fear to finally take control of his actions. I felt the call of the predator within my heart. The lure of the chase had begun. He acted as clumsy as a wounded deer who tried to elude the hunter. The scent of fear filled the air. I could not resist pushing it to the limits.

Time after time I appeared before him. It forced him to run in circles; however, each time I would appear his heart would begin to push itself harder. More and more narrow were the circles. He had no choice in making the path. Panic finally overtook him as he tripped over the corpse of one of those he considered a friend. He tried to stumble to stand a last time. Yet it was in vein.

The moment was over. I felt their blood coarse through my body. All of my thoughts turned to the girl again.

Silence. No screams. No thoughts of danger or worry about my hunger that had broken loose. She had fainted sometime during the conflict that I had so desired. Carefully, as to not wake her, I scooped her up within my arms. I removed her from the scene of the carnage. I brought her back to my camp where I had lived for the past two months.

Upon a bed of green moss she lays now. She still sleeps peacefully as a child near its mother. The sun will rise soon. I know that I must be cleaned of most of the blood. I know she will wish to return to the life that is normal to her in the morning.

October 4, 1784

It is far too true that time does change all. When time is the one thing that someone has plenty of, change usually holds off, only then coming into your life all at once.

I now find myself inside of a tavern room with what few possessions I have. All expenses were taken care of.

The girl awoke the next morning. She was partially in shock at finding herself in front of a smoldering fire with a complete stranger. The look of panic told me that she expected her pursuers from only hours before instead.

"Who are you?" Her voice rang with an accent that I had not heard since the time I lived on the Emerald Isle.

The accent I had purposely been suppressing for well over a century came back without effort. "I am known as Rowan Rasland."

The worry seemed to subside within her mind and heart as my voice filled her ears.

"The last thing I remember was running away from four fur traders who got thrown out of my father's tavern for being disrespectful to everyone. Including myself. They thought that because they had gold to spend everything was for sale." She stood and brushed some of the derbies from the skirt of her dress, looking puzzled as she continued. "Then someone, I think someone saved me." Her eyes looked up at me while she smiled. "I thought you were Robin Red Cap or another spirit by what you said."

I quickly rationalized that if she remembered the slaughter she would have been running in terror by that time. Casually I laughed at her comment. I reached for my leather travel pack that showed signs of being exposed to the elements for months, and placed it over my shoulder.

"Where are you going? Have I offended you in some way?" I could hear the thought of being left in the untamed wild, in which she had no clue how to survive.

"I am taking you back to your life, seeing as how you are not at home within these surroundings."

She glanced around at the pure nature I had found beauty in. She cringed slightly before she followed quick in my footsteps.

"Have you always lived like this? I mean if you have there is nothing wrong with it. Why have I never seen you in town before?"

She was young and as full of life as she was questions. The only answer I could pry from her was her name, Kyra.

Kyra could have easily turned the short hike into a complicated process of attempting to dissect each answer I gave, only to ask yet another question until my entire life was know to her. Luckily the town had organized a search party led by her father. When we had found them they all looked nearly as lost as Kyra the night before.

"Halt!" The now familiar click of flint locks rang through the air. I peered over the mass of people, which had to number at least twenty if not more.

A uneasy silence had fallen between us all. It was as if they now had found someone they knew not what to do with.

"Father! Do not point that rifle at Mr. Rasland; and that goes for the rest of ya as well. A fine welcome and thanks you give to the gentleman who saved my life when the rest of ya were either drunk or asleep."

The long rifles lowered one by one. Dumbfounded looks passed amongst the group of men. I took a secret pleasure as I viewed this side of Kyra taking over the inquisitive nature that I thought ruled her personality.

"I thought you were dead, Kyra. We found those traders shredded by some kind of animal...Well um.... I suppose I owe you an apology, Mr. Rasland was it?"

The accent was heavy in her father's voice, heavier than her own. Then I understood why Kyra had asked so many questions of me and my past. Her father, like myself, was born in Ireland. Her accent resembled a pure one; she had been around the other settlers most if not all of her life.

"No need to apologize. You were just acting in the best interest of your daughter. Any respectable man would be expected to do the same."

His hand ran through the graying brown hair upon his head as he smiled. "Ahh!...an Irish lad! I should have known that a fine lad like yourself would have been coming to Heritage to return my feisty daughter. The name is

Amus…Amus McGreger. Rasland is a strange name…What part of Ireland did ya say you were from?"

I knew for certain then, as we all started to walk toward town, where Kyra's nature of not being afraid of asking a question came from. We arrived at Heritage near nine in the morning. For the first time I had the chance to experience the town, unlike what I had during my normal nocturnal hours.

Travelers filled the street. Some with only travel packs. Others with full wagons pulled by horses, mules, and the occasional donkey. Hens and roosters ran in and out of main street. They dodged the feet of visitors and town dwellers alike. It was a true settlement trying to establish itself within the monitory world; though bartering still was the most accepted form of payment.

It was life…normal life with worries of survival, wealth, love. It was what I had craved for so long but held back from out of fear, rage, and the desire for revenge. Yet as I was led to the simple tavern Amus owned I realized that I was willing to forget my fears and anger. But not forget what caused them, all for the chance of truly starting a new one here. If Audrius was still alive he would have made a move by now, or I would have found him at least.

I sat in the tavern all day while I talked to both Amus and Kyra in shifts. They would take turns caring for the patrons' needs. When night fell not only did the travelers come in to fill themselves with food and drink, so did most of the townsmen and women. Everyone wanted to relax after a long day. I was ready to take my leave and sort through my thoughts by penning them here; however, as I walked for the door I was stopped by a strong feminine hand upon the back of my neck.

"And where do ya think your going, Mr. Rasland? Surely not back out into those dark woods at this hour. There's still a wild animal prowling through those trees looking for its next feast. Besides, my father has already set aside the best room for you this evening."

That is how I have found myself here in the beginning of a new chapter of my life. But this is not before Amus visited me after closing. He felt the need to share his best bottle of whiskey in reverence to my deeds.

He did mention an interesting idea of forming a partnership with someone. I do believe that the coins I have been collecting from my victims may do more than just secure me a chance at a new start. They may be able to buy me a place in Heritage as well.

October 10, 1784

The partnership is now present in the tavern. I have talked Amus into renaming it the Emerald Inn. But these events did not transpire without difficulty. It seems the coins I have been collecting since 1498 are still worth the value of the precious metals they are made of; however, coins formed nearly three centuries ago are not recognized by their realm of origin here. When I attempted to purchase more suitable clothing for a man of my wealth, to begin my business venture, I found too many questions were arising from my gold and silver.

Therefore, I have decided to safely guard these coins, for they should prove useful in the future. Yet I was still faced with the dilemma of how to acquire a large sum of modern currency quickly. All without drawing suspicion to my means of doing so.

I must admit that my thoughts were very narrow in the beginning. I used the same plan I had devised centuries ago. Take the coins, gold, and possessions of my victims. It was not until I killed two who fit my taste that I remembered that the ones I hunted rarely had something to call theirs.

It was clear I had to set my sights on a higher-prized game. Yet, I had never hunted within nobility because their loss would be too widely felt and questioned even in the general populace.

Nonetheless, I thought the answer was known then. I had to pick my prey well.

He was the son of an English duke who wore purchased buck skins. He sought adventure in the wilderness of the Americas. Yet for such an adventure seeker his skins were remarkably spotless. I still believe that it was due to the servants that rode with him on horseback.

I tracked him through the trails that were used by the traders to come and go from Heritage via the forest and mountain trails. That was before they stopped at the tavern for the evening. I had to wait patiently for the right moment when he could disappear without notice. Yet as the night drew on I began to believe this was going to be impossible.

Laughing and drinking was the highlight of the early night. He tried to impress the locals with his stories of adventures with natives and widely respected members of the new American government. Most of the people bought into his tales; however, as I sat in the shadows I listened to his thoughts and found that they contradicted his spoken words. I have grown too accustomed to listening to thoughts since I found this ability.

Then, as if it were pre-rehearsed, the cards were brought out and the games of chance began. I watched for over an hour as Heritage shop owners lost their entire lives to this boyhood man. My heart sank when Amus finally got involved. Then, as if it were second nature, I began to listen to the players' thoughts. I found that I could easily know who was bluffing. Who had what pair or straight and so on. It only took four hours of play before everyone in the tavern had lost what they had worked so hard to earn. Farms, the general store, and even the tavern he now owned. The people were almost ready to kill him themselves. I knew that I could not have that happening. Not now.

"Well I do believe I have won all that I can from here. It is time for me to take my leave, good people of Heritage."

It was clear to me then how to defeat him. As well as how to amass the wealth and loyalty I needed here in Heritage.

"Wait," I said as I came out of the shadows with my old coin purse in hand. "I have something to wager that the rest of the town cannot offer."

"Really? Let us see it, old boy. Maybe it might interest me."

I moved to the table where he had been most of the night and allowed my coins to spill out onto the table top. "These are an assortment of antique coins my family has gathered since the late fifteenth century."

"I can see that, you poor, pathetic fool; my family has a far greater abundance of these such coins in England. But I cannot resist taking money from anyone who is so eager to give it away. Please sit. I'll keep the bidding low so that you will feel that you have at least had a fair chance to win."

He knew how to push anyone's temper out of hiding. I did think about killing him. I restrained from doing so. We played nonstop until dawn. But it did not take long for his gloating to cease after time and time again of losing.

The townsmen and women who normally would have been starting their day before daybreak had not even slept. They watched hand after hand be dealt until I won all that they had lost. However, I could not stop there. I also won the possessions of the noble boy.

The second to last hand I won his horse, and the horses of his servants. The last hand I won the buck skins off of his back. The tavern erupted in cheers as the boy began to scream and pout about cheating. But this did not matter because he insisted on dealing. He was stripped against his will and thrown out of the tavern as he screamed like a baby. This was especially so when the fall air nipped at his exposed skin.

"How am I to continue my travels without gear or a horse!"

I could only think to myself, *Why do you not use the skills you learned from the natives and travel how I traveled most of Europe, by foot.*

The conversation I had with those who lost what they owned went generally well. I allowed them to retain their land, homes, and shops. This was with the understanding that it now became a partnership. A partnership where they still remained in control of their goods and services while I collected a small percentage of the return, if any. It did not please them at first, but then I explained that if there were financial cost or loss I would pay half. To sweeten the deal more I also made it known that if there were ever a financial urgency I would take full responsibility. Needless to say this pleased everyone. This insurance made them feel safer in their lives here in Heritage. Also Amus and Kyra were very pleased to see that I was willing to protect them and their friends. Finally I had a place where I belonged. A home.

December 24, 1787

Three years, two months and fourteen days have passed since I last thought about making an entry for myself to look back upon in the future. This is because things have been going so very well. The partnerships that started three years ago have flourished. It has made the community, and myself, a large amount of money. The question is why am I going through the troubles of bringing my journal, quill and ink out of hiding just to make note of this?

The reasons are simple, at least simple in mortal life. But are not so simple in the life of an immortal.

Little time had passed after the fleecing of the noble boy when I had begun to court Kyra. Amus was inflamed at the idea of his daughter being involved with a "resourceful lad who managed to become of such high standing in no time." But as time passed, bringing us all into this present, it has become expected of me to follow through with such a long courtship with the next obvious step. That is as they see it.

I cannot help but to relive the events that transpired with Elania. It seems to me like it only happened yesterday. I thought I had long since learned to deal with the pain of her loss, not knowing what may have happened in our lives if we could have been together, or what would have been if I had not walked into her life. Would she have married? Would she have bore children? Had grandchildren and so on?

Yet I also have been reminded of the dream. Or at least what I still believe was a dream, though I sometimes find myself questioning if Elania's spirit was talking of Kyra.

It is a humorous thought. Kyra willing to accept the truth of my nature when she still carries so many superstitions about spirits and demons, these things that her father had taught her as a child. But still I rationalized. I believed at one time in a higher power, a thing I could not see. I have to force myself to remember as well that I, too, am a creature only thought of as superstition. That is, except for the few who remain loyal to ways forgotten by most long ago.

Nonetheless, Christmas is only hours away. Amus raised Kyra to be God fearing and respectful. Within these three years she has become more respectful; however, the curious, mouthy girl is dying out.

I find it hard to imagine being with Kyra without her knowing of my life, my secrets. I would look as I always have. Though it would not be noticed at first, Kyra would begin to show the signs of age with graying hair and lines being etched ever so deeper into her now smooth face. She would question why I had remained the same as would the rest of Heritage.

The chances of being cast out or tried as a witch, or even the devil himself, are great. If I choose Kyra I will eventually lose her either by my own choice or by her own. Yet if I choose to keep things as they are, or attempt to do so, I will still lose her in time to another.

I hate to admit this now. Especially since I cannot, nor will ever truly agree with Audrius, I can at least see what could have caused him to believe the way that he did. Or even still does.

February 3, 1788

I married Kyra on January 22. Though I have tried to tell her countless times what I am her response is the same. "Rowan, you know I don't want to talk of the devil's work in the house." Unfortunately a time has settled upon Heritage that I never thought would. A strange illness has been striking members of the community. By far it has not been at random. There is talk of witchcraft and curses at every corner. It has become far greater than the gossip of housewives. Each night I have attempted to guard the town. This is while I avoid those who have made it their missions to search for strange happenings at night. They at first would split up and meet every hour to ensure they were all still alive. Within the past two nights four well adapted men of the wild have been found dead without explanation. At least without explanation within normal means of explaining death.

They were perfectly healthy in life, and completely without blood in their veins when found dead. I am lucky that no one besides myself has checked, otherwise the town of Heritage would be claiming someone is a vampire. But being charged as a witch is still dangerous when people fear enough to allow their common sense to fade.

Tonight I travel outside of the town's boundaries to the graveyard. It is a far too obvious place to find he who preys upon the town. Sometimes the obvious is the right answer. I have to take into consideration that whoever is to blame has to be new at this life. Why else would they leave the corpses of their victims to be discovered in the light of day?

February 4, 1788

They were starving. More like a pack of feral dogs than they were blood drinkers. Every townsman and woman who had died from the supposed curse were not truly dead. All of them must have been given the dark blood before they took their last breath of human life.

The first had to be the farmer, Christopher. He had died before this completely started becoming a plague. I am theorizing that he was schooled, if you will, in the means of creating others. This would explain why his family and friends were the first to be found dead after his death. Yet whoever taught him to do this did not tell him to feed only enough to make the heart slow to the point of stopping, thus not creating a night breed of savage killers. This also explains why the four who recently died have not risen. They were slaughtered with no concern of questions that may arise with the corpses.

The problem of the savages has been solved. No deaths occurred last night; however, now I am forced to think of Christopher and where he now may be. But more importantly I am forced with the thought of the clear possibility that Audrius has returned to my life to complete his lessons. This would put all that I care for in danger. That is, if he was the one who thought this plot through and began the series of mindless killing with one innocent farmer—a man who only wanted to be with his family and friends no matter what.

February 6, 1788

Within mere days of the past events, the life I have made here has started to fall apart at the seams. The methods of deception that I used to live amongst these people are being questioned. The day of the fifth Kyra announced to me that she is with child. Though I knew this child would not be normal, I was still filled with joy.

The night had brought a new and unexpected development. Christopher appeared at the tavern as if he were not dead. This placed the entire town into fear. I was summoned quickly about the matter of a man who was dead and stood within the tavern of which I now owned half. He had talked of how I was to blame for the plague upon Heritage.

I entered the tavern quickly, still keeping my human persona. Christopher drank bottle after bottle of liquor without Amus questioning payment.

"Two living dead men in the same tavern." He stood and moved toward me. "To think this town thought you were a savior of some kind. Hell, I even thought it. Look at me now. I'm the same thing you are."

Amus looked at me with eyes that questioned as I looked Christopher eye to eye. "And what is it that you think I am? A killer who goes about by night slaughtering those who I am closest to. I only wonder how did you fake your own death, and also if you truly believe what you say."

The tavern erupted in a nervous laughter. It informed me that, though they were still afraid, they believed my words over his.

Christopher's face had begun to change; I knew what was about to happen. I could have easily defended myself and everyone in the tavern. Yet I also knew that if I did so Christopher's words would have been proven true.

He lunged for me and knocked me to the floor. His jaws snapped repeatedly, looking for just one mouthful of my blood. I knew he wanted to weaken me from blood loss. Christopher was still young. He was very easy for me to hold back. But I had to at least make it look as if it were a daring effort to hold him at bay.

The sound of glass being broken was followed with the shards of glass and liquor. It had covered my face and burned my eyes. Before I could have clear sight again, Christopher was off of me. I heard musket fire followed with Amus moaning in pain.

I sprung to my feet. Christopher tried to keep his hold upon Amus' neck while those who chose to be heroes attempted to make him release. Another musket shot. Christopher released Amus as this ball ripped through the bend of his knee. It shattered bone, and ripped flesh alike. Amus fell to the ground. He lacked the strength to support his own frame as Christopher scrambled to get back to the wound that still gushed forth blood.

Before he could make it back to Amus' bleeding body I flipped him onto his back. The rage that had flared in me had been released. Each time my fist hit his head I heard more bone crack from the force of my blows.

When I stopped, Christopher lay upon the wooden floor covered by graveyard dirt and blood. He was motionless and appeared to be dead, but this was only to those who did not know the truth; however, it was heard with their own ears.

Though the tavern was still filled with individuals, complete silence was all that could be heard. I ended it there, at that moment. I refused to give Christopher the time needed to heal so that the fight could continue. With one hand I grabbed all the liquor I could hold and Christopher's ankle in the other. I cared not if I was followed into the street. This was because no one could have persuaded me to change my mind.

With precision, I made sure every inch of his body was covered with the brown and clear substances. From a small fire I kept outside so patrons could warm themselves before entering or leaving I took a single flaming log and set him a blaze.

The stench of his burnt flesh rolled up through the air with the smoke. I turned to go back to Amus and found all had followed me. As I walked toward the door they parted.

Their thoughts were heard clearly as I walked past: *Is it true? Could there be a chance? But I've seen him in the sun personally. Rowan does squint sometimes. But we all do. I've never seen him actually eat anything. The same day he was found the bodies of those four poor mangled traders were found...I was there, I remember.*

Amus lay on the floor. His body had turned pale white while he gasped for breath. His eyes had grown ever more blank in their look. Death approached him quickly. "Rowan...Rowan...Lad, come close. My...time is growing short."

I quickly knelt down to his face. "I am here, Amus."

"I've known, lad...I knew from...the beginning. But you're still a...fine...lad."

My mind flashed to how Elania's father had died. How Father McDonnell died. How Elania was tortured. I now had a new name to add to my list. "I am sorry. I wish I could ..."

"I know..." His last breath was spent with those words.

Kyra shoved her way through the masses as she screamed. "Out of the way, you oxen. Move!" Her eyes locked upon her dead father who rested within my arms. Even now her cries of sorrow still fill my ears. Even more, fear fills her heart. The monsters she was taught to fear as a child have now been confirmed in her mind. But she still refuses what was said of me. Love is both blind and deaf.

The tavern has lost enough business since the night before that it is not worth my time nor money to continue its trade.

The townsmen of Heritage no longer speak to me when I am out during the day. At night I am followed. It is as if I am expected to be caught in the act of a dark feast.

I now close this entry and prepare to place this volume into hiding. The evidence within these pages is enough to condemn me without a trial, though I think it will be done regardless.

December 27, 1788

Normality. I crave it as a poor man craves power and wealth. If I could be rid of my unnatural side my heart would not be left with a hole in it again. My life would still be perfect in Heritage. Friends I have made there would not fear or shun me.

Yet, I have been cursed with this existence. I question that maybe in a past life I took part in some dark deed that required my punishment to be eternal in this existence.

The rumors of witchcraft and monsters that stalk by night ran wild in Heritage long after Christopher was disposed of. Though there were no more murders of traders or townsmen, every time a simple accident took place— a broken toe, an unfaithful husband or wife—witchcraft was the sole blame. There were no witches publicly accused. The people of Heritage attempted to keep their accusations secret and it was clear that Kyra was being blamed.

It was common knowledge that I was the one who found Kyra so many nights ago in the woodlands that surrounded Heritage. But even this became perverted because I had never been known before that night. The four who died that evening were now rumored to be the sacrifices made by Kyra in the name of Lucifer to seal my creation to serve evil.

At first the rumors were just that. Yet as Kyra's pregnancy became known by the public the tales began to grow. Fear began to breed belief; soon thereafter I was the father of the antichrist that was growing every day within Kyra's body.

The habits of my dear Kyra had changed as the nature of our child began to take a toll upon her body. During hours of light Kyra rested soundly. Her eyes ached with any light greater than that of a single candle. When night fell she would awaken and crave the raw flesh of an animal. It was a craving that I had no choice but to fulfill each evening. I stalked the wilderness for deer, rabbit, wolves, anything I could find.

It was one of such nights when Kyra's hunger could no longer be ignored that I left to find some prey to ease the suffering. I was foolish to leave Kyra alone. But I felt confident that she would be safe. I left knowing that our home was being watched so that I could be followed. This had become common practice. Normally they would track me through town, then attempt to do so in the woodland; yet they could not do so because of my speed.

All was as it should have been, except for the guards. They were normally composed of common townsmen. I had heard casual conversations and thoughts of two experienced trackers who were due to arrive days before this night. The scent that emanated from them was of the wild, untouched and pure—the kind of wild that could not be found near cities, townships or what was considered civilized settlements.

They watched me measure them to my standards. I viewed them as a challenge just by their scents. Yet it was more of a game. Even now there is a desire for the hunt. The opportunities to make the hunters the hunted. To turn their abilities against them. To change their confidence into doubt. Shape their courage into fear.

I moved to the tree line and heard their dogs unleashed. They barked as if wanting to chase me like a fox. Their masters followed as close and quickly as they could. The dogs had found little trouble tracking my scent. It was due to the smell of lavender that Kyra had grown accustomed to. I assured that I was far enough from town before I turned for the dogs. They continued to bark until I growled deep at them. Instantly it caused them to stop in their tracks as they whimpered. I moved forward, still growling. The dogs knew they were outmatched. The sounds of their whimpering yelps filled the air as they ran past their masters.

"What the hell was that?"

"I don't know. Remember he's supposed to be a tricky one. Keep your eyes open."

It was then a matter of skill against skill, experienced predators against each other as each tried to gain the upper hand. I gave them sounds of branches snapping and footsteps to follow. It caused them to frantically rush from point of origin to point of origin. There they would find the tracks I wanted them to find.

"This is impossible! No one can move that damn quick!"

"Stay focused! We've been paid to do a job and we're going to do it. I don't care if this man really is a demon. We are going to track it, find it, and by God's will we will kill it if need arises."

Honestly it was more enjoyment than I had experienced in months. They were oblivious to the fact that they were being led farther and farther away from the town, as well as paths cut into the forest for travel. I had long lost track of the hours that had passed since my original venture into the wild. The only thing that reminded me of the task that should have been completed shortly after I entered the woodlands was a lone doe that had wandered from the herd.

My eyes widened as my memory returned to the more serious matters at hand. As quick as my body could move I took the dear down and dressed it messily. The wild blood covered my body. With the bloody carcass then over my shoulder, I ran back toward my home. I had forgotten the trackers until I ran past them.

"What in the hell was that?"

"It looked like a doe running on two legs!"

"There are some things that man was never intended on understanding, let alone hunt. This job is over, let's go back to that town."

"But which way is the town?"

I laughed silently to myself as their words faded from my ears. They were maybe three hours walk away from town. Yet even in the light of day it would test all of their skills to follow their own tracks out. But that would only be after they learned that my tracks were only to confuse them more. I had wasted far too much time with my escapades. I felt horrible at the thought of Kyra suffering as the craving became increasingly worse, all due to my chance to forget the restlessness that had become a common part of each day.

As I approached the tree line that bordered our home, I slowed, still making sure that my secret was somewhat secure. I composed myself to walk out into the open. Then the scents first filled my nose. Wood smoke was predominate. But it was not the type of wood smoke that rose off of a fire to warm yourself by. No. It was the type that rose off of torches, the type of smoke that mixed with the scent of scorched cloth soaked in oil. Underlying scents of a mass of people filled the walkway to the door.

The carcass I dropped at the door. I expected to find a situation where I had no choice but to unleash all I had kept hidden. With all of my might I flung open the door. It crashed into the adjoining wall and caused the door to rattle on its hinges. The scents were stronger there. An entire mob of people had entered into our home. But the scents had already started to fade from the air. It caused my heart to sink.

I tried to remain hopeful; however, the scent that had become stronger was of fresh death. It seemed as if my steps were slower and more heavy. I walked to the bedroom Kyra usually occupied during the hours of light.

The door was partially open. Instead of hearing Kyra's breath or movements I heard the sobs of the one who was due to be Kyra's midwife. She had resided with us for a few weeks prior. Slowly I pushed the door open. It creaked eerily as my sight filled with a bed covered with blood. It had started to dry and turn the normal dark color of dried human blood.

"Mr. Rasland! I tried to stop them. They wouldn't listen. I tried. I honestly did try."

There was no need for me to question her sincerity. The tears and the mournful way her words trembled out beyond her lips was enough of a sign of truth.

I grasped the top of the extremely thick covers we used for our bedding. Kyra always complained of how cold I remained, even during sleep. With a quick tug they flew down to the foot posts. The midwife wailed like a mad woman. I dropped to my knees and buried my face into the bed as I tried to muffle my screams.

What I record now I have no desire to remember; however, I cannot ever forget the horrors men are capable of if they are provoked in the right manner, where our unborn child had been growing and preparing to join this world was no more. The wound was sloppy. It gave evidence of how hard Kyra had fought her abductors. The wound alone was enough to kill her in the weakened state she had been surviving in. Yet this alone was not enough. They slashed her wrists to ensure she would die.

My child, who I had only dreamed of seeing, was plucked from Kyra's life-giving body. It was to prove we were of evil origins. They had expected to find the flesh and blood embodiment of their Satan; however, they found only an innocent life, a life who could not have harmed even the youngest of their children. Still they fed the small body to their purifying flames. But this is only what the midwife recalled them saying. Their excuse was that the Devil can take on many forms, even the forms of the small and harmless.

How I wanted to strike out in vengeance against the entire town. If only to quench the rage that burned in my heart with blood. Yet I knew that the town of Heritage needed someone to stand behind. Someone to follow as they had followed me before. They could not act out any such plan alone.

The midwife knew of a wandering "preacher of the word" who had happened upon the town. With no money or material influence he gave his gospel in the streets. It took no time for the people to find faith in his words. So much so that a large wooden crucifix had been erected in the town's square. It was to "show their loyalty to God" or at least that was the word of the preacher. When the rumors of Kyra and myself were made known to him it gave the perfect chance to ensure God's will be done. In reality it gave him the perfect chance to seal those who followed his word into mindless obedience. He now had an enemy of the people to point his finger at. He claimed that God had judged what should be done. He also claimed that it was up to him to make God's will manifest; however, I knew well that the only judge present was himself.

Just as he had past judgment against Kyra and myself, I intended to do the same to him. It was late in the evening of the same night. Heritage was fast asleep. Some felt secure that they had accomplished the will of God. To them it made all of the horrors they had partaken in seem just. I knew that somewhere mingled within the cottages and shops was a man who had committed the actions, the actions that prevented me from attempting to live the life I had struggled to establish here.

Building by building I searched. I would enter like a specter, unseen and unknown to still exist in the form I had last been seen in. Some slept soundly as if nothing had taken place only hours ago. Others had the events return to them. It caused their minds to scream out from re-witnessing something they did not truly agree with. They had partaken of it only out of fear, fear that their family would be accused next if they did not do so.

I know now that I pitied them all because of their fears, because it was so easy for someone whom they did not know to walk into their lives—to allow someone to take over completely the most basic choices they could make in their lives.

From one end of the town to the other I searched. It was not until I came upon the evermore dilapidated Emerald Tavern that I noticed things were out of place. The sign that Amus designed and that I had spent many good hours on the construction and painting of was no more. It was as if the event that led to its precision creation were nothing more than events of my imagination. A spark and the flicker of a flame-kissed candle wick shown through the thick glass of the windows. The door that was once there was replaced with a new one with detailed iron hinges. A wooden crucifix hung from the door. Though

I am sure it was to act as a deterrent for any unnatural force, I saw it as an invitation that screamed to me. It was a sign to me that the focus of my anger was within.

The door I found was bolted from within. Surely it would have kept out the normal man who wanted to enter; however, nothing was going to keep me from getting to him. The bolt broke with a loud crack and thud as half of it fell to the floor.

"Who's there? I've got a musket! I'm not afraid to use it!…I'm warning you!"

His voice was shaken and terrified. I moved into the shadows to avoid his candle light that was dimmed because of his rapid movement. His eyes fell upon the smashed-in door that allowed the night air to rush in upon his bear legs. His breath quickened as his body froze in place.

"Forgive me for I have sinned." My voice must have seemed as if it came from thin air to him. He gasped as if an unseen force was talking to him. His head darted around as he searched for me. When his eyes met me as I stepped from the shadows, he looked as if I had walked out of his worst nightmares.

"I…I do not care, sir, if you are covered in blood. You will pay for the damage you have done to my home. That is, before you are tried for whatever murder you have committed."

His confidence grew as he saw me to be nothing more than an insane man covered with dried blood. Something that the hand musket could easily make fall in his eyes.

"I have only taken one life tonight. That was the life of a deer. You are the one who has taken the life of an innocent child and mother. A wife whom you ripped the child from, unborn, and you convinced an entire town of the evil it never was."

He began to back away into the night due to my confrontation of his actions.

"It had to be done! God's will demanded that the seed of evil was to be destroyed! It was done in God's name and to question me is to question God himself."

He spoke the words as if it were a gospel, if they were to strike fear into my soul for even daring to question what was done; yet he did not know who I was.

"You have no right to pass judgment upon me or my family! You see me as being evil, and for what reason? Because I am different? Or because it fits into your plan of using this town for everything you can get out of it before they all realize they are being used?"

His eyes widened in terror as my words rang within his ears. He had never seen my face before that moment. But he knew all too well who I was.

"You're him!...But we paid..."

"Yes, paid experienced trackers to follow me. Hoped that they would kill me. Only because the townsmen who volunteered were never good enough to find me after I reached the forest boundary."

He turned to run; however, before he could get too far under the night sky I stood before him. I awaited his body to plunge into my open arms.

"As I have said, I have only taken one life tonight. That was of a deer. However, the night is still young enough for me to have made my judgment as you have made yours."

A gasp and many mumbled prayers were all I heard from his mouth. But his mind tossed and turned at what I was going to do with him. Before I appeared before him I was nothing more than a simple man, a simple man who just happened to have many rumors spoken about him. Someone who just happened to be at the right place at the wrong time.

His mind told this all to me, as I was worked upon tying his limbs upon the crucifix he had erected in the town. I raped his mind for all knowledge that I may have needed to know before his departure from this world. He began to cry out for help only twice; however, each of those two times his eyes locked with mine. I reminded him without using spoken words that it could be far more painful if he alarmed the entire town of Heritage to his future demise.

From that point on he looked like a horse who's spirit had been broken in the cruelest of manners. He did not offer to continue with mumbled, hollow words. The words that he truly thought would help him out of his situation. His left arm was the last to be tied in place. As I watched him using every muscle in his body to breathe I knew that he would tire. Soon thereafter he would begin to die from lack of what was all around him. Air.

It seemed a fitting fate to befall someone like himself. Someone who used the words of a man who died in the same manner like a weapon. A weapon that was more terrifying than the weapons of common and uncommon men alike. Still my heart longed for more vengeance, more pain to be inflicted. I continued to think of the senseless pain Kyra was put through. Not to mention that of my child if it took its first breath.

The hour of first light drew near. Soon the people would awaken to go about their daily lives. They would act as if nothing had happened only hours before in the night. Anger filled the man who used the people. He realized there was no escape from his death. His mind then screamed to me: *I will see you burn in the pits of hell. There will be no mercy for you because even God cannot forgive someone who degrades the symbol of Jesus.*

I looked upon him once again as the sweat poured from his brow. A sadistic smile grew across my face. I knew that he would not scream out for help. He clung onto life desperately out of fear. The wasted breaths of screaming would surely cause him to blackout. I hurried into my next chore because I knew time had grown short. Anything that could catch with flame quickly, I grasped by the armful. Cloth from the stores, oil, brush and dry derbies. Nothing was safe from my rampaged search. It all found its way to the base of the crucifix.

Dawn was breaking over the horizon. Roosters began to crow their songs of morning. I heard people stirring as they woke. It was the time to end the life of a murderer, a real monster who the public had chosen to hear over their own reason. Be it because of fear, or a search for someone to blame for their problems, it mattered not to me.

The kiln caught a blaze fast and hot as it licked at his flesh. Screams of pure pain erupted through the air. They alarmed those who were waking and awakened those who still slumbered. I felt emotionless as I walked away from the horrific scene. Townsfolk rushed to the blaze and at once they began to work at extinguishing the flames, though it was far too late.

The ropes gave way and left the limp body to fall within the dying flames. But by the time questions arose I had already departed. The only thing that had mattered to me in a long time was dead. I used all of my speed to gather Kyra from our home. We then left into the woods before anyone could come calling to see if the "demon or witch" had survived.

I doubted anyone would attempt to follow me. So far it has been three long, restless days since these events transpired. I have erected a headstone crudely for Kyra and myself from a large limestone rock. It reads: *Rowan and Kyra Rasland. Till death do us part, 1788.* I used nothing but my bear hands to dig two graves, one of which I have already laid Kyra to rest peacefully in. The other I plan to use for myself. I may not be able to die but perhaps if I lay here long enough I will never awaken again. Or at least until the world ends. I now prepare myself to lay within the earth with only this book layered in cloth and hides. Clothes with coin purse at my side in the grave, I refuse to leave the coins behind to fund someone who betrayed me in Heritage.

I watch over my last view of light now, still unable to accept that Audrius is not involved in all that has happened. Yet somewhere in my mind I can hear his voice asking me if I have learned my lesson yet.

Darkness had enveloped me in its icy, cold grasp. No light. No warmth. No air. With no one to interact with my mind began to feed upon itself. Visions of family, friends, and the possibilities of what could have been tormented my every thought. Yet, at times there were brief moments of clarity. I would know where I truly was. I would also know why I had buried myself deep within the earth. During those moments of knowing I felt time shifting forward. I knew not how many years I had spent in this personal limbo; however, I had never before felt time speed past. For three hundred seventeen years I had lived above the surface. I acted as if I were human, yet knew that I would never truly be like those surrounding me.

The moment of questioning had come before me.

My intentions were to stay within my earthly slumber far away from the world of mortals. This was to ensure that no harm could befall another who I had come to care for. Yet progress had chosen a different plan for the locations of our grave sites that I had made in days past.

At first the voices did not stir me from my slumber; however, the vibrations of digging and falling trees that shook the ground caused my mind to come to itself.

The voices were muffled through the earth and stone, yet they could still be heard. "I don't know why we have to dig up these two graves. After all, they're over a hundred years old. There won't be anything left but dust and maybe some bone."

My senses came completely to me when I heard their words. They had caused my eyes to attempt opening; however, the earth had compacted hard over my face.

"It's a job. Let's start with the woman's grave first. Maybe there will be some jewelry, or something we can compensate ourselves with."

Grave robbers was my first thought. Then my mind turned to the thoughts of Kyra's grave being desecrated by two common thieves. Men who did not have the courage to prey upon living victims.

I struggled against the weight of the earth that surrounded me. Slowly I made slightly larger pockets for my body to move. Each time I heard a shovel pierce the ground to scoop away another layer of soil more rage filled me. I felt the ground bulge upward from my forceful thrashings.

"What was that?"

"I don't know. But I'm not sticking around to find out."

The last sound I heard was that of footsteps running farther away. I relaxed when I heard them become faint in the distance. I had exhausted myself, and could no longer fight against the soil. Hours, perhaps even days passed. I continued to lay their between the conscious world and that of sleep. There was a chance that I would have returned to my slumber. That is, if it were not for the rain that soaked through the dry soil. As it soaked through the soil the cracks I had made allowed the rain to soak my body.

Again I thrashed and forced the soil off of my body. Finally I built up enough force, and pierced through the ground. My lungs then took the first breath of fresh the night air. My vision was blurred under the light of the moon; however, it cleared quickly. I looked around slowly and found myself in strange surroundings. The only thing that was familiar was a weathered limestone rock. It scarcely had the remains of poorly chiseled names and the date 1788.

The forest that once thrived was nothing more than a small grove of trees. Even this grove was being dwindled due to human hands. Strange buildings had been erected along what I then considered to be a new form of cobblestone road.

After I completely pulled myself from the grave, I fished for this volume through the soil that had caved inward as I had sprung forth. Surprisingly it was still well intact. That was unlike my clothing. They were little more than rags after my slumber within the earth.

Hunger filled me to the point of pain; however, I knew that I had to find suitable clothing as well. There was no way I was willing to refuse the chance offered to explore the world that had developed around me.

Music then caught my ear. It led me closer to an odd carriage. There was no horse before it to pull the thing along its path.

"It's about bloody time you showed up. Do you have any idea how long I've been waiting around here for you? Get in the car. We're late as it is."

His accent screamed origins of Britain. Or perhaps some English settled colony. But the accent was not the old sound of English that I remembered well.

"Do you even know who I am?"

"Of course I know who you bloody are. You're the infamous Rowan Rasland, murderer of your own family and kind. Now get in the bloody car!"

He removed his dark blue hat that matched his clothing, with exception to the undershirt, which was white. Each small movement he made was an attempt at my intimidation, which I found humorous to say the least.

"How old are you? I only ask because you are lacking in certain knowledge that comes either with an experienced teacher, or with time."

"I'm old enough to know that even a pure blood, like yourself, is unable to put up much of a fight after a sleep like yours."

He opened what I know now to be a door to an automobile. Also I knew that he had called my bluff and was right, for that moment in time at least. It had taken me a week to pull myself from the grave that I rested within. Even now as I am scribing these pages I still am recovering my strength.

I climbed into the soft seat that smelled of well-maintained leather. The automobile rumbled as it pulled off onto the road. The music I found to be louder within there, music that I could not compare to anything that I had ever heard.

I spoke over the music to ask, "Where are you taking me?"

"A simple, and fair question. You are to stand before the vampire council. First they want to have a word with you. Then they will decide what should become of you."

The rumbling of the engine and the sound of the music was soothing. So soothing that once again I dosed into a slumber. At least I knew what was taking place. A trial.

May 12, 1952

I arrived on the night of the eleventh, the night I had completely awoken. I wish that I could say that I knew where I was; however, that fact escaped me, for I slumbered the entire time it took for my unwanted escort to get me here. Though I doubt it would have done me little good to remain awake. The entire area has had time to change and develop beyond my memories of one hundred seventy-four years ago.

The automobile had stopped within a building. I was quickly led to a room by another of my kind, younger I do believe. The room was very well furnished, in an old way familiar to me. A chilled wine bottle filled with blood was upon a table beside a soft, satin-covered chair. A single crystal wine glass accompanied the bottle. Books lined the wall upon dark wooden shelves. A door upon my left opened to a bed. The bed was large enough that it had to belong to royalty at one point in history or another.

Needless to say I took full advantage of the contents of the bottle. I totally ignored the glass that would have made it look more proper. It was still living, though un-tastefully cold; however, it did cure the edge of my hunger to make it bearable. A quick search of the bed chamber revealed more suitable clothing than the rags that hung off my frame after awakening. Though they are of a different cut than what I would usually choose the clothing is still comfortable.

I checked the door that brought me to these furnishings and it confirmed my suspicions. The door had been firmly locked. Though I knew that it could quickly be opened with force, I decided to allow it to remain so. This was only due to the elegant hospitality of my unknown host or hosts as it may be.

Therefore, I wisely used my time. I began to read the volumes of knowledge at my disposal.

The night of the eleventh quickly transformed into the morning of the twelfth as I read of wars in foreign countries, new inventions, inoculation against disease, deciphering of Egyptian scrip, paintings being created through mechanical wonders called cameras, and so forth.

Though I did find these things to be fascinating, sometimes very difficult to take seriously or believe, one event has captured my mind. A simple monk, named Gregor Mendel, found discrete, hereditary elements by crossing various types of peas with one another in 1865. This and Charles Darwin's theory of evolution support one another. It is of no matter how strange and odd I think it may be as of now. It offers me a chance to ponder what I am. How a creature like myself could come to be after countless centuries of evolution had taken place after who or whatever was the first.

The sun now begins to set. Footsteps are drawing near. Now must be the time for me to meet those who have provided for me. Strange though how these judges would treat me so well just to have a trial over my past actions.

May 14, 1952

The entire night I spent with the unknown council while we traded questions and answers; however, I must begin where I left off.

The footsteps stopped at the wood-engraved door. A loud click, followed by the door opening, revealed the same vampire that brought me to these strange surroundings.

"I see you decided to stay. It shows good character to be willing to face those who are going to judge you."

I still do believe that I was expected to be nervous about this meeting. I still do not know why. Simply put, the council tries to govern the affairs of all vampires, even those beyond its control, with little success. But this I did not know yet.

I was led through a long, dark hall, unlike that of a manor or castle; however, it would still send a chill that would bother those of mundane mortal lines. The hall gave way to a large chamber with its walls covered with heavy drapes and ancient tapestries. These tapestries depicted battles I knew not of. Others still displayed animals and creatures now thought to be mere myths.

A long table, almost the span of the room itself, sat in the middle with thirteen chairs behind it, all occupied. A fourteenth chair sat in front of this table isolated from all other furniture.

"Please take the seat, Rowan."

No audible words were spoken purposely. It was to display the power that was in the room behind the table. I politely followed through with the request. Only then did I project a word of sincere gratefulness to them all. However, it was not done one at a time. I did so all at once as a counter move, as if we were playing a mental version of chess.

As if it were an unexpected move to be played, they all stopped. They then glared at me, hoping to catch a glimpse of my soul. When it was found to be a wasted effort they began to look at one another, questioning what should be done now.

Then the one in the center spoke. I deduced that he had to be the leader. "Enough games. Do you know why we have brought you here?"

"According to the escort that you provided for me it is because I am the infamous Rowan. The one who has little qualms of killing my own kind when the need arises."

Silence. Their faces did not hold shock; however, I was sure that they did not expect the answer I had given.

"What of you family? Your mother and father? What of your chosen mate and protector? Were their deaths senseless or were they a necessity?"

"I did not kill them."

"Not with your hands. But was it not you who ran to the humans? Did you not tell them of your dark blood lines in attempts to save your own soul? Hatred is the cause I see for this. Hatred of your parents and yourself."

"No! I did not wish to save my soul because of where my lineage came from. I instead wished to save the life of an innocent infant who was to be a sacrifice to ensure my continuing changes. I could not hate my parents, or even Margrette. They were my family. However, fear at that time was a different subject. I did fear what I was destined to become."

"And what of Audrius, Lucious and William? The three most feared of our kind. Do you deny that you lived with them? Do you deny that you followed the teachings of that lunatic Audrius willingly?"

"Audrius has in one way or another been the direct and sometimes indirect cause of my entire life falling apart. He forced me to become what I am. His entire lessons went against my entire beliefs about life and love. Audrius killed my first true love, and my second true friend ever. He ordered William and Lucious to kill me because I refused to live as he taught. I did slaughter them both. I took their lives as I would have any other prey. I would do it again to Audrius. In fact, I have searched for him for this exact purpose for almost three hundred years."

"Fear can be the root of many actions. But are you also claiming that fear drove you to kill Lucious and William?"

"No, rage induced by the torture and death of love is what drove me to kill them. You may call it murder. I say it was a just punishment, though it was not painful enough I am sure."

"You have admitted to killing without remorse. Is this not heartlessness?"

"Enough of your questions. You are all repeating my statements as inquiry. Pass your judgment if you truly deem yourselves to be in positions to do so. Just know I will not lay down and die like someone who fears your decisions."

"You are greatly outnumbered here, and yet you would fight us all?"

"Yes, though the odds are in your favor. Thirteen to one. I am sure that I would fall under your blows. But my question is how many will I take with me? Two? Three? Perhaps even four if I am lucky. Who here wants to be in these numbers? Who here wishes to perish beside me? Who wishes to perish due to a choice made because you all who feel that a right has been given unto you to judge another? The only person who has right to judge me here is myself."

The silence had fallen over the room again. I would catch a stray thought here and there. The ones that I heard focused upon possibility of me bluffing. They were all very strong. Almost strong enough to have covered their mental bickering; however, I still managed to hear those occasional words that passed between them. I stood and removed my overcoat. It was placed neatly upon the chair behind me.

"I am by far not bluffing! Let it be known by the survivors of this conflict that I was the first who directly opposed your judgments. These happenings shall spread among those who follow only because they fear a punishment given by their equals of blood. It may take centuries to have another do what is about to be done. However, have faith that another will come. They will keep coming until this ideal is abandoned."

"Wait. Our choice has been made. We find that your actions, past and present, were a matter of survival. The same survival that drives us all to feed upon man as a parasite. You are free to go, Rowan; however, we would like for you to stay and feast with us this evening."

My trial ended there with no further questions asked of my deeds of the past. They then wished to focus upon my future. But this questioning lacked the harassment of the trial. They all offered current events to bring me completely up to speed with their world. Possible professions were offered. As well as collectors of antiquities. "For surely a vampire of my age has at least some relics stashed away in secret."

An endless supply of their chilled blood in wine bottles were emptied and so progressed the night. Dawn now approaches as I finish penning this down. Today I rest here not knowing what awaits me in the setting of this sun.

May 17, 1952

I had woken early on the fifteenth. So early that the sun still hung in the sky. I knew my welcome had ended. I dressed myself within another suite offered by my host. After I clasped this book in my hand I prepared to take my leave; however, I felt that it was only proper that I informed someone of my departure. Therefore, I set out of my quarters to do exactly that. Traveling the way I was escorted the previous evening, I thought that the council room was the first and best place to encounter at least a servant. Yet, as I entered the room that once held the decor of ancient tapestries and elegant furniture, I found it was barren and dust covered.

There was not even as much as a footstep within the thin layer of dirt that covered the floor. It was as if it was nothing more than a dream. Not even a slight scent, including my own, could be found to disagree with what my eyes told me. I simply dismissed it as if they all left after the festivities, taking everything with them except for the furnishings of the room I occupied. And so I turned to take my leave, which would cause me to pass the guest room. At first glance I found it odd that the door was open. It was and always had been a habit of mine to close doors behind me. I checked the air as I walked forward. All that I found was the same damp musk scent that clung to every surface.

I intended to correct a mistake I obviously had made. Yet when I walked by I found that the door I had thought to be so painstakingly hand-carved to detail was no longer there. There was not even a sign of its hinges. The room I had left only moments ago was no more. It was devoid. Untouched by mortal or immortal hands for years so that the dust and cobwebs could have gathered as they had done.

I did not attempt to explain how this was so. I had seen strange things before; however, this was beyond all I had witnessed. I left the building confused and uncertain of anything that had happened. For hours I wandered the streets. I silently thought over the evidence to support the trial. Every possibility went through my mind as I tried to explain what had happened. Even thoughts of it being a dream, or me going crazy from such a long slumber, entered the realm of possibilities.

I continued to wander aimlessly with these thoughts that weighed upon my mind. I even questioned how I knew the date, and if it, too, was nothing more than a figment of imagination. Yet a stand with an old man behind it held the answer to this question. Periodicals filled the shelves that surrounded him. In front of him laid newspapers that all bore the name of *The Heritage Times* and the date of May 15, 1952.

I spun around and looked at all of the lights and buildings. I thought, *This is my Heritage?* What a massive township she had grown into. It was almost enough to drive me to laughter. I continued to think about the small trade town I helped to firmly set its roots down. Had it grown into such a sight?

I neared the brink of insanity when I heard a voice out of nowhere speak to me.

"This is not your Heritage anymore."

The voice was female, and very pleasant to listen to; however, when I spun around to look for the source I found men and women who stared at me. It was as if I were strangely out of place. This caused me to look over my own body. I found that the suit I knew I had dressed myself in only hours ago was nothing more than the rags I had brought with me from the grave.

I had been pushed to the point of collapsing to my knees, to laugh like an African hyena at my appearance, at my experiences, and at my very existence. I questioned who I really was and what I really was flooded my mind. Was I nothing more than an insane human? Or was I truly an insane vampire?

"Enough of this."

Two strong, yet smooth, hands of silk spun me round. She glared at me with blue eyes.

"Do you not see that this is what they planned for you? They knew facing you with force would only cause you to react in a manner that would endanger them. However, after a sleep as long as yours it leaves your mind vulnerable to be manipulated. It is like that of a child who has been kept in a cage for most of its life, only to then be set free in a world it does not know."

Her eyes were so very soft; however, every minute the light shifting caused them to change colors from the blue to yellow then red and so forth. Her eyes I found were the only thing I was able to focus upon. All else was nonexistent, like we stood outside of time's forever forward motion.

"Come with me, my poor child. Do not ask questions right now. Just come with me."

And so it was as if I were a child who was led away by a protective parent come to save the day, or night as it was.

No other words were given to me. Just her satin smooth hand within mine that carefully guided me on a path I felt she knew well.

That evening was spent with her in yet again an unknown location. However, this time I was not left alone. I fell asleep with my head comfortably upon her leg while she gently stroked my hair. She hummed ever so softly. The sound filled my thoughts and dreams. She reminded me of a siren of legend who would lure sailors to their doom. Even my slumber within the earth was not as peaceful as this sleep. Nor can I remember a time since my childhood when I did not have a care or a memory haunt me to the point of waking.

I awoke on the night of the sixteenth and found my mind was swimming. Nothing made sense. The woman who had come to my aid was no longer with me. I had been laid to rest upon a bed trimmed in gold and crimson. The rags I had proudly wore as a suit of common fashion now were stripped of me. There were no signs of the existence of such foul things about me in this place. Had I been dreaming? Was I dead? Had any of it ever been real? I could not answer my own simple questions. I sat up and pushed the coverings off of my body. I felt the madness seep back into my mind through the dark cracks of uncertainty.

"Reality is a strange thing to question, let alone live in. Some things are far simpler to not question. Nor seek out the truths of. But this is very hard for us to understand. We defy all that reality has been thought to be."

The sweet voice yet again forced my madness away. I forced myself to look away from only her eyes. I wanted to study each detail that complimented and completed this figure. Her face was that of a painted masterpiece. It was without flaw, with soft, delicate features that matched her thin body. Thin, crimson cloth hung from her frame trimmed in gold lace. I questioned if she were a goddess of ancient times. The only accessory she lacked was a string of flowers woven in her light golden hair. Even it bore many highlights of white and silver.

"Who are you?" This was all I could ask. Her mere presence made me feel as if I had little right to question her.

"I am known as Xillis, and I came to save you from yourself."

"Why?"

"Because I, like yourself, have defied the ones who try to make law where survival is all that matters."

"The council."

"Yes, the council. That is what they like to call themselves. It is such a hypocritical term to use. They counsel no one. Try to help no one. Yet they do not resist temptations to judge all who they deem have broken their laws and traditions that only its members adhere to."

"Why not just kill me? Why torture me with the magic they used on me?"

"You were willing to fight them physically. You bypassed the grandeur that was intended to intimidate you into submission of their will. They would have lost power by physical force due to the feral nature that you still possess deep inside."

"You are saying they are domesticated like an animal then."

She laughed as if my words were intended to be humorous and jest for amusement.

"Domesticated...I have never heard it spoken of like that. But yes. By their own choice it is so. There is no question that we as a race are far different than the race of normal man. We are predators, and like predators we have to fight each other. Sometimes these fights are to the death to ensure our own survival. However, the council sees the race as being more sophisticated than the predator nature we all have. They have suppressed this nature so much by drinking their chilled blood in bottles, blood given by willing human donors so that they have become domesticated as you have put it."

Xillis sat upon the edge of the bed as we continued this talk.

"How long has this been happening?"

"The chilled blood is only recent; however, the willing donors and this council of the sophisticated judges began ninety-six years ago. This is all I know. The exact cause of this way of thinking has never been made known to me. Nor anyone else outside of this party.

"They tried to judge you? Or am I incorrect by assuming this?"

"Yes, they did try in the beginning. This was before they realized that all of their ages were still young to me."

I questioned if my own age was a youth to her; however, I did not ask out of respect. Yet I still received an answer.

"I am far older than you, Rowan. But your power is far stronger than what it should be for only four hundred eighty years."

"How can this be?"

"It is a simple matter to explain. You were born a pure blood and not darkened like so many others of this time. Also I believe their names were William and Lucious, if I am not mistaken."

My mind flashed to all those many years ago when my beloved Elania was taken from me. When she was butchered like a common piece of meat.

"Yes, you fought them. You killed them. You killed them like prey and took their blood. Their power became yours that night and it will always be this way."

I shook off the memory. I wanted to keep myself from reliving the pain of her loss. That would only lead from memory to memory of pain. It was pointless to relive all of them. As I thought of this Xillis laid her hand upon my knee.

"Such pain you still have in your heart. Not just for her, but for them all. I only wish that I had found you instead of Audrius. Your memories would still be sad sometimes. But you would at least have happier thoughts of them. Instead of thoughts of them being stained in blood."

I shot off of the bed and looked at her with a mixed expression of disbelief and rage.

"Yes, I know of him. Audrius came to me ages ago. It was when he was younger than you are now. He sought after support and approval of the beliefs he was taught by his master."

The emotions faded and left only more questions that I did not know the answers to.

"He never told you? Rowan, he is not like you and I. He was not born into this existence. Audrius is a darkened soul; however, this does not mean he is weak. As far as I now he is the oldest darkened one to date."

"What of the master?"

"This is enough for now. We are going to have plenty of time to continue this conversation. I have a gift for you."

Xillis stood and glided across the floor. She looked as if she never took a step. She disappeared behind a delicate hand-painted changing screen. When she reemerged her arms held a suit of black. It was cut with a hint of the old styles I had witnessed come and go. Footwear that shined like a black mirror.

A pocket watch of new craftsmanship. Last but not least a ring that was far older than I.

"I cannot accept such things, though they are very nice."

"What else would you do? Continue to cover yourself with remnants of grave cloth. Besides, this is the first step I can take in helping you adjust to these surroundings. Do not refuse the offer of help out of pride. There are no strings attached."

I could not argue a counter point. Xillis was very aware of this as we both smiled. Each article I adorned until I tied the last shoe lace. I then stood before her looking like a new man.

"It is all very nice. I would ask how you happened across everything that feels it was made for me personally; however, it would be impolite."

"Every woman has to have some secrets. This is true even with vampires. Now then, if you would check your coat pocket you will find the real gift."

It puzzled me; however, I could tell by the look within her eyes that she enjoyed the game that had started. I kept my eyes upon Xillis as she watched my movements with anticipation. My hand emerged with a crisp folded paper in it. The excitement built within her to the point that I knew she could take no more delays. I unfolded it. I read it quickly. The document told me it was a land deed. Other than this fact, the location meant little to me.

"You now have ownership of the grave you came from and the grave of Kyra."

My eyes lifted from the paper to her smiling face.

"You read my thoughts when we first met?"

"No. You talked in your sleep. After a bit of searching I found where they were at. It was good timing. A new city hall is going to be built no more than eighty yards away. No one had claimed responsibility for them thus far and she was to be relocated. I also took the liberty of purchasing a half acre of surrounding land. You never can tell if you may need more space for reasons of disappearing in the future."

It was truly a touching gift to give; however, I am sure a morbid one to give a normal person. I could not find words enough to show my gratitude. Yet this alone seemed to have made all effort invested worth while to Xillis. She then excused herself. She told me that she would return in a few days. I could not question her, nor attempt to tell her to stay with me; therefore, I now wait patiently. While I wait there can be time taken to learn what I can about this strange new world through printed periodicals.

Also, recording this in such detail has taken at least a few hours of concentration. It always does to remember exact conversations and usage of words. I end this by saying I am, and always will be grateful to Xillis. However, I get the distinct impression that I am the first person she has had contact with in untold ages. At least, contact that is of a benevolent nature.

February 19, 1962

Time passes so very quickly when you are happy. Also there is little to record about one's life when there are no worries or concerns to eat away at thoughts of the future. No nightmarish memories or dreams have haunted me since my rescue by Xillis. For nine years, three months and two days we have lived together. During this time we have shared our darkest secrets and desires. She has been like an older sister to me all of this time; however, like all things time does bring an end to them.

My time of rehabilitation has ended. As well has my time of learning the secrets that the council had used against me. The secrets that made me question my own sanity.

My heart aches to think about being separated from Xillis. The pain within her eyes confirms that she feels the same. Yet to quote her: "There comes a time when we must stand upon our own two feet and continue to walk the path chosen either by us or for us."

We also had our final talk of Audrius. I now understand why he is the way he was.

"Rowan, do you remember when you first arrived in my home, you asked what of the master of Audrius?"

"Yes."

"Here is the tale as I know it to be. As it was told to me centuries ago. He was only known as the Ancient. Rumors said he was older than myself now. The last of a clan long forgotten. A clan who thought themselves to be gods over all life. This belief is what sealed the destruction of the clan. Far too many humans and vampires had been angered by them. Thus, as the humans sought out all vampires, we sought out the clan to element the problems at hand. Our hunt lasted far longer than the humans. It lasted until only one remained. He was thought to be harmless, a child in appearance. He played the part well from the stories that are sometimes told. He was left for dead with no one having the suspicion that he was already like we are and of untold age. Using the fact that he appeared to be a child, the Ancient wandered as an orphan. He also used all of the charm and mental prows he was taught. It did not take long for a family of higher standards to adopt him out of projected pity. The family's oldest son was the only one who could see through the guise. The thought of a human seeing through what he showed himself to be is intriguing to me. It had to be the same for the Ancient. He planned the move well.

"On an evening when even the slaves were asleep, no one survived the night except for the oldest son who still fell victim by being forced to be an immortal servant. It took years for this darkened soul to plot his revenge. All the while he learned of his new self. On a night near dawn's break when the thunder clapped loud the son made his move. His master sat asleep in what was the favorite chair of the son's father. The sword had been sharpened so that it sliced through the air quietly. The master's eyes opened only after the blade cut through his throat; however, by then there was no way of stopping the momentum of the blow. The Ancient's physical body died in those early morning hours. But the son had refused the hunger within him since his creation. The blood that gushed from his master's decapitated body sang to him with power and promise of ending the suffering. This is the moment that all becomes unclear. It is not known if the blood of his master drove him to insanity, or if Audrius is the embodiment of the Ancient possessed by such potent and dark-natured blood."

The possibilities presented by Xillis have made me question exactly who I have hated this entire time. Whether it be insanity or possession in the form that I have known all of this time almost makes me feel pity for him. Yet the memories of how my life was taken from me time and time again sometimes directly and sometimes not refuses to allow me to forgive and forget.

The time has come. The belongings that I have acquired from Xillis are all packed. I have already went to say my goodbyes to her. I was still unsure of where to go or what to do; however, Xillis was nowhere to be found. Only an envelope was in her bed chambers with my name upon it. Opening it has revealed more of Xillis' compassion. Though I have been questioning what to do she has already taken steps to ensure a firm stepping stone within the outside world. The documents of my identity have me as of now being Samuel Rasland. The money she left for my beginning, though uncounted, appears to at least be two thousand American dollars. If not more.

A letter of well wishing written by her hand expresses more emotion than I have ever known her to show. I would record it verbatim, like so many things I do, if it were not for secrets I know she does not wish to leave me about her true self. Instead I choose to only say I have destroyed it. I keep the written contents locked deep within my mind where none shall pry it loose. I shall deeply miss you, Xillis.

February 22, 1962

I once again find myself by fireside for light; however, it is now different than before. For three nights I have wandered in search of a place to bring my new emergence into this world. Until this night only hours before, I felt as if I would continue to be lost without Xillis by my side. However, a single discovery has filled me with confidence that I will continue on. A dilapidated church built in old-fashioned stone I now call home. Though it truly needs the hands of experienced craftsmen to restore it to what it once was, the building reminds me of myself being lost in a world that has forgotten about its existence.

There are no roadways running here. An overgrowth of trees and various plant life have overtaken the grounds; however, this shrouds the place in an air of mystery. I see great potential for this home. Yet the repairs and upkeep afterward are not going to be a cheap undertaking. If only I had saved more than a book and the same purse of old coins.

The coins. I never took the coins out of the grave.

February 24, 1962

I rushed back to my own grave sight. I dreaded the sight of Kyra's grave; however, I hoped that I could still retrieve these pieces of history that had to be rare now. Some of them are far older than myself. I expected to have difficulty locating where I had rested. Yet as I neared the area of the limestone rock I saw how much had changed.

The new city hall for this small town of Heritage Landing had been completed. It looked as if it had been used for years now. To the left of the city hall now was fenced with hand-forged steel with spear points at the tips. The rock had been removed. A chiseled headstone sat in its place.

As I opened the gate the cold steel creaked and popped loudly. It echoed through the night air. The ground where I emerged had been filled and made to look as if I had never slept there. I thought it was to be another dig that I hated to make. Xillis had been the one to pay for this and I knew it; however, she never told me. It was as if it were a final going-away present that I was meant to find as a surprise. It was a terrible thought to have, having to upset it after so much work was put into it. I knelt and prepared to claw up the earth when a voice came from behind me.

"I knew you would be back for these."

I stood and turned slowly. I already knew who was going to be behind me. His blond hair was still cut short; however, it had been greased back as he continued to wear clothing that was out of date—just like the first time that I had met him. He did not know how to change and adjust to the years that passed. In his hand he held a simple black cloth bag. It rung with the sound of silver and gold as he placed it within his coat pocket.

"Let me guess, the council wants another meeting to find out why I am not insane or dead by now."

"Not quite, old chap. I'm here to kill you. To send a message to Xillis to stay out of the affairs of the council. To let her know next time it will be her answering instead of the product of her actions."

"Typical. One person does not conform to a set belief and they are considered dangerous to the whole. I have seen churches and kingdoms alike fall for the same reason throughout the course of time. I am feeling rather generous, so here is the deal I am willing to make with you. Give me my rightful property. Then turn, walk away and I will let you live to see tomorrow."

"Courageous words. But is the speaker courageous enough, or ignorant enough to attempt to back them up?"

"Courage has nothing to do with this situation. This is nothing more than primal survival of the fittest in the purest of conditions. Indulge me by telling me your name so I at least know who I am about to kill."

"Devon…Devon the Dark as I like to be called."

It was so very hard to contain my laughter. Devon had already provided me with so much amusement. Yet the laughter was easily forgotten as he made a leap for me. He had actually thought that it was going to be so easy to strike me down. The shocked look upon Devon's face when his feet touched the ground told me that he expected me to still be standing still. He then spun around for another attack. But as his eyes reached my face I struck with a closed fist upon his face. The force of the impact threw him back upon Kyra's headstone.

"Tisk, tisk, Devon the Dark. You actually expected this to be an easy feat to undertake. You really are new at this, are you not?"

His anger had grown far too great for common sense to say stop or run. With what can only be compared to a war cry, he was up again. He leapt through the air like a cat who tried pouncing upon a bird. His hands were stretched above his head as the wail continued. This time, however, it ended. Before Devon's feet touched the earth my hand was around his throat to redirect his motion so that he landed upon his back. He tore at my hair and pounded upon my back; however, it was too late. My fangs had already pierced his throat. I drained him as quickly as I could. Only when his body went limp did my grasp lessen. I reached for the black bag that held my coins.

I stood back upon my feet. I felt the heaviness within my body once again like I had when I was still new at this game; however, it faded quickly and then I knew there was a difference between Devon and the two companions of Audrius. Devon was only a darkened one, a young one at that.

His body looked as dry as that of a mummy in a museum display. Though I had already retrieved my property there was now unfinished business at hand.

While I still had the empty streets and shadows of night to work with, I scooped the husk onto my shoulder and ran as fast as I could back to Heritage.

It took hours for me to scour over the city before I found the scent of Devon that faded. It also had the scent of chilled blood upon it. I tracked through damp and dark alleyways. Some areas it seemed even the rats were afraid to travel. Finally I had found a building that once appeared to be a large apartment complex. A large sign nailed across the door read: CONDEMNED.

To the senses of other people I am sure that it appeared as if the building was truly vacant. Even boards covered the windows from the inside. No detail had been overlooked. Yet with my eyes and ears I could tell that there was much more. I saw the faint glow of light between the cracks of the boards. I heard the voices of those who thought they were safe within their home.

I kicked the door in by physical force. It caused a thundering echo that traveled through the building to announce my arrival. The lobby was empty, showing no signs of anything alive or dead near. When I neared the stairwell a slender, well-dressed young man met me. He tried to adjust his suit into place as he stumbled down the last few stairs.

"I am terribly sorry, sir. But I must ask you to leave. This is private property and you are trespassing."

The sweet stench of fear rolled off of his body as his heart pounded with terror. His eyes widened as he realized whom I carried on my shoulder, lifeless.

"Where are your masters? What floor are they on?"

"Would you be so kind to wait here while I announce your presence to the lords and ladies properly."

He turned to rush up the stairs; however, before his foot could land upon the first step I stopped him.

"No. You take me to them now, or I will have two corpses to deliver at their feet."

Until this moment I had not known how fear-filled a mortal soul could be. He answered me with a very simple answer after the choking sensation left his throat.

"Very well, sir. Please follow me."

His steps were deliberately slow. When I read his thoughts I knew why: *If I don't bring him to the lords and ladies then he will kill me. But if bring him up there I am a dead man still.*

I realized how their servants were treated. I placed a firm hand upon his shoulder to stop him from the continued climb upward.

"If you have been threatened with death by them then why do you continue to serve them? Why not leave here and start a life where it is not necessary to fear those you work for? What payment could be worth such torment?"

"I am provided free room and board here, sir. It's much better than a street life. Plus, if I serve faithfully long enough I have been promised to be given their type of power."

"Have you ever seen anyone who has served well enough to receive what you speak of as a reward?"

"No, sir. I am told Devon was the last one. But that was long before my time."

"You have proven my point. It is true that Devon here was not always the way he was a few hours ago. But even after this reward was given to him he still served them. It was just in a different manner than you. It is slavery with death being the only true freedom."

"Even if what you say is true, if I tried to leave then I would be hunted and killed. If by some miracle I was not found and had the chance to settle down and start a family it would only be a matter of time before my children, grandchildren and so on would be stalked and made to pay for my choice of treason."

"Let me worry about that. That is, if you want to escape this life of eternal servitude."

"Follow me, sir. Those who you seek are up here."

Confusion had set into his eyes as he turned and led me up the fourth flight of stairs. He paused before leading me on. He was not sure what fate would be worse to accept. I am sure it appeared to him that damnation lay within either path. Once again he ensured that the tail suit was in place. Then he walked in through the doorway with me at his heels.

"Lords, ladies, presenting…"

His upright formal face went blank as he looked back at me. He realized that terror had made him forget to ask for my title.

"There is no need for introductions, Patrick. We all know the exploits of this Rowan all too well."

A female was the one who spoke—a female I had never seen before. My eyes scanned the large room made by removing many walls of what would have been separate apartments. I counted the other thirteen plus this new one.

"What brings you here, Rowan?"

I slammed the husk of Devon upon the floor. The force caused a hard vibration that could be felt by everyone's feet.

"I have brought you back the executioner and a message. The message is this: You all have failed. I am still alive and far from insane thanks to another who defies your will."

"Yes. Xillis. She can be annoying when interfering in our affairs. Yet out of respect of her age we allow it from time to time."

"You lie poorly. It is not out of respect that you allow it. It is out of fear. The same fear that prevents all of you from attempting to attack me now."

The room felt as if it had started to shift. A tingling crept over my mind. Vertigo was trying to take hold of me. Her eyes never left me. However, before I lost comprehension of my environment I summoned all of my will. My eyes locked with hers and all I focused upon was searing, hot pain. It seemed like eternity was passing us by. When I thought that I could not stand the disorientation longer, it ceased. A high-pitched scream caused what little glass that remained in the windows to quiver, then crack and shatter.

The room returned to what it should have been. The woman clinched her head within her hands.

"Sorry to disappoint all of you. But I have learned a few new tricks myself. Now that my point has been made to where none of you can question my intentions of surviving my own way, I will take my leave."

I turned to leave and found Patrick behind me in disbelief. He had never seen someone confront them and live through such an event.

"Rowan! We will never...stop hunting you!"

I turned back and found that the woman had stood to her feet. She still tried to recover from the spike of mental pain. I smiled at what I still feel was an empty threat.

"To tell you the truth, I would not have it any other way. After all, where else could I find so many people so tightly wrapped up within their own egos."

With nothing else to say I turned back to the stairwell and started to make my departure.

"Well, Patrick my boy, it seems as if we now have a new position needing to be filled. Tonight is your lucky night."

I heard his heart begin to pound. The scent of nervous sweat rolled through the air.

"With all due respect, lords and ladies, I have been made a better offer. So I must decline your offer and also resign."

I had frozen in mid-step as I listened to thoughts of how he should be punished for refusal of such an honor.

He was trapped. He had known that he would be, yet he still had taken the first step to be rid of burdens that should never have been placed upon him. They would have done many unspeakable horrors to his body. All slowly till his death finally released him if it were not for my final words.

"Come, Patrick. Dawn is quickly approaching. We have many affairs to tend to before the next night falls."

He stayed so close to me as we left that I felt his breath on the back of my neck. We both walked out under a sky painted in hues of pink and ever-so-slight highlights of orange. Patrick sighed a deep breath of relief. I knew he had expected to die walking away; however, he expected that I was his new employer, as he called it.

"Mr. Rowan, where is it I will be staying now that I am within your services?"

"First just call me Rowan. No mister, no lord, no master, just Rowan. Second, here is the situation I am currently in. I have very little money. The place I call home is a church, falling apart and forgotten by time. Much like myself. I have no fortune or wealth of ancient artifacts to fall back on. All I possess is a small bag of coins I have had for centuries. I doubt they will bring much. This is my life as it stands currently. No luxuries, and no real means of acquiring them quickly. I cannot guarantee what tomorrow or the next day will bring. You are much better off starting a new life. A life better suited for someone who does not have the curse of constant time."

"But…I don't have anywhere else to go. I'm not even sure who my parents are. Or where they are. I'm an orphan."

I had attempted to drive him away. To make him see that life around an unnatural like myself is not pleasant; however, I learned I was now all he had to look to for aid of any kind. I sighed deeply before I turned away again.

"Come along. Come along. For now we will be together until we both can get ourselves into a better position."

Now I must admit that Patrick was very useful to have at my side. At daybreak when the entire city began coming to life after its deep slumber, he was able to take me to the different services. The same services that his keepers had used over and over again, though some were very deceptive. I found that the coins possessed were indeed rare. But it would be pointless to attempt to sell them without an auction, to highly reputable private collectors of high wealth. The deceptive means were best for now.

I choose not to list how and exactly where these events transpired; however, I will say I intend to repay the banks involved in the loans.

By early afternoon I had the funds to begin restoration of my chosen home. After a few well-placed phone calls all was ready. The restoration was due to start immediately. The property the church sat upon, as well as a great amount of the forest that surrounded the building, was officially mine.

Patrick made the comment that with such powers at my disposal we should make a trip to Las Vegas. Discussing this with him told me that gambling was too much like work to his old employers. Therefore I end this here by saying I used my advantages once upon a noble. Why not do it again upon a noble of different breed and time.

April 30, 1962

Las Vegas was a dreadfully noisy and bright place. It was truly a city that never sleeps. Perhaps I still have too many old values of peace at night, when all is still except for the night creatures.

Yet this is beside the point of this record. I am now back in Heritage, and back to an almost completed home. Though I have made changes to the original design, there was still time to add the wings I desired. Obviously the trip was a successful one. I am now rid of Patrick. I split the winnings with him, 75/25. This I think was more than enough to make him be considered a wealthy man; however, it was not a moment too soon. I caught him reading this volume as if it were his right to do so.

I could have killed him for such intrusion; however, I could not because of guilt. It was, after all, I who had placed him here in this situation to begin with. I have now learned a valuable lesson of trusting people in this day and age. A man's word is no longer as good as gold; therefore, I now plan on keeping this book in hiding again. I will only record key events that should be remembered—not only by me, but by anyone reading this. If that time ever comes.

I now prepare to use my powers to help others in need. To make the best out of what I have viewed too long as a curse. Laws were made for everyone. Yet I am seeing that only the rich benefit from them. Perhaps I can change this one person at a time as a lawyer.

March 12, 1976

My life as Samuel Rasland was going well until a few days ago. The law office I opened has been a great benefit to those in need of justice at a fair price. I assured that even the poorest of people could afford these services. That is, depending upon the severity of need involved.

Yet I luckily have seen the possibilities of such events happening; therefore, I have already prepared for the untimely death of Samuel. He will leave all possessions to his father, Rowan.

Let me begin with what made me make such decisions.

After Patrick received his part of the winnings, he did move on. He settled down with a fine young woman by the name of Heather in the small town of Heritage Landing. They married quickly, before 1962 was over. By early in 1963 they had a son named Jon. I believe he was named after Heather's father, perhaps grandfather? However, the money I had given Patrick had corrupted him. Not to forget the abuse he had suffered from the council. For thirteen years poor Heather took the abuse he gave her. All the while she tried to protect Jon from it. October 5, 1975 was when Mrs. Heather Dunn walked into my office with her twelve-year-old son, Jon. She sought a divorce from Patrick.

I thought of refusing the case; however, when she removed her sunglasses and the purple, blue, and black shades of bruised flesh were exposed to me, I knew I could not do such a thing. I in part had made him this way.

I used all of my resources and favors I had acquired while being involved with the field of law to push Heather's divorce through quickly. On January 15, 1976, it was finalized. It left Jon in custody of his mother. Patrick was only to have visitations for Jon's protection.

February passed quickly without worry. Then on the tenth day of March, Patrick found his way into my office, intoxicated. He tried to bargain the life of his ex-wife for his silence. He threatened to tell of my darker half that was unseen to the general public, the public who thought of me as a very good member of the population.

With Patrick's first appearance I tried to pass it off to myself that it was only the alcohol that talked, that he would not remember the conversation when he sobered. Yet it was only wishful thinking. He returned the next day to reinforce his deal while his words did not slur together in a drunken manner.

While Patrick ranted to me, showing me the type of person he had become, I decided no matter the cost at hand I was not going to be played as a pawn. No words that I could have spoken would have pleased Patrick's ears; therefore, I sat silent until he finished.

"I'll give you to the twelfth to meet my demands. Otherwise, the headlines of the paper will read interesting when I expose you."

This was on the morning of the tenth. It left me with only two days to get all of the affairs of a dead man in order. Samuel Rasland's will was easy enough to write and make legal. It had been done long before this matter. It was bringing his father, Rowan, back to life that would have proven to be difficult. But I have been one to prepare for the next move long before it had to be made. After all was taken care of, on the morning of the eleventh there was a phone call made by Samuel. He complained of chest pains. By the time I was found, there was no questioning medical science about my death.

The will I left upon my body stated that I was to be rushed to the funeral home of my choice. Of course there was only one in town. Instructions were left for my immediate burial the next day. This was to be done without preparation of the body or wake to allow the public to view the corpse. It was a simple task to sneak away from the casket. It left me to attend to matters that needed to be brought to an end.

It was late afternoon when I began to stalk my prey. He was leaving the bar in Heritage when I found him. Patrick was barely able to walk. It made him a very easy target to follow. I am unsure of the time when he finally arrived at the apartment he called home.

Patrick was so drunk that he did not even close the door behind him. Silently I followed his stumbling frame until he fell upon the bed. He already seemed to be lifeless.

TIMELESS: AS THE WORLD STANDS STILL

"Hello, Patrick."

He pushed himself up and glared at me with red eyes blinking. He probably tried to rid himself of blurred sight.

"Samuel? That is what you call yourself? Right? Oh…who cares. Have you finished the job?"

The stench of his breath was unbelievable. He had to be near the point of poisoning himself with what smelled like cheap gin.

"Almost. You see, my poor drunken orphan, Samuel is dead. I just have to tie up loose ends that could prove otherwise. That is, if anyone would listen to such babbling."

He started to fall over into a drunken slumber when I caught him by the shirt collar. I then lifted him off of the bed.

"I saved you from injustice just for you to become worse than those who I saved you from. But there is no need to explain such things to you because you will never remember. Especially now."

Patrick's eyes rolled back into his head. I thought that at least he would feel no pain. I did not want him to feel pain because I still blamed myself for his new behavior. With a flash of speed I ripped open his throat. I let his alcohol-thinned blood spill onto my tongue. A gasp then made me pull away.

I am unsure how long he had watched my actions and listened to my words. Jon, Patrick's twelve-year-old son, turned to run from the scene that I thought had been planned so well. He stumbled over his own feet as he tried to get away from the grizzly scene. But it had given me the few seconds I needed to appear before him like a ghost. With his father's blood running down my face I snatched him by the neck and brought him to my eye level.

"You have seen nothing here, boy. You heard nothing. Do not say a word about this or else a curse will befall you for the rest of your days, child."

I do not believe I will ever forget the look of terror within his eyes as I let him go. He ran without looking back once. I knew I had to be quick. My time was limited because of this. Luckily Patrick kept an empty steamer trunk by bedside. It took very little to position his body to fit perfectly along with the throw rug he bled upon. I lifted the trunk and rushed from the one-bedroom apartment. I was forced to hide within the shadows. I heard the faint sounds of sirens. If I tried to move the trunk I would be found.

It was grueling to wait for nightfall to come before I continued on; however, I did so to guarantee that I would have an easier time. The funeral home was empty of life when I returned. I placed Patrick's corpse into my coffin. He would be buried tomorrow morning. I knew all was well.

The morning headlines of the *Heritage Times* read: *Respected lawyer, Samuel Rasland, accused of murder and disappearance of client's ex-husband.* It was an unexplained mystery. How could a dead man kill another? According to the police, the investigation would remain open. Samuel was accused by young Jon of the supposed butchering of his father. Yet Samuel had died the same morning. It was impossible for Samuel to have committed the crime in question. Also, with no body it was difficult to prove there was truly a homicide to investigate.

If my plan does work, nothing more should come from these events.

November 25, 1988

The 1970s had passed quickly. The 1980s came into full force with loud, heavy music. It seemed as if it would carry over into the birth of the 1990s. For twelve years now I have existed only at night. I have been very careful to stay as far as I can out of the public's eye. I was now a quiet, tax-paying citizen of Heritage who made money through stock trade. Though a dull existence, it ensured that I would be able to let the events that were still fresh in my mind die forever. No one had looked back upon what took place with questioning eyes and I was thankful of this.

I found myself more often wandering through quiet streets, sometimes of areas that begged for someone to cause trouble. On such a street nights ago I wandered; however, unlike the times before someone began to stalk me. This one was unlike the normal street creatures that now make a consistent appearance on my menu. Blocks passed as he kept his distance from me. I carefully picked through his thoughts and found that his deepest fears weighed heavily upon his mind. Even though he understood the crime that was about to take place.

His fears are what intrigued me the most. They mainly all consisted of how he was to spend his life. He really did not want to survive the way he did. He did not wish to prey upon those weaker than his own six-foot-two-inch muscular body; however, this was all that was known to him. He was a true product of a dysfunctional society. A society that did not know how to prepare a youth now considered to be an adult by the government. There was a drive within him. A drive to change if only a means was provided. It was these thoughts that saved his young life. There were no worries of where he was going to obtain his next fix. Or next drink. There were just worries of how to turn his life around.

I neared a blind alley. It was the perfect place for him to be cornered. There would be no chance of him attempting to run once confronted. His footsteps quickened as I turned into the alley just beyond his sight. I used the shadows to totally conceal my movements. I waited until he stepped far enough in between the brick buildings that I could rush past him. I did so without his notice of being penned there.

I heard thoughts of confusion as he carefully looked into each shadow. He was completely unsure of what had happened. Or what he had really seen. He then turned to give up the chase. As his eyes met me they widened in shock. He found that I patiently awaited his attention.

Run. This thought filled his mind. It caused his body to tense in preparation of attempting what seemed to be a sound option. But when I shook my head in disagreement his body relaxed. Needless to say the thought quickly escaped him. I moved closer to him while I looked deep into his eyes. I listened to his thoughts turn to a popular novel. It was about a man who had the chance to record the life of an immortal and those who interacted with him for I believe two hundred or so years. It made a perfect chance to use a book considered fictitious to my advantage. It had opened a doorway of unknown possibilities in his mind.

"You have not been following me. I have been leading you here since you first took notice of me. In life sometimes the predator is the prey. They never know it until they are blocked into a corner with no place to run or hide. You could be so much more if only there was the chance for you to develop yourself. Come with me and let us talk. I have an offer you cannot possibly refuse."

Silence. However, it was not the uneasy silence left between two people when words are spoken that are not liked. I turned and walked away. There was a pause before he started to follow me. But he did follow, nonetheless.

A café I frequented in the late evenings was where I intended to take him; however, after a mile of walking on foot I heard his breath becoming deeper. Sweat had begun to build upon his brow. I stopped at a pay phone and looked at my new shadow.

"I do suppose we will need a taxi so you will not have to walk the entire way."

Laughter erupted from deep within him as if I were insane.

"You're joking! People are afraid to drive through these streets just in

case their car breaks down or has a flat tire. And you expect to make a call and
have a taxi come for us."

"Yes."

I drew a coin from my pocket. Quickly I dialed the number to the company
I used on a nightly bases.

"This is Rowan Rasland. I need a cab at the corner of 8th Avenue and
Broad Street as quickly as you can manage…Five minutes is fine."

Another snicker erupted from him as I sat on the curb patiently. The story
from the book faded from his mind. He then wondered if I were actually
insane. Still he stayed to see if there was a chance that a taxi would come.

In the distance of the barren street, a single car of bright yellow
approached. When it neared us it slowed to a stop. I stood and climbed in the
back. With the door left open I called to the one who finally had said his name
in thought.

"You can come now, Norman, and have your future change for the better.
Or you can stay here and continue this path. Mind you that it will eventually
catch up with you in death or incarceration. It is your choice to make."

There was hesitation that had built in his step. He questioned if I was
serious; however, he soon decided that it was a chance worth taking. The door
closed behind him. After I had told the destination to the driver, we were off.
Norman kept watch of me out of the corner of his eye. He did so until he could
not stand the sound of silence.

"I have to know. Who in the hell are you?"

"Someone who sees untapped potential. Someone who is willing to care.
A friend if you will."

"But that doesn't answer a thing."

"Not all answers come easily, and when they do come they are not always
accepted with gentle repose."

"You're still not answering the question."

"In due time. Mind you I am not saying tonight or tomorrow. But in due
time you will have the answers you seek."

And with due time we arrived at the Java Rose Café. I gave the driver three
hundred dollars and told him to wait for us to finish. In the café I gave Norman
free rein to order whatever he wished. After two cheeseburgers, two double
orders of French fries, four cups of coffee, and three slices of apple pie, he had
finally had his fill of food.

"Do you always eat this way?"

"Yeah. When you live on the streets you eat as much as you can, when you can. You never know when the next chance to eat will come along."

"That changes as of tonight. First let us talk about your job responsibilities."

"What do you mean responsibilities? We haven't even talked about pay. Not to mention that not everything has a price, Mr. Rasland. If you're looking for a partner in some strange sexual escapade then you definitely have the wrong guy. I may be desperate at times but not that desperate."

I laughed at his open boldness with no concern of my personal emotions on any subject. However, I did not take into consideration that even though Norman had lived a hard life on the streets he still wore his heart on his sleeve.

"I don't have to take this."

He had started to leave; however, while his hand was still braced upon the booth table I grabbed hold of his wrist to halt his movement.

"No, please sit down. I apologize for my sudden laughter; however, I do enjoy someone who is without worry about being brutally honest."

Though he still wore a hurt expression upon his face, Norman still sat back down. He then looked me in the eye.

"Okay, what's the deal?"

"First you go to collage or a technical school to better yourself. After that we will see what happens from there. But while you are still in school you will live with me in my mansion. There you will have no worries of money or food; therefore, you will be able to focus upon your studies."

He started to question my intentions. He then stopped as I counted money from my clip that I kept in my coat pocket.

"Consider this thousand dollars your first week of pay in advance. As for tuition and materials, they will be fully paid for. Any questions?"

"Yeah. Are you serious, or is this some kind of perverted joke?"

"I do not joke about matters of money. Nor in offering a chance to bring about a new life. Yet I can understand how this offer would be hard to believe; therefore, you can take the money now and come with me to my home. Once there, if you decide to leave then you are free to do so. But you will still be a thousand dollars richer. If you find this to be agreeable then we can go."

"What do I have to lose?"

"Exactly. You only have everything to gain."

It was like magic. His eyes widened at the sight of the church that had an added north and south wing.

"Oh my dear God! You're serious."

That evening I gave him the grand tour. I told him he was welcome to

168

anything and everywhere within the mansion. But this excluded the south wing. I made it very clear that these were my personal rooms and quarters.

As of now Norman is making sure our bargain is being kept. He has already enrolled in a state university. He is expected to graduate in 1992. That is, if he does not lose the drive that I first liked about him.

July 4, 1992

Norman's graduation day had come and passed by. It left him with a strong sense of accomplishment. He graduated at the head of his class with a degree in business management. There was never a question in my mind about him being able to do it. But this had only caused our agreement to close. It meant he was free to go with the money he had earned by our agreement.

I never thought that I would grow so close to someone; however, within the past four years Norman has become like a son to me. And though I have only watched him grow through education it has been a fulfilling experience. Yet I hate to see it end. Only hours ago I had what I thought would be my last conversation with him. I told him that he was more than welcome to stay. My home had become his home as well.

"I know, Mr. Rasland. I know. But before anything happens don't you think I am long overdue for certain answers? The ones that you said I would get in due time."

"Yes, I cannot deny you an explanation after four years of loyalty. Especially when you have never questioned certain habits of mine."

I walked from Norman's room in the north wing to the south wing. The lock clicked open without a key being placed in the key hole. It was something that I had learned to do with concentration. I looked over my shoulder to see Norman's face, not to ensure that he had followed, but to attempt reading his expression, for his mind told me nothing. There was not shock or disbelief to be found. Only the normal mellow expression that I had found he kept most of the time.

I led him through the dimly-lit hallway of stonework I had left unaltered, unlike the south wing. It reminded me of the past construction that caused me to feel more at home.

My study door stood opened, and was lit by replicas of old oil lamps. I sat in the large, wooden chair behind my desk. Without being told, Norman followed my example as he pulled up a chair.

"I am not like you, Norman. Though I cannot think of an easy way to tell this, I still intend on being honest. I was born in 1471 and have lived for the past five hundred twenty-one years. I have watched the world change endlessly while I have remained the same in appearance. I am a night creature. A blood drinker. I am a vampire. That is the truth about me without diving deep into detail."

I watched as a smile formed across Norman's face. He looked like a child who had just played a prank.

"I know. As a matter of fact I've known for about three years you were a vampire. I wasn't sure about your age. But I wanted to hear you say it."

"How?"

"I've lived with you for four years. You barely eat, except on rare occasions. You never get sick. Most of all I only see you at night, except for a few times that it required you to be awake in the day. Do the math and it leads you to believe there is a supernatural force at work."

"It does not scare you? Does it not bother you to know what I must do to survive?"

"Why would it? So you're different, it doesn't make you an evil or bad person."

I had never heard those words from someone unlike myself. I must admit it was nice to have heard them from another.

After what I had believed to be a secret was out in the open, Norman then talked business. He wished to put his education to work in the form of a night club, a night club that would cater to the taste of everyone who defined themselves with a form of popular music.

A partnership was born that night. One in which I would handle the funds needed to get started. All profits would be split evenly after expenses were taken care of. This involved Norman's newfound degree.

The designs flowed from both of us. It allowed a touch of old-world class to be combined with the taste of the modern world. Yet Norman did not wish to be known as a partner or owner. I learned that he had a fear of public relations. The idea for what we call the Club Unknown has been born. Most importantly, though, our living arrangements will not change.

December 18, 1997

As of two nights ago the Club Unknown is no longer an idea written down upon paper. It is now a reality, though it is a risky venture that took a large amount of the money I had acquired; however, judging from the opening night it was a wise investment. After expenses were taken out and profits divided I have already made a quarter of the money back.

However, it seems as if fate has thrown another twist into my life. A life that is already inconceivable by most people. The club had a line on the outside that stretched half the length of the old theater that I had purchased and remodeled into what it is now. It took four hours to get the line more manageable. It took that long just so that I could tour the rooms to see how they were all doing.

I had just started to look over the lobby when a man with a balding head, graying hair and mustache staggered past me. He never would have drawn my attention normally. Yet he was very free with his thoughts.

"I'm drunk enough. I can't even feel my feet. I can blow my brains out and not even care."

I grabbed him and tossed his limp body over my shoulder. He was a man of questionable size. But he could not fight back even if he wished to. By the time we reached my office in the back of the club he had passed out. I did not believe he would wake before we had to close.

For the rest of the club's open hours I sat with him. I listened to the drunken, mumbled words in his sleep as well as nightmares. I heard enough of the story to have made me feel pity for him. He had lost everything. This included the woman he loved. All due to the actions of teenage kids who thought they knew all there was to know. They obviously believed that they were indestructible.

When he finally woke he found himself in strange surroundings. Norman and I had gathered him up and brought him home with us.

"Where am I, and who are you two?"

"I am Rowan. This fellow is Norman. Right now you are within one of the many guest rooms in our home. Earlier you were a patron at our club. But some unfortunate events have caused you to be brought here."

"So you make a habit out of bringing strange drunks back to your home."

"No, Clifford. Just the ones who intend on ending their lives in my parking lot after a few hours of drinking."

Clifford sprung up out of the bed and searched his pockets. He looked for a .32 caliber revolver that he had planned on using upon himself.

"Looking for this? I have taken the liberty of removing all but one bullet from the gun."

Quickly I looked over to Norman.

"You may want to leave the room for this."

Norman left the room as I had asked him to do, and shut the door behind him.

"Now then, Clifford, here is your gun. You have one shot to attempt to kill yourself as you planned. But be warned that I will not allow that. Or you can shoot me, take the other five bullets, then kill yourself. That is, if you think you can manage killing me."

"You don't want to push me, man…I don't have anything to lose, so your life doesn't mean much to me."

"I know, and that is what I am counting on, my friend."

The word friend seemed to rip through his soul. It caused tears to swell within his eyes. Anger flooded his heart. The shot rung out and his aim had been true to its mark. The smoke from the shot filled the room with a sulfur stench. It burned his eyes and caused him to blink repeatedly. His vision cleared. He found me still standing before him. The wound in my chest slowly bled, though it had already begun to heal. He then stumbled backward and tried to get away from me. He landed upon the end table, knocking over one of the two lamps that illuminated the room. The door was thrown open as Norman rushed. I could tell that he had expected the worst to have happened.

"I shot you! I can't believe I shot you!"

The shock of his desperation wore off quickly. He then noticed where the bullet had struck me.

"I shot you! What are you? You should be dead! If not dead then at least not standing!"

I walked over to him and offered a hand to help him out of the queer position he had managed to get himself into. It shocked Norman and myself that he did not refuse it.

"Consider me to be a guardian angel of sorts. You did not meet the requirements of our agreement, Clifford; therefore, I do not believe you need the gun anymore."

"No. Please take the gun. I'm sorry I shot you! I'll do anything, just please don't kill me."

"I have no intention or desire to kill you. Yet you must pay the price for your actions; therefore, be happy I am very easy in my nature."

"Oh dear God…"

I reached into my pocket. It caused him to squint his eyes. He expected me to pull forth some type of weapon or bullet for the revolver. The jingle of the keys caused him to look and see what his fate held. As I handed them over to him, puzzlement filled his mind.

"In all of my years I have never found the need for a driver's license before. However, I am finding that the expense of taxi companies at night in certain areas are quite steep. I know you were a professional driver; therefore, that is what you shall do for me."

"But?"

"I do not wish to hear excuses or reasons why it cannot be done. Norman will handle all of the details, including doubling your original pay."

I turned to leave the room and stopped as I reached the door.

"And, Norman, you may wish to explain things to him. After all, it is not every day someone sees such things as what just took place."

Two nights have passed since. I know that Norman has told him the truth. Yet it is not out of fear that he continues to stay. Within his mind there is nothing more than a very deep respect for me.

Two people now hold within their minds the secret of my survival. Yet they do not judge nor question me of it. The people of this age are quite interesting. They lack the fear that their ancestors always kept close in mind. Perhaps one day the world will come to accept those like myself; however, if they do I believe that it will still be far within the future.

December 16, 1998, 2:45 A.M.

The veil of sorrow has parted, showing me a small ray of light. Her name should be that of a goddess from the old times forgotten, yet for one so beautiful the name is so simple. A new life has been set before me. A life that until only hours ago I thought was lost from me until the end of all days.

A chance meeting brought me before her. Though Rabecca's makeup resembled those in the room of darkness, her likeness to Kyra is uncanny. Yet within her heart burns a fire unlike what was possessed by Kyra so many years ago.

I cannot keep my mind from wandering to her, and the unbridled desire to see her yet again. I await her call in anticipation. But it is not from thoughts of having Kyra in my life once more—though I will confess to her that this was my original thought—yet a dream I feel is coming true. The voice of prediction that I once passed off as fantasy is now echoing from the past to remind me that it may be possible.

If I could only ask one thing of God right now it would be to let Rabecca be the one I have secretly hoped would come along. Please, let the voice of Elania be true.

Chapter Six

The first rays of sunlight had started to break through the cold, gray, lifeless clouds of winter. A new day was born. Rabecca rubbed her tired eyes. She neared the final pages of the extensive volume of history. A history that had been told unlike any ever seen before by scholar or student alike. Within only hours she felt as if she had lived lifetimes filled by war, death, sorrow, and sometimes, but rarely, love.

She now knew of Rowan's past in almost complete detail. She had lived his victories and losses. All within the pages that revealed how time's grasp had aged all, except the author.

Rabecca's emotions swelled as she reached the final words of what Rowan had lived through. Her eyes ached from the amount of tears that she held back for him. She closed her eyes to collect herself as her hand closed the cover. The breeze caused by the cover made her nose become engulfed in the musky smell of the yellowed pages. Only one thought now resided in her mind: *Go to him.* Quickly Rabecca sprung from her seat as she snatched up the lifelong collection of history.

If it were not for the slight sound of a piece of paper that landed upon the tile, Rabecca would have sprinted out the door. Yet this slight sound drew her attention downward. There she found a single envelope that had fallen to rest at her feet. Her name had been written upon it in the same flowing script as within the leather-bound volume.

She was somewhat dumbfounded by the fact that she had overlooked the envelope. Rabecca slowly bent down and retrieved the fallen letter. Slowly she opened the envelope and read the words addressed to her:

My dearest Rabecca,

Upon finding this letter you should now know my deepest and darkest secrets that I have kept hidden for a countless time now. Kyra, my first wife, was very dear to me. There is not a doubt in my mind that you now understand. Yet there remains one confession that must be told before you can make a decision about our future together.

The night of our first meeting, what attracted me to you was indeed the fact that you resembled her so much. For a brief moment I thought that God had forgiven me. That perhaps I had been smiled upon one last time by Kyra returning to me. I will admit openly that this was very arrogant of me to say the least.

However, once I began to understand you, I realized that even though you do favor my long-departed love, you are so much more than she was. Times are different now. Your spirit is wild and free.

I do not wish for you to be with me and feel as if you must live up to my expectations. Nor do I wish for you to attempt to fill the hole in my heart by changing yourself to Kyra in a false way.

No, all I ask of you is to be yourself, unbridled and free. Do not have regard of what people may think of you. This is what I wish for you if your decision involves us sharing our lives together.

No matter what, though, always know that I love you. Even if you go your own way, at least remember that once upon a time you found a monster who could love. A monster who loved enough that he wished he could trade his immortal soul for a life. A life in which he could grow old and die with you.

Eternally your love,
Rowan

The fresh white paper showed signs of tear stains. It seemed to her as if Rowan had spoken his last farewells. He had expected her to run for her life. To run far from the hideous, bloodthirsty beast of the ages that he considered himself to be.

Slowly she moved as if she sleepwalked. Rabecca walked to the cash register where she paid her check. No matter what went on about her, Rabecca heard only her own deep thoughts. Her face remained expressionless and her lips silent. Rabecca found her way back into the limousine. She showed little signs of consciousness within her emerald eyes. The deafening silence caused by her mind did not end until a firm hand grasped her shoulder.

"Rabecca, are you okay?"

The sensation caused by the warm touch caused her to realize where she was. Rabecca's eyes took notice of the concerned look upon Clifford's kind face. Though her mind was in turmoil, caused by the emotional madness she had read, somehow she managed to smile.

"Yes. Yes, I'm fine. I'm just exhausted is all. Regardless, I want you to take me to him."

"As you wish, Ms. Hollyard. as you wish."

"Brian, we've been searching all night. Give it a rest for now. I'm sure that she's safe wherever she is." Rachel rested her head against the passenger side door as she watched the sky being painted with the colors of the sun rise.

"Wherever Rabecca is, that thing is with her. That monster! How can anyone be safe around something like that?" Brian's bloodshot eyes continued to search the road side for any sign of Rabecca as he slowly drove along the streets in the early morning.

"Brian, are you telling me that you believed that nut case?" Rachel forced herself to become more awake as she stared at Brian, awaiting an answer.

"Rachel, damn it, you saw the newspaper with your own eyes! Tell me that you haven't considered that it could be true!"

"Of course I've thought about that possibility. But I've also taken into consideration that I know there are a dozen novelty shops that will print anything. They'll make it look authentic if you are willing to pay the right price!"

Brian slammed on the breaks. It caused the car to halt. It also caused what few cars were on the country road to almost wreck into them; however, they maneuvered while sliding across the dew-moistened asphalt.

"Don't you see?! Okay, so what if Jon is crazy? Don't you think there could be some reason why he thinks this Rowan is a monster? So maybe Rowan isn't some kind of movie monster. But there are still monsters who look just like everyday people. What's to say he isn't some kind of murderer?"

Rachel sighed deeply as she placed a tender hand upon Brian's knee. She then looked him deep within his eyes.

"I know you're worried about her. So am I. I've never been able to trust anyone who rides in like a prince charming to save the day. Even if there is a reason for them to do so."

Her hand lifted from his leg. She then began to gently caress his razor-stubbled face. Words were not needed because of the touch. It was enough confirmation of what both desired internally within a moment of pure, overwhelming lust. Their lips met gently at first, like hands pressed together for prayers; however, it only caused the blood to rush faster through their veins. Their movements then became quicker and filled with more passion. Their hands started to explore one another without a moment of shame. There was nothing that seemed like it could prevent this one moment. A moment of lustful desire that could easily climax to the highest peak of pleasure. The cars that passed them did not hold concern. Nor did the few wintertime birds that sung in the tree branches hung high above the road. The lust would have been brought to climax if not for a waking soul who stirred in the back. Porter continued to lay cramped on the back seat of the car as he spoke in a tired voice. "What's wrong? Why have we stopped?"

The moment was crushed like a crystal being shattered with a hammer. They quickly broke each other's hold and arranged themselves. They wanted it as if what had happened was only a lustful dream recalled from the deepest of sleeps.

Rachel took a deep breath. She tried to cool the spark that had been fanned into an inferno before she spoke with a nervous voice. "Nothing, Porter. Brian is just tired of driving and we pulled over so we could switch places."

Before any questions could be asked, Rachel stepped from the car. She moved to the driver's side where she met Brian who towered over her.

Their eyes locked only for seconds; however, it was enough for both to realize that there was no regret of what happened. They both knew that it was far from over. They switched places as if nothing had been out of place and continued on their search.

Porter sat up and rubbed Rachel's neck with such loving grace. It caused her to want to pull away from the pure warmth of its meaning. The love could be felt within each stroke; however, love only filled the heart. It was not enough to fulfill the lust of a body that tingled with anticipation.

The limousine pulled to a stop in front of the well-aged converted church. Rabecca remained in the back. She continued to sit within a daze until Clifford opened the door beside her. He then escorted her through the door of her awaiting palace. She said nothing to Clifford as he opened the door to the south wing.

"I cannot follow you any farther and I cannot show you the way. Mr. Rasland is very protective of his sleeping chamber. Go through the third door on the left. But please be careful not to wake him suddenly."

Rabecca glanced at Clifford. He knew that it was a sign of acknowledgment to his warning. She then walked down the dark corridor that she had been in only a sunset ago. The passage had remained dark and sinister to her eyes; however, it felt as if it had changed somehow. It had not changed physically, like a picture being hung or a new decor being added. Instead it had changed with emotion that she felt for Rowan's chosen reminders of life.

Rabecca neared the door to which she had been instructed to go. There she found the faint glimmer of a light that streamed beneath the door. Her hand reached for the door knob. She still expected to find this door, like so many others here, locked from the inside. Yet when her wrist twisted a click rang through the stone halls and echoed. The door had been balanced so perfectly that the slightest breeze could have caused it to be swung back upon its hinges.

Her eyes were then met by pale candlelight. The candlestick rested upon a table near the door. Within the center of the dully-lit room a large bed stood. Rabecca softly walked to the bed side and peered down at Rowan. He remained motionless with his dark eyes closed.

She studied him intently and watched for movement caused by breathing. Or another sign that proved there was still a spark of mortal life left within his body.

He looked like a flawless marble statue that had been placed within the bed. If Rabecca had not believed the words that she had read, this would have seemed to be the center of a perfectly-planned practical joke. Rabecca carefully placed her finger tips upon him as she felt for a pulse. She waited patiently, as if she knew that with any second something would disprove Rowan's words.

"My dear, I have written only the truth within my journal. I have only spoken the same truth to you; however, if you wish to stand there until you feel something that resembles a heartbeat you may do so. But I am afraid that you will be waiting for a very long time."

The sudden sound of his voice caused Rabecca to dart back in fear. Rowan then raised himself so that he could view her with more ease.

Rabecca gasped for breath as she searched for words that could explain her actions. Rowan looked at her and smiled. The candlelight reflected off of his pale, muscular chest.

"Shh. You need not explain yourself or your actions. But tell me, have you read the book in its entirety?"

Rabecca searched for words that she could not find. She searched until she had given up. Then she nodded her head, which caused her self expression to look rather simplistic.

"Good. Did you find the letter of my last confession at the end?" Rowan arose from the bed and moved to where he was only inches away from Rabecca's face.

She wanted to answer him in some way. In any way so that an end could be brought to her silence. But she knew that words alone could not express what she felt. Rabecca then fell into his arms and held him tight. Rowan's hand stroked her hair as she wept. Through the sobs Rabecca confessed all that she hoped.

"I never doubted what you told me. Never! It's just after reading that, learning of your life through your own emotions, I just hoped that you were lying to me! No one deserves to suffer so much!"

Rabecca could no longer control herself. Her words had turned into a jumbled sound of sobs and moans. Through this emotion she showed him how much she wanted to be lied to. Rabecca knew that it would have been far easier to cope with instead of knowing how he had died emotionally over and over again.

"I am sorry, Rabecca. I am sorry that I cannot lie to you. I am also sorry that I had to tell you this way. How I wish that I could have taken more time to tell you; however, time was not something we could spare for such things. If I had not told you everything then there was a chance of losing you. I cannot bear to lose love again. I cannot—"

Rabecca cut his words short as she forced a kiss upon his lips. The kiss allowed both of their tears to pool as one around their lips.

With only one kiss they stopped. They gazed into the other's red, tear-

182

stained eyes. Rabecca grasped his hand tight before she collected herself to speak.

"Don't lose my love. No matter what may happen today, tomorrow, or whenever. I may not be immortal, but the love that pours from my heart is. No matter what, my heart will always belong to you."

As she finished speaking the words' heartfelt honesty, a deep yawn sprung from her core. It was a reminder of how tired she was.

Rowan gently moved her to the bed. There they lay, holding each other. They both hoped that it was not a dream; however, Rabecca's mind had been put to rest. The silent hand of sleep caused her eyes to close. Rowan held her for hours as he watched her breathe. He continued to watch until the candle flickered lower and lower. Finally the flame had disappeared in a small rolling puff of gray smoke.

Only then did Rowan allow his eyes to rest. He knew that upon the next moon rise he must have the energy needed to begin building a new life with her.

"Can't we just go? We've already looked over this same street three times now!" Porter whined as if he were a child who sought unneeded help from his mother.

The look of frustration continued to grow on Brian's face until he leaned to Rachel. He then whispered, "If he whines one more time I swear I'll throw him out of this car and watch him roll down the damn street!"

Rachel smirked at the thought of Porter being tossed out of the car. In her mind he'd bounce almost like a ball.

"Okay, guys, I think we should call it a day. We've looked everywhere. Plus it seems like Rowan is a night person. So first thing tonight we should check the club."

"Finally! I can sleep on a real bed instead of the back seat of this thing." Porter stretched out and tried to become as comfortable as the given space would allow.

Brian turned and prepared to punch Porter; however, he was met by a sly smile. A hand had started to wander. Her hand rubbed higher along his inner thigh.

Chapter Seven

The sun had fallen behind the horizon. It allowed the gray, colorless day to be replaced with a cold night. The sky had been painted in dark hues of blue and purple. Porter had just begun to wake from a restless day of sleep. His slumber had been filled with nightmares of the one he loved betraying him. His eyes opened and were met with the faint red glow of the alarm clock that sat within the bookshelf headboard of Rachel's bed.

He took a moment to rub his eyes and shake off the nightmares. Porter then rolled over to gently kiss Rachel. He intended to wake her, yet found that she was no longer there. His hand reached for the bedside lamp. Porter quickly switched it on and caused light to flood the room. It revealed that there were no signs of her departure.

Porter sat up in the bed and slowly collected his thoughts. He tried to rationalize his nightmares from reality.

She never wakes up before me. Usually I have to fight with her to get up unless she's had over ten hours of sleep. What am I doing? It was just a nightmare. Sometimes I even make myself wonder why I think the things that I do.

Quietly he laughed as he stretched. He then started to dress himself. As he placed the final shoe upon his foot, Porter's nose was met with the unmistakable smell of a home-cooked meal. His stomach raged and reminded him of how long it had been since he had eaten, which had been due to Brian's relentless search. Porter's thoughts now turned very simple and primal. They consisted of only two rooms in the entire house: the bathroom followed by the kitchen.

Porter opened the door and stepped into the hall. He could see steam that poured from the open bathroom door. As he walked to the door his thoughts turned to the hypnotic smell of the food. He rounded the corner of the door and found Rachel. She stood in front of the fogged mirror while she towel dried her short hair

"Hey there, sexy. I was wondering where you had run off to."

The sudden sound of Porter's voice caused Rachel to jump in shock. It also caused her to almost lose the short towel that covered her pleasuring parts.

"Porter! You scared the hell out of me! You could have at least knocked or something."

Porter looked at Rachel, puzzled. His eyes slowly traced over her body from head to toe. "Why knock? The door was wide open. It's not like I haven't seen you with less on than a towel before."

The blood in her veins boiled as he continued to gaze upon her. It was a look that she had always thought to be a sign of his ignorance. The simple sound of Porter's voice irritated her. She tried to find words to not only justify the way she felt, but to also explain the disgust she now felt toward him. Her emotions had cast aside all rational forms of thought and communication; however, her actions spoke louder than any words. She picked up her clothing and stormed out of the small bathroom. Porter stood there as he watched Rachel slam the door to her bedroom shut. It caused the hall to echo with the brute sound of anger.

A hand appeared on Porter's shoulder. It caused him to turn his head quickly. He found that Brian stood behind him.

"What's wrong with her?" Brian asked, his hair still dripping water upon his shoulders.

"I'm not exactly sure. Well, except that I startled her when she was drying her hair. Other than that sometimes she just gets this way."

Brian's face looked as if he thought hard before he next spoke. "Rachel's mom is finishing dinner. Why don't you get ready while I talk to her. I'll see if I can find out what is wrong."

Porter looked at him with sincere eyes. "Thank you, man. It could just be this Rabecca thing getting to all of us. But see what you can do."

Porter walked into the bathroom and shut the door. Concern of what he had done still filled his mind. He lifted the lid to the toilet and prepared to relieve himself. Porter looked down as he tried to rid himself of the events; however, his eyes found a new concern that floated upon the water of the white porcelain. A single condom and wrapper floated upon the water's surface. The nightmares rushed back into his mind. The cold truth of reality had set strong within his mind. His athletic body collapsed upon the floor as he cried. He felt as if each tear was a separate piece of his broken heart. In low, mumbled words he talked to himself. "They both had wet hair. They both had wet hair..."

Porter stared into the toilet with tear-filled eyes. He would have continued to stare if it were not for Rachel who knocked on the door.

"Porter, I'm sorry. I'm just really stressed out. I don't mean to take it out on you."

He quickly flushed the evidence away as he dried his eyes upon his shirt. "It's okay. I'll be out of here in a few minutes. Tell everyone not to wait for me."

Silence had fallen on the opposite side of the door. Porter collected his emotions and pushed away the remaining tears. But his heart beat in pain while his mind flourished with anger. A few moments passed before Porter attempted to step forth from the walls of the bathroom. He then began the grueling journey to the kitchen. Each step made toward her was a step of agony. A step in the direction that his heart did not want to go in.

Yet, with persistence, Porter found himself seated before the love that betrayed. A plate of steaming food awaited his long-lost appetite.

Emotional breakdown radiated off of his very presence. It caused everyone to remain silent within the tension. Rachel tried to look into Porter's mournful eyes once; however, she found rejection as he lowered his head downward in a shameful manner.

Though Porter's heart had been broken beyond that of a crystal shattered, he managed one small conversation. It was a conversation with Rachel's mother in a moment of heart-broken madness.

"Ms. Duffy, I really do love your house. But have you ever thought of having an addition built? Perhaps a second bathroom?" Porter's eyes cut upward. He glared at Rachel who suddenly choked while she took a drink.

"Actually, Porter, I have. But only when I have a house full of guests. Not to mention it is so costly."

His eyes remained upon Rachel with a cold, emotionless look. The color had drained from her face.

"Well you know, Ms. Duffy, I have taken several building trades classes. I could do most of the work myself."

Rachel's mother smiled. She looked upon her daughter with hopeful eyes that involved Rachel's future. "Honey, it sounds like you've really got a catch here. A football player, a carpenter, and good-looking! What else could a woman want?"

Porter suddenly stood up and pushed his chair under the table; however, he never took his eyes off of Rachel.

"We will talk over all of the details later. I don't think I'll have much else to do this summer. But if you will excuse me, I have some thinking I need to do."

Rabecca's eyes fluttered open. She found that her head was gently resting upon Rowan's pale chest. He held her close as he continued to stroke her hair. Her head tilted slightly upward as she wanted her eyes to meet his. A small grin crept across Rowan's face that caused Rabecca to push herself upward to see his face better.

"How long have you been watching me?" Rabecca asked as Rowan arose out of the bed. He still gazed in her eyes as if they were the center of all the living in this world. "Long enough. But I still had to step out for a few moments to redecorate for you."

Rabecca's eyes narrowed as a large smile shone across her face. "What do you mean redecorate for me?"

Rowan said nothing as he motioned with one arm for her to look about the room. Her eyes followed the motion of his arm. She found that the room that once only held a bed and a single glowing candle had been filled with the flames of dozens of candles. These candles were surrounded with countless long-stem roses from every band of the color spectrum.

Her eyes filled with the faint mist of tears as she looked back at Rowan's loving gaze. "They're absolutely beautiful. I'm not going to ask where you found all of them. But I can say this is the most romantic thing anyone has ever done for me."

Rowan then knelt down to her eye level. "I've been told that sometimes one rose is more meaningful than a dozen. That one rose, I would give my life just to gaze upon its beauty for a few peaceful moments."

Rabecca's arms moved outward and caught Rowan's neck. She pulled him close as she showed that all worries about the monster he claimed to be had vanished from her mind. Before Rowan could find the self control he needed, his arms wrapped around Rabecca. His head lowered to the base of her neck. Rabecca's body tensed and began to quiver with each breath. Rowan traced her neck line up to her moist lips as he slowly kissed each inch as he did so.

Rabecca's arms pulled him in with each kiss. Then Rowan gently pushed himself away from her. "We cannot do this. Or should I say I cannot do this to you."

Rabecca opened her eyes. The look she gave showed how much her body ached with desire. The desire for the touch that she had waited so very long for. She tried to speak as Rowan gazed deeply into her eyes; however, she could not find words filled with enough passion to express what was felt with each heartbeat.

Rowan lifted a hand and placed two fingers upon her soft, inviting lips. He then spoke to her from his heart.

"You don't have to say anything. I already know. I know you think you are ready but I don't want you to be mistaken."

Rabecca smiled as Rowan stood. Carefully he picked a rose from the many that filled the room. "Take this with you tonight when we go out. That is, after we get you a new wardrobe."

"Jon here. This better be pretty damn important." His voice sounded tired as if he had not slept in days.

Brian cleared his throat as he tried to regain the nerve about calling him. "This is Brian. I'm calling to see if you have any news to report about Rabecca."

"Rabecca...Rabecca...Oh, you mean the vampire fodder! No, I haven't seen hide or fang from either one of them. I'm staking out the club again tonight. If she is still alive then she'll be here later when the spawn of satanic shit makes his nightly appearance. If you want to possibly see her alive then you better get down here soon. Otherwise you may miss out."

Then as suddenly as Jon had answered the phone he ended the conversation. It left Brian to listen only to the low static of silence. Slowly he hung up the phone as Ms. Duffy gazed upon him with a sympathetic look upon her face.

"No one has found her yet?"

Brian shook his head in a slow, pitiful manner. He attempted to give the impression that there were true emotions of loving concern embedded in his heart. Emotions that clawed their way to the surface.

"Not yet. I have a guy at the club keeping an eye out. He seems to think that she will be there sometime tonight. I'm going to get everyone together to go down there and hopefully talk some sense into her. That is, if she even shows."

Ms. Duffy lowered her eyes, unsure of what kind words could be said. Words that would make him believe that the pain she thought seen would subside. Seconds of silence passed before she gave up hope on finding the words. She then stood and looked at Brian again.

"I'm going to start on these dishes. But I hope you find her. I can tell how much she means to you."

Ms. Duffy collected the dishes as Brain turned his back to find Rachel and Porter. Brian had almost made it to the room that Porter and Rachel shared when he heard them. The beginning of words that he knew would come sooner or later.

"Porter, I promise I can explain everything." The sound of fear-filled tension was unmistakable within Rachel's voice. It tempted Brian to peep around the corner unseen. Porter had ignored her words. He continued to pack the few belongings that he had brought with him into a worn backpack that had seen better days.

"I know it looks a little suspicious. But what you think happened isn't what really took place."

Porter turned and looked at her. His eyes showed that the flood gate he stored all of his anger behind had broken.

"Oh, I see. The poor, slow-thinking jock has to be told what really happened. Even though all the evidence has been seen! Well, then tell me what really happened. Just remember to go real slow and use small words so that I can keep up!"

Rachel's fear vanished as shock overwhelmed her. Porter had never talked to her in such a way. Though she had heard it with her own ears it took time for it to set into her mind completely.

"What do you mean evidence? The only evidence I've seen is that you have lost what little mind you had to begin with! Well, mister big bad ass, what evidence have you seen?"

Porter's passive nature disappeared as he zipped the backpack. Only then did he list all that was on his mind.

"We will start from the beginning, and I do mean the very beginning. When we first met, you felt like you had to take the dominant roll. I never really had a problem with this. Even though it meant having to live with a picky, bitchy you. I've gotten used to your mood swings. Which usually always happens when I do something you don't approve of. But after I woke up all I did was talk to you and you snapped at me. It was different but I could have let it go. But the dumb jock noticed something strange. Your hair was wet and so was Brian's."

Before Porter had time to finish, Rachel's attitude once again had overtaken her actions. "That's it! You're saying that something happened between Brian and me because of my permanent P.M.S. and wet hair! Now I understand why jocks can only get athletic scholarships!"

Porter moved silently to the edge of the door. It caused Brian to jump back before he turned and looked Rachel in the eyes one last time.

"Like always you assume that I can never find a fault in you. But this time, Rachel, things are different. True, both Brian and you had wet hair and you could have used separate bathrooms. But wait, your mother only has one bathroom. I guess you took a shower after Brian."

Porter walked back to Rachel and patted her on the head gently. It made her feel like he dealt with her like a child. A child who could not understand why she had gotten caught with her hand in the cookie jar.

"I'm sorry, Rachel. I'm sorry that even a jock on an athletic scholarship, such as myself, can still realize what a used condom floating in a toilet looks like. Come see me when you're ready for a grown-up relationship. Perhaps then, if I can forgive you, we can give us another try."

Porter smiled a small smile of victory. He watched the flushed color of anger drain from Rachel's face. She had realized that, though she wanted one of her fulfilled lusts to remain a secret, a pleasurable moment, it caused her to overlook the smallest of details. A detail that ended an otherwise perfect cover up.

Porter turned to the door. He tried to hide the pain of the emptiness that now flourished where his once love-filled heart had beat. Though he felt as if he were mortally wounded and could never forgive her, a small part of desire caused him to ache to hold her. He found that it was harder to fight off as his ears filled with the sound of Rachel weeping since their first time together. Yet he pushed himself to walk through the door. Porter knew that he left behind his first and only true love.

He wiped a single tear from his eye. He then stared at the evil smile that Brian wore as they exchanged glances. Porter continued to walk past him. He believed that he had nothing left to say to anyone; however, a small memory from only two days before caused him to stop. Without turning, Porter spoke to Brian with a chilled tone in his voice.

"You know, the day will come when all the pain and suffering you have caused everyone will return to you. Hopefully when that day does come everyone who you have fooled will realize that the person they see is just a front. A front that hides a person who cannot be happy unless all happiness around him is destroyed. Then the entire world will know that you are the person Rabecca said you were."

With one last deep breath, Porter walked away. He left as if only a memory of the past soon forgotten as the front door closed tight. The demonic grin remained upon Brian's face. He enjoyed listening to the sound of victory that had come in the form of Rachel's muffled sobs.

After he carefully composed his face to resemble an expression of shocked questioning, Brian went to Rachel. He found Rachel with her face buried in the soft blue fur of a plush bunny that had become more tear-soaked.

With a low, almost believable, sympathetic voice Brian asked, "What's going on? Why did Porter just leave with his backpack?"

Rachel's face lifted from the stained fur and exposed her swollen, red eyes.

"Why do you think he left?! He found out about us! You told me that there was no way he could find out!"

Brian's perfectly-prepared face melted in an instant as he defended himself.

"Now wait a minute. I'm not the one who engaged this to begin with. I'm not the one who said Porter wouldn't find out. You were!"

Her puffy eyes filled with more tears. She repeated, "You bastard…you bastard."

Brian forced his arms around Rachel. She fought him with every ounce of energy, but she was not strong enough to have matched his strength.

"I know it's hard to accept that it's over. I know that it is easier if someone else is at fault. But it is not your fault or mine. What happened between us happened for a reason. I don't regret it. I believe that for anyone to have sex with someone you have to love them. Even if you don't realize it at the time."

Rachel pulled away as she sniffled. Her tears had begun to stop as she listened to Brian's words.

"You heard me right, Rachel. There has to be something drawing us together. If you feel you have to blame someone then blame Porter. After all, he is the one who has been trying all this time to be something that he isn't, just to be with you."

Rachel rubbed her eyes and dried her face. Her emotions had been calmed while she listened to Brian's words of comfort.

"Sometimes you just need someone to point these things out to you. Do you understand where this conversation is leading?"

Rachel cleared her throat, which had started to become sore. In a hoarse voice she answered, "Yes."

Brian smiled charmingly as he took her hand in his.

"Good. But we need to get ready. I just talked to that crazy guy from the club and he says that Rowan usually shows up there every night."

Rachel's eyes filled with tears once more as she turned her face from Brian's view.

"But I thought there was something between us. I thought…"

Her voice cracked from the hurt she felt. It made her unable to finish her words. Brian's hand lifted her face and gently turned her head. He made her look toward him.

"There is something between us. I just want us to find Rabecca so that we can tell her that everything is okay. You know, to wish her a happy life if she wants to stay there with Rowan."

Clifford stood behind the open door of the limousine with open arms. Rabecca climbed into the back while Rowan handed over bags upon bags to him. The mall that they had walked out of closed after they had exited.

"Like normal, I see that you were not joking about buying her anything she wanted."

Rowan smiled. It allowed the street lamps to reflect off of his unnaturally white teeth. "You have to realize that she has never been given free rein like this. In time Rabecca will grow accustomed to this life just like a certain driver I know."

Rowan placed the last bag into Clifford's hand. "Well, I just hope she has better taste than I had. I still don't know what I'm going to do with all of those tacky tropical shirts. I really did think that they were so great when I was in her place."

Rowan chuckled as he climbed within the limo beside Rabecca. Clifford placed the bags within the trunk. He then rushed to take his place behind the wheel of the car. Without spoken instructions, Clifford began to drive toward the club. Rowan picked up the built-in phone in the back of the limousine and made a quick call.

"This is Norm, and this had better be important 'cause I'm kinda busy."

"Sorry to interrupt you…"

Before Rowan had finished the simple sentence, Norman's voice changed from its normal, rough tone to a softer, apologetic one.

"Mr. Rasland! I'm so sorry, it's just you never call me on this phone."

"No need for excuses. I'm just wanting to inform you that Rabecca and myself are going to enjoy the evening together at the club."

"I understand, sir. I'll be sure to inform the crew to keep their eyes open for any of the undesirables."

"Good. As long as we understand one another, farewell."

Rowan ended the call as Rabecca gazed upon him with inquiring eyes. "What was all that about?"

His hand gently landed upon Rabecca's knee. "Just business, my dear. Business to ensure our evening is flawless."

Rabecca smiled as she saw the lights of the club. They grew larger and brighter with each breath that she took.

"Rowan, no matter what happens, as long as you are with me the evening will be perfect. You see, my love, I could die on this night and have only one confession to make. That would be that my life could not have been more complete."

He smiled as their hands joined. The physical bond represented the emotional and spiritual bond that could never be broken between them.

The limousine slowed as it joined the line of vehicles that stretched the length of the building's front. All of which waited for the passengers to be let out at the front doors, as if they were persons of great importance. Slowly the limousine stopped in front of the club. Norman stepped away from his duties to open the door and help Rabecca out, followed by Rowan.

Norman casually leaned toward Rowan's ear. He whispered so that only he could hear through the senseless noises of others talking over the sounds of the mixed music.

"Sir, two of the undesirables have been spotted here with that lunatic, Jon."

Rowan sighed deeply as he acknowledged the problem that would soon be at hand. "When and where were they last spotted?"

Norman stepped away and looked toward the extensive parking lot. "Well, to be honest, they are heading this way right now."

"Inform security to be ready for anything. Try to discourage them to come back; however, if they resist then you know what to do."

Rowan stepped from Norman. He placed his arm around Rabecca to pull her close. He then led her to the door. "My dear, it looks as if your words are to be tested on this very evening. Your friends, if you will, are approaching as we speak. I've told Norman to handle the problem. That is, unless you wish differently."

Rabecca turned and saw Brian and Rachel as rapidly they approached. With them was a figure that was familiar, though she had almost forgotten about him. "I at least feel as if I owe it to them to tell them about us. If nothing else, to let them know that I am happy here with you and that I am staying."

Rowan kissed her lips as softly as a gentle breeze could have blown. "As you wish. But if you should need me all you have to do is call my name. I will be there before you can take your next breath."

Rabecca smiled lovingly as she hugged him. She then walked toward them as security rushed from the open door of the club.

Rowan casually held his hand up and said, "Wait! There has been a change of plans. She wishes to speak with them one last time. After that, escort them away and tell them that they are no longer welcome here. But look sharp just in case."

Security stopped without hesitation. They joined Rowan as he watched and waited for any signs of trouble that brewed. Rabecca walked calmly to the first row of cars in the parking lot. There, Brian and Rachel stopped. Jon continued to move forward until he stood between Rowan and his love.

"Rabecca, I know we've had our problems in the past. But you have to listen to me! That man is a monster. You're not safe with him!"

Rabecca shook her head, disappointed. She also tried not to laugh at Brian's words. "Look, I'll try to make this simple so that maybe this time you will take the hint. I'm staying here with Rowan. He loves me for who I am. Not for what I may do for him or his image. And as far as him being a monster, perhaps you need to take a long, hard look in the mirror before you pass judgment on somebody else. I only see one monster here, and that's you,

Brian. Now if you will excuse me I have a date that is waiting for me."

As Rabecca turned and began to walk away, Brain released one last hopeful call. "But I love you for who you are. Please don't let it end like this."

His words that filled the air caused a spark of anger within Rachel. Anger that made her forget about the pain of her parched throat.

"You bastard! You told me that we were coming here so that you could tell her about us. Because of you I betrayed Porter. I lost him along with all self respect that I had for myself. Find your own damn way back to whatever hell you call home!"

Rabecca stopped and turned to face Brian once more. Her face wore a look of total disgust. It was a look that he knew all too well. "I see that you have made my point for me. I at least should thank you for showing me what misery is. At least I can recognize true happiness when I finally found it. Perhaps one day someone, or something, will take pity on you. Maybe then you can learn what it means to be truly happy. I'll pray for you."

Rabecca turned to walk past Jon as the final strand of sanity had broken within Brian's mind. It left only the dark side that had been so well hidden. It emerged and controlled his actions without any hesitation. Before the first step could be taken in attempts to place enough distance between Rabecca and her one-time controller, a hand grasped her wrist. It was almost enough force to have crushed her petite bones.

"You don't get it, do you? No matter what you think, no matter what you do, you're mine! No one can stop it! Not you or your bloodsucking boyfriend! We're leaving this instant, like it or not, little girl!"

Rabecca tried to resist with all of her might; however, she could not stop herself from being drug away to wherever he intended on going.

Jon shouted. "Yes, my boy! She is not yet tainted with the foul demon's curse. Take her from here and I'll deal with the beast!"

Jon glanced back to where Rowan had been standing only moments ago. He found only the club's security team that rushed toward him, led by Norman. Then a sinister voice that almost growled caught his attention. The voice was followed by a whimper of pain. It sounded as if it had sprung forth from a grown man.

"I do not think things are going to go as you planned! Release her before I show everyone what color your blood is!"

When Jon's eyes jumped back to Brian he sprung toward him. While Jon moved as quickly as he could, he drew a silver, jewel-inlaid dagger from his stained coat. The look upon his face told that he had prepared to combat the monster from his living nightmare.

"I had this made especially for you, you black-hearted son of a bitch!" With the end of Jon's war-cry-type words, he plunged the blade into Rowan's back with all of his might. He hoped that it was enough force to pierce the heart in Rowan's breast.

The pain had become more evident to him. The sensation of the cold spike wore away. It left only a dull throb as blood trickled down both front and back. Rowan's grasp around Brian's neck loosened. It allowed Brian to feel the life return to him. The life that was slowly being crushed out of him.

Rowan's cold, black eyes met Jon's terrified face. He then shook off the pain that remained caused by the deadly item within his back.

"If only you could remember the way your father treated your poor dear mother. Perhaps then the hatred you feel for me would be directed to the truth. He did die at my hands. But only for the well being of your mother and yourself. Yet I am the reason why you chose the life you did; therefore, it is my responsibility to bring your torture to an end."

Rowan released Brian completely as he reached for the dagger hilt. He then slowly pulled its blade from his flesh. The dagger's sharp blade flashed through the air. It caused Jon's eyes to widen as the kiss of the blade made its way to his chest.

Rowan then lowered his head. "God forgive us both; however, I hope you find a better place."

Jon fell to his knees as the final essence of life poured out from his body. Steam began to rise, caused by the warm blood in the cold night air. With the last breath within his body, Jon struggled to say, "Thank you."

Overwhelming grief and regret could have engulfed Rowan in this instant. But Rabecca's anger-filled scream would not allow him to.

"I said let me go!"

Her bare knee slammed into Brian's groin. He fell to the ground in agony and her eyes found Rowan with a great relief.

Every instinct within her body caused her to ache to be held within his arms. Rabecca's eyes had seen nothing but Rowan. Her ears knew only the sound of her own heartbeat, which grew stronger as she moved closer to him.

Rowan called out and tried to warn her; nothing could be done as the car sped away. It left Rabecca's bashed and bleeding body upon the asphalt. Rowan ran to cradle her within his arms as words that faded filled his ears.

"You always have gotten what you want, Rabecca. Now it's my turn."

The source had been one who he thought a friend of Rabecca's only days ago.

"This is Norman at the Unknown Club. I've got a woman who has just been hit by a speeding car in the parking lot. Also there's a man who has a stab wound in the chest. I think he's already dead." Norman knelt beside Rowan as he continued to hold Rabecca close. Tears left his eyes and washed over her face.

"Rowan, the paramedics are on their way. So are the police. You have to go."

His eyes flashed upward with anger directed at Norman. The type of anger that no man should ever know.

"Boss, I'm talking as your friend right now. You can't help her if the entire world learns about you. Especially starting with the police knowing first. For Rabecca's sake, go."

Rowan kissed her motionless lips. He had tasted how strong her life's blood was before he lowered her to the ground carefully. With a friendly touch he grasped Norman's hand and said, "Thank you, my friend. Thank you." Then, as if all had been nothing more than a dream, Rowan disappeared within the open arms of the night.

The hospital room was dim and quiet as the late-night shift took over. Rabecca lay lifeless upon the bed. Each wound had been cleaned and dressed appropriately. Brian had fallen asleep in a corner chair. The steady pace of the heart monitor had been the only sound within the room for hours. The door opened slightly. A soft-voiced female spoke as she tried not to disturb anyone. "She's in here, Mr. Rasland, with her fiancé. But I'm afraid the impact of the car has caused her to slip into a coma."

"I understand. Is it okay if I go in? Or should I come back later?"

"Oh, it's okay. She's in a private room so you can stay all night if you want."

The door opened completely and allowed more light to spill into the room as Rowan stepped through the doorway. His eyes locked on Brian's sleeping body. The sight caused hatred to swell in his heart. Yet, as his eyes lowered, he found Rabecca. She was barely able to breathe. Her appearance was as if she were already dead.

He opened her pale hand and placed a gold pendant within the palm. Rowan then whispered in her ear, "I don't have much time." Just then a voice erupted over the intercom system. "Security report to the ICU."

With a sigh he continued. "I took a life tonight that I had ruined. It is only right that I save yours so that I have not ruined yours as well."

Rowan then stood, and made a precise cut upon his finger tip. He then carefully gave Rabecca a few precious drops of his dark, electric blood. It caused the heart monitor to race. Rabecca's eyes opened and found Rowan's, which smiled. "I love you," he said.

Suddenly the door flung open as security and police alike flooded the room. They frantically looked from left to right until their nerves calmed.

Rabecca sat and looked at them confused. She looked at Brian who had been forced awake due to the alarm. "Who am I?"

Chapter Eight

December 18, 1999

Dear Diary,

Well, it has been a year since I lost my memory. Even though I thought it would drive Brian and me apart, it actually has brought us closer than what I feel we ever were. It's taken a lot of work. But if it wasn't for Brian I'm afraid I'd be more lost than what I am now. It took a while to learn to love and trust him again. But I don't think I could find a kinder, more understanding man.

But sometimes I feel like he's hiding something from me. I know that it's just because I can't remember myself. I sometimes expect him to know everything about me. The only thing I think he does know about, and is not being honest with me about, is my dark angel.

I see him each night in my dreams. It's almost like he is calling for me. I can't begin to count the many nights that I have woke up crying. It's like I can feel his loneliness and despair.

Is he the answer to the pendant? Is he the one who wants me to remember that true love never dies?

What am I doing? I'm writing to you like you can answer the question of the inscription left to me by R.R.

I just wish I could find some clue. Something so that I could remember everything. Then I could stop putting off setting a wedding date for Brian's sake.

All of the doctors say that my memory will come back in time. But how do they know? They've never been forced to live a life of a person who doesn't *remember their friends and family. Let alone themselves.*

At least I still have one person to help me through these difficult times. Speaking of whom, Brian is going to be home from work anytime now. So I better start dinner.

> *Your absentminded friend,*
> *Rabecca*

Her hand gently closed the black cover to the spiral notebook she had been using as a makeshift diary, and she tucked it beneath the mattress of the bed for safekeeping. Rabecca sighed deeply as she looked over the cramped, run down efficiency apartment that she called home. Something deep within her knew and told her that there was a better place meant for her somewhere in the world; however, she smiled, knowing that at least she was well loved if nothing else.

She walked to the small kitchen. There Rabecca began to prepare the most extravagant meal that her budget allowed. The broken air conditioner and multiple fans offered little relief from the heat. It had built up within the main room that was the apartment due to the use of the stove.

She had toiled over the hot stove, with sweat that poured from her face staining the thin shirt that she wore. The meal was completed and laid to rest upon the only two matching plates she had found at the local thrift store.

Now we just have to add the finishing touches, Rabecca thought as she spread a red linen table cloth across the small table for two. Then with a pair of candlesticks and a single match the room was lit with a dim romantic light, though it added to the heat.

There she sat with candles that flickered and the constant ticking of a clock to keep her company. However, she still waited patiently for Brain to return home after his long day of work.

The candles burned lower and lower. Then with a quick breath Rabecca blew out the flames. Yet she did so carefully because she did not want to cause wax to be splattered upon the only table cloth she had.

"Where is he? Brian is never any later than 4:30 getting home. Here it is seven already! He must be stuck at the store again. I'll just give him a call to let him know that dinner is waiting for him."

Rabecca pushed aside the fear of Brian angered by her if she called. With a slightly hesitant hand, she picked up the phone and dialed.

"Gill's Hardware. This is Richard. How can I help you?"

Rabecca then nervously spoke. "Hi, Rich, this is Becca. Is Brian still around or has he left to come home already?"

"Sorry, Becca, Brian left early today. He said something about having a lunch date with his sweetie, but…oh, I thought he was talking about you. I'm sorry…I have to go."

Rabecca remained silent for a few seconds before she said, "That's…okay. I'm sure that there is an explanation for it." Yet her ears were met only with the fumbled sound of the phone being hung up at the other end.

Complete silence filled Rabecca as she hung up the phone. Tears swelled within her eyes as different ideas filled her mind. Each would be worse than the last. As the tears flowed more and more in number the sudden fear left her. It then started being replaced with the flame of anger. Anger that seemed familiar while directed toward Brian.

Suddenly, as the anger made her common judgment blinded by an unexplained feeling of hatred and betrayal, the phone rang and caused the emotions that felt like returning memories to be put on hold.

"Hello," she said with a voice that could have caused all but the bravest of men to cringe.

"Sounds like you've been having a bad day, baby. I'm sorry but I don't think my news will make it any better."

"Brian," she sighed. "I've been worried sick about you!"

"I'm sorry. But I've been so busy at the store I wasn't able to call earlier. Listen, don't worry about dinner tonight. I've got to stay here till closing."

"That's okay. Dinner is already waiting for you when you get here. Did you at least have a nice lunch?"

"Becca, I've been so busy that I haven't had time for lunch. I've got to go. I have a customer waiting for me. Love you, bye."

The dull sound of the dial tone echoed through Rabecca's ears. She tried to contain herself from letting a scream of anger loose.

"Why is he lying to me? And I hate being called Becca! I've hated it since the first time my grandmother called me that!"

Her anger quickly got pushed aside as she realized what she had said. She knew that somehow it had sprung from within her own memory.

"My grandmother called me Becca. After…after she took me in. I remember that. I also remember that I have always had a diary. That means that I may have an old diary around here! I might be able to remember more if I can find it!"

She moved through the small apartment like a human tornado. She ripped through each cupboard and box until the area looked as if it had been ransacked by thieves. Tired, and with even more sweat covering her than before, Rabecca collapsed upon the bed. She was unable to continue her search. She panted for breath as she looked at the mess that her quest for the past had left.

"I've searched everywhere! Maybe…it wasn't a memory."

Rabecca's head lowered in disappointment. She sat upon the bedside that Brian had claimed since they had moved to this place. From the corner of her eye a silver glint caught her attention. A silver metal briefcase sat between the bed and the night stand.

"Brian's briefcase…He never wants me to be around when he opens it. I know he's hiding something. After all, look what he's doing tonight."

Several moments of self justification came before her choice was finally made. She then reached out to take hold of the box of secrets. Her subconscious caused her hand to jump as it touched the cool, textured surface.

He'll never know, she thought as she quickly grabbed the black, plastic handle and lifted it to her lap. The combination clasps were shut securely. It allowed the box a more formidable appearance.

"Well, at least there's not that many combinations to go through." Rabecca tried different number sequences until she heard the rattle of keys at the front door. Fear rushed through her body. It caused Rabecca to fling the briefcase back into place. She then ran to the door to meet Brian. When he stepped through the door Brian saw the nervous smile that Rabecca wore. He also noticed what seemed to be an endless room of disorder.

"Honey! You're home earlier than what I thought you would be," Rabecca spouted out in a fake tired voice.

"Becca, it's a little cold for spring cleaning," he said in a frigid, cynical voice.

Rabecca hid a cringe at the sound of the name and continued. "I had a memory come back to me today."

Brian paid her little attention as he unbuttoned his shirt. "That's nice. So what's for dinner?"

"Didn't you hear me? I said I had part of my past come back to me! I'm starting to remember things slowly like the doctors said I would."

Brian glared at her. "I heard you already. I'm just tired. I want to eat then go to sleep, Becca."

"Stop calling me that! I hate being called Becca! My grandmother used to call me that. You should know I hate it!"

Brian stopped when she finished her speech. He nervously looked into Rabecca's eyes while the color drained from his face. "You weren't joking about a memory coming back were you?"

Rabecca stood and faced him. He recognized the spark of anger in her eyes. The same anger that he hoped would never rise forth again. With only a single word Rabecca answered and caused Brian to swallow deeply. "No."

"That's...well great, Bec...I mean, Rabecca. How much have you remembered?"

"Enough to know that I really dislike the woman. Also enough to know that something just doesn't feel right. I'm not sure exactly what. But I know it's lingering there just waiting to be found one way or another."

Brian walked past her as he watched for anything that could break upon the floor. He moved to the small kitchen table and found the cold meal that awaited him. "You did all of this for me? I'm sorry that I didn't get off work on time again. If I would have known..."

Rabecca sat opposite from him and continued to peer with heartless eyes. "What are you hiding from me?"

"Nothing!" Brian stopped and cleared his throat. "I'm sorry for being short with you. It's just I can't tell you everything about your life. I wasn't there for all of it. Remember?"

"No, that's my point! I don't remember. For all I know you could be my cousin, or brother for that matter."

Brian took a bite off of the plate and chewed twice as long as needed. She noticed that he looked for a reason not to speak again. Finally, after the delay, he spoke with a loving voice. "I'll do anything in my power to help you remember. But some things will be painful to hear. Ask whatever you want to know about."

Rabecca closed her eyes. She used every bit of mental ability as she recalled exact details. "There is a man in my dreams. A man with dark black, no, brown hair. He looks so sad. Even though he looks like he could have anyone or anything that he wants. Who is he?"

After another sigh following a long pause Brian told his version of the truth. All within a hesitant and mournful voice.

"His name is Rowan. To be honest he is someone I hoped you would never remember. A year ago we took a trip with another couple who we were friends with. While on this trip this man found you at a local hot spot. He started to enchant you with his charm. He was a very hard act to follow, if you know what I mean. At that night's end Rowan invited you to his home and gave you his phone number. Later I finally worked up the nerve to say something about it to you. It caused a big fight. We were in a different town. Hell, a different state, and you had nowhere else to go. So you called him. He offered you a shoulder to cry on. That is until you wanted to come back. That's when things took a turn for the worst. He forced himself upon you. He raped you and tried to keep you prisoner in his house. Somehow you escaped and made it back to me. After you told me what had happened I went crazy. I tracked him back to the same hot spot. There we began to fight. He pulled a knife and tried to kill me. But you stopped him. During the moment of rage that bastard threw you into the path of a speeding car. He made you this way. He almost killed us both. But I've looked at your memory loss as a sort of mixed blessing. At least this way you didn't have to live with the pain of the truth. That is, until now."

Rabecca's face streamed with tears as she listened to the tale. "Why didn't you tell me this sooner?"

Brian reached for her hand in an embracing manner. "How could I? I just didn't want you to have to live through that nightmare again."

Rabecca dried her eyes as she tried to find a smile; however, she could not hide that the tale had scared her. "I'm sorry that I snapped. I was hoping that we could have a nice romantic evening." Rabecca sniffled.

"Not tonight. I just want to go to bed after I eat. Plus I don't want you to feel like you have to do something. Especially after this skeleton has come out of the closet."

He stood before her as she turned and ran. From door to door she ran through the stone hallway. She found each locked until she came to a room filled with candles. Quickly Rabecca shut and bolted the door. She braced it with all of her weight as she repeated to herself, "Please just go away."

Her crying echoed within the hard walls of the room until she screamed, "Quit haunting me!" Yet, as she did so, she noticed there was still the sound of crying that was not her own. Fear filled her as she slowly turned from the door. She found the figure in black knelt upon the center of the floor, his face buried within his hands.

Rabecca spun around and began to unlock the door when he spoke.

"Why do you run from me? Why do you fear me? Why do you come to me just to run and disappear like a phantom at night?"

Rabecca slowly turned again and found the cold, sad face looking up to her. His dark eyes had turned red and were filled with questioning.

He stood slowly as he continued to speak. "All of my life I have searched for the other half of my soul. The person who could make me complete. I love you even now, though seeing your presence torments me. I know you will awake thinking it was simply a dream."

Rabecca stepped forward reluctantly as she asked, "Who are you?"

"Remember, true love never dies. No matter what happens I will always love you." Gently he placed his hand upon her face as he looked deep within her eyes. "Don't believe him, Rabecca. He will tell you anything to keep you from searching out the truth about yourself, and me. Find me."

Suddenly Rabecca felt herself being pulled away from the scene by a supernatural force. All went black. She then shot upward in bed. The only light in the room came from the red numbers of the digital alarm clock that sat at her bedside. She breathed deeply as she pushed the faint echo of his last words from her head. She sought relief as she lay back down and rolled to snuggle up to Brian. She found only a sheet of paper on his pillow where his head should have rested.

Still tired from her restless sleep, Rabecca slowly stretched for the lamp. With a click it turned on and caused her eyes to ache for a brief moment. After she rubbed her eyes she tried to focus on the paper. She read carefully due to her blurred vision:

Rabecca,

I've went in early to open the store. Hopefully I'll be able to get out of there early today. I'll call and let you know.

Love, Brian

Her eyes stared at the word love. She wondered if the word written by Brian's hand was as hollow as what it felt. The paper fell to rest upon the bed once more as Rabecca stood and stretched her entire body. She started to talk to herself out loud. "Oh, it's too early. I need a cigarette."

Rabecca then froze immediately as she heard her own words. She then thought, *I smoke? Brian never said anything about me smoking. But it sounds right for some reason.* After she tried to remember, Rabecca shook her head and went to the closet. One by one she pulled out different shirts, all of which were as brightly colored as spring wildflowers growing in a meadow.

"What am I? Ms. Prep U.S.A. or something? I mean who would buy stuff like this besides cheerleaders?"

Every garment that had been upon a hanger found its way to a pile on the floor. Rabecca looked down and sighed. Disappointed she bent over and began to pick up the hangers. Then a suitcase that sat within the shadows of the closet caught her eye.

"Where did this come from?" Her hand reached into the closet and she pulled the suitcase out. She walked to the bed and sat down, her eyes never left the stained, faded blue canvass. Her fingers continued to run over the edges until curiosity forced her to open it.

She smiled when her eyes were met first with an unopened pack of cigarettes and a lighter. Before she thought about her actions Rabecca found the tan filter in her mouth as the tip was kissed by flame. As she exhaled the smoke Rabecca realized what she was doing. Though she had loathed the smell before she found that the taste was familiar and tasted good.

She continued to smoke as her hands eagerly dug through the neat packing job. From within the suitcase she pulled out clothes of a darker nature. An hour had almost passed as she now looked at the bed. The white sheets had been covered with clothes styled in a way that pleased her as she lit another cigarette.

"Let's see. We have makeup, a violet and black velvet dress, which I love. A few silky shirts that are okay because they're almost transparent. Some black jeans, one small black purse, and I can't forget the makeup. Oh yes, and these black leather boots that compliment everything so well! I wonder why Brian never told me about these."

She did not ponder long as she snatched up the dress and put it on. Rabecca found herself as she looked at her reflection within the mirror. Her hands reached for the makeup case. Almost as if it were second nature, her hands worked. Slow and steady her hands moved as Rabecca's face transformed. She knew that she had finished after her naturally pale face was accented with black that surrounded her eyes and dark red lips.

"Now this feels right," she said as she packed up the makeup and went to the bed to pack the suitcase. Neatly she folded all of the clothes and placed everything within the suitcase, excluding the cigarettes and purse. After she had finished she once again reached for the silver briefcase. "Now where were we yesterday when we were so rudely interrupted?"

Again she tried different combinations; however, it did not take long before frustration overwhelmed her patient side. "This damn thing is going to open one way or another!" Rabecca stormed to the kitchen. She dug through junk drawers and returned with a long flathead screwdriver. With very little pressure applied to the locks the briefcase was opened. Her eyes gazed over its contents, which she thought rather odd.

A crucifix laid on top of a cloth, which covered garlic. Beneath the cloves she found bottles marked holy water, and wooden stakes. "Great, Brian thinks he's a vampire hunter. But for some reason it doesn't shock me." At the bottom of the briefcase she found bank statements for a savings account in her name. Newspaper clippings and an opened letter, clipped together, covered a small flower-covered book. "More than likely a list of all of the vampires he has killed. I wonder if Dracula is at the top of the list." Rabecca picked up the book and flipped through the pages. She then found herself reading her own thoughts, feelings. Rabecca continued to let her mind absorb each word until she reached the events that had led up to her last diary entry.

"That bastard has been hiding this from me all this time! How dare Brian do this just because he wanted me to do and be what he wanted! That does it! I may not remember everything. But by my own words I know something isn't right. I'm going to go down there and give him a piece of what mind I've gotten back!"

Anger drove Rabecca as she picked up the phone and called a taxi. She quickly packed the diary, bank statements, and letter with newspaper clippings in the suitcase and walked to the door.

"Damn it!" Rabecca dropped the suitcase at the door's edge as she turned around for the cigarettes and purse. She tried to put the cigarettes inside of the purse as she rushed to the door; however, something blocked the zippered entrance of the purse.

"Now what? Am I going to find the birth certificate for a child I don't even know I have?" Her opposite hand reached inside and pulled out a half pack of cigarettes. A debit card had been stuffed within the plastic wrapper. "That's never a bad thing," she said before she pulled the card out with teeth. Then almost as if it were in slow motion, a white card fell through the air followed by a fifty dollar bill. She knelt down to snatch up the money and then noticed the name printed upon the card.

"Rowan Rasland? *Remember True Love Never Dies - R.R.* That explains this thing!" Her hand grasped the pendant that hung around her neck. Rabecca placed the card with the money into the purse with no hesitation. After the delay of arranging her purse Rabecca grabbed the suitcase and walked through the door. Her heart raced as she reached the main entrance of the apartment building. There the cab was awaiting her arrival.

The driver stood propped against the passenger side of the car. He wore a tacky tropical shirt and had been reading a newspaper until Rabecca walked out and said, "I need you to take me to Gill's Hardware. From there I'm not really sure." The driver folded the paper, took one look at Rabecca and smiled. "Not a problem, let's go."

Rabecca climbed in the back with suitcase in hand and the cab took off. Rabecca's anger had clouded every sense she had. It caused the trip to feel as if it had taken place instantaneously.

"We're here, Ms. Hollyard." Rabecca looked up quickly. She found that the cab had come to a stop and the driver looked at her through the rearview mirror.

"Thanks. I'll be back." She opened the door and stepped out; however, she then stopped and looked back at the driver. "What did you call me?" she asked, puzzled.

"Ms. Hollyard. At least that's what you said your name was in the back while I was driving up here."

Rabecca shook her head as she rationalized not remembering the conversation due to the state of mind she was in. "I'm so mad I don't even remember saying anything."

She stepped from the cab and had walked to the automatic doors when Brian stepped out with a young blonde. He had kissed her before she turned and walked away. Brian stood at the doors and watched her walk away. He had been so blinded by lust that he never noticed Rabecca who stood only a few steps away.

"Hello, Brian," Rabecca said with a scornful voice.

Brian's eyes glanced at Rabecca and then nervously cut back at the blonde. She had just begun to drive away.

"Rabecca, honey." He then looked her over. "What the hell happened to you?"

"You know, that's exactly what I am wondering. Oh! You mean the way I look, right? I decided to give myself an old make over with the clothes in my suitcase that was hidden from me."

"And what makes you sure it is your suitcase?" Brian asked as Rabecca lit a cigarette.

"Well, the last time I checked I was the only one who smoked these. So who was your bimbo?"

The nervousness blended with shock as he watched the smoke pour from her mouth. "She was a customer! What are you doing smoking those things?" Brian snatched the cigarette from her lips and broke it in half.

"Oh, I see. You always kiss your customers. Forgive me, Brian. I forgot that was in your job description. Why am I smoking? Gee, let me think. It could be because I'm a smoker. You know, something you failed to tell me before!"

Brian glared at Rabecca. He allowed the anger to be seen in his eyes and heard within his voice as he almost screamed.

"It's a bad habit that I've always hated! I didn't tell you so that you wouldn't start again! Forgive me for trying to save you from cancer!"

"It's a bad habit that YOU'VE always hated. I understand now! You took advantage of my memory loss. It gave you the chance to mold and shape me into the person that you've wanted me to be since day one!"

Brian stumbled over his own words because of Rabecca. He never thought that she would confront him about his hidden agenda.

"Give it a rest! You've lost!" Rabecca turned and walked back to the cab. She then stopped at the back passenger door and looked at Brian once again. "If I were you I would either get fast food after work or call that little toy that you've been having an affair with. I hope she can cook because I won't be there when you go home."

Brian jumped forward in anger as he shouted, "Where are you going to go, Rabecca? You have no one. It's like your memory, nonexistent. Who are you going to go to? That slut Rachel? Sorry, she's got a slight case of death right now! Or perhaps that meat head, Porter? Never mind, you can't do that! Rachel caught her slight case of death from Porter!"

Rabecca climbed into the back and then rolled down the window. "I'd rather have no one than be stuck here with you. At least then I can be myself without being brainwashed by a two-timing loser like you!"

Rabecca quickly rolled up the window as Brian made a mad dash for the cab. Just as he was within arm's length Rabecca looked at the driver, panicked. "Get me away from him please." The driver nodded and stomped on the gas. The tires screeched across the asphalt as the cab almost ran over Brian's foot.

"Where to now?" the driver asked as he darted through traffic. He looked through the rearview mirror to ensure that they were not followed.

"I don't care, just get me away from here. I just need to find the place where I feel that I belong. I know that's not here." Rabecca sighed.

"Not a problem. To the bus station it is then."

Rabecca leaned over the passenger seat and studied his kind, somewhat familiar face. "You might find this odd, but have we met before?"

The driver laughed as he prepared for a turn. "We very well could have. But after you've been driving as long as I have then it seems like almost everyone you see you've met before."

Rabecca moved back in the seat. She wore a grim sign of bewilderment as she continued. "I don't even know if who I'm looking for is a real man. Or if he's some fairy tale built up around someone very dangerous."

Her mind folded inward upon itself. She wondered what the next piece of her puzzle was. Rabecca looked for some sign of what was next as she went through her purse. Her eyes examined the white card as she hoped to find an address; however, her hopes were crushed as she found only the name followed by three phone numbers. They were listed in the order of office, home and limo.

At least I have these numbers to guide me, she thought as she replaced the card. She then reached for the suitcase.

The bank statements were found to be boring. But she was grateful to learn she was at least not totally broke. She tucked them away safely before she looked at the letter.

The handwriting looked feminine on the envelope. It caused her to sigh as she threw away hopes of it being penned by the one, Rowan. Rabecca carefully unfolded the letter as she took it from the envelope. She treated it as if it were a precious artifact that was priceless. Something that could never be replaced. Her eyes then read each neatly-written word:

Dear Rabecca,

How I wish that I was only writing this to tell you that I found your diary in the guest room after Brian rudely packed up and left abruptly.

I'm not sure if you still care, but you were friends at one time with Rachel and Porter so I thought you should at least know. Three weeks after you left Heritage Landing Rachel got an emergency phone call from Porter.

I tried to tell her to have him come here. But like normal Rachel always did what she wanted to. That night I had a terrible feeling. But Rachel hadn't called so I didn't worry too much. The next morning I found that she didn't come home. I tried calling the police, but they said I had to wait forty-eight hours to fill out a missing person's report. Also they said she was over the age of eighteen and it was considered moving out, not running away.

Finally they listened to me after the second day. They found Rachel's car sitting outside of an abandoned motel nearly two counties away.

The police found them laying arm in arm, dead, with a note written on a page from "Romeo and Juliet." It said something to the effect of they had lost each other once. At least this way the would never lose each other again.

An autopsy showed that they had both drank wine laced with some kind of poison. I know my Rachel would have never done that willingly. But as much as I hated Brian for what he had done to them I have tried to forgive him. I had Rachel and Porter buried beside each other after consulting Porter's parents.

I hope you can forget the past and will someday visit them and me. But leave that low-down jerk at home.

I hope to see you soon,

Carol Duffy

Rabecca's eyes were flooded with tears. It caused the ink to blur more than what it already was from the tear stains of the author. She quickly dried her eyes and crammed the letter back into the large brown envelope. Rabecca then noticed the cab driver watching her through the rearview mirror.

"Are you okay?" he asked as the cab stopped in front of the bus station.

With a sniffle Rabecca blurted, "I'm fine." She put the letter in the suitcase and fastened the lid tightly. "How much do I owe you?"

The driver turned around in his seat and smiled. "Well, that really all depends on where you are going to be heading from here."

"I'm not exactly sure just yet. I was thinking about a place called Heritage Landing but I'm not sure if I should chase after a dream or not."

The driver laughed uncontrollably and caused Rabecca to become more infuriated with every breath. She tried to ask him why he laughed, but each time he laughed harder. He laughed until Rabecca climbed out of the taxi with suitcase in hand.

After she dug through her purse she tossed the fifty dollar bill at him. "Keep the change, asshole!" Only when Rabecca stormed off did he stop laughing and chase after her.

"Wait a minute," he called. He hoped that Rabecca would actually listen to him. He wove through people as he continued to peruse her through the crowd.

He pushed and shoved people, and caused them to curse him; however, he caught up with Rabecca. He then darted in front of her and said, "Wait a minute now. I'm getting too old to be chasing after a young thing like you."

Her eyes glared at him evilly. "You can say that again." Rabecca walked around him as her fury continued to grow.

With a loud huff he ran behind her. "I'm sorry that I was laughing. But I found something funny."

"Can't you take a hint? I've had enough happen to me today. Somebody laughing at me doesn't help my disposition too much!"

He stopped and shouted in a tired voice, "You won't be able to get a ticket to Heritage Landing, Ms. Hollyard!"

Rabecca turned around with cat's grace and walked back to the exhausted driver. "What do you mean that I won't be able to get a bus ticket to Heritage Landing? This is the bus station, right? Or have they just suddenly stopped selling them because I'm wanting one?"

He wiped the sweat from his brow. "No. You see, the only bus that runs through Heritage Landing is a small church bus. It takes the city's elderly residents to their weekly bingo meeting."

Rabecca looked at him in disbelief. "Yeah. Whatever. Like I'm going to take the word of a cab driver who doesn't live there."

She turned to walk away when the driver jumped in front of her yet again. "You're right. I don't live there, now. I just grew up there and spent most of my life there."

Rabecca had reached the point of screaming as she stopped for him the third time. "Okay, fine! I'll get a ticket to the nearest stop and take a cab from there. That is if it is okay with you? You know your opinion means so much to me."

He gave a parental-like look as he said, "I'm just trying to be helpful. You have two options you can choose from. Option one, you take a bus to Heritage, which is thirty miles from Heritage Landing. Spend more money than you have just to get where you are going. Or there's option two: you can take back your money, come with me and we can go there together."

"Now why would a cab driver, states away, offer to take me all the way to Heritage Landing for free? I think it could be because he is looking for an easy victim. Don't you think I read the newspaper? I know I look like a target.

Trust me, I may live in my own world, but I still keep up with what happens in the world you live in!"

He placed his hand on her shoulder as she turned to leave. "I'm not going out of my way. I'm driving the cab there with or without you. You could say I'm taking a vacation to visit an old friend who called a few nights ago. Just think, Rabecca, we could be looking for the same person."

She stopped and asked, "What do you mean? This time just tell me what is going on."

"I was instructed to pick you up today while I was sleeping by my old friend."

Rabecca turned around. Her wide eyes were filled partially with fear and excitement. "You're talking about Rowan, aren't you?"

"Let's get going, we'll talk in the car." The driver turned and walked away with Rabecca right on his heels.

"But I don't even know your name," she said as she matched his footsteps.

"Cliff, just call me Cliff. Here, let me carry that bag for you."

A moment of clarity. How long has my mind been feeding upon itself this time? A week, month or longer? I see her face. I hear her voice as if she were with me. Am I going insane? Rabecca, is that you?

Chapter Nine

The door quickly swung open to the small apartment. "Rabecca, enough is enough. I know we have to come to an understanding. Rabecca?"

Brian stood alone in the doorway as he glared at the lifeless apartment. Hastily he moved to check if Rabecca's clothes were missing from the closet. He found each article that he had purchased for her within the last year upon the floor in one large pile. It looked as if they had been prepared for a funeral pyre.

"Well, if she didn't take them, she cannot be too far away." Brian knelt to clean up the mess of fabric when his mind echoed her words. With a quick dart of his head Brian searched the back corner of the closet for the suitcase.

"Damn!" He turned and almost slipped as he ran for the bedside. His eyes no sooner laid sight upon the bed when he realized what had happened. "The diary." Brian dove across the bed. The contents of the briefcase spilled upon the sheets and floor. Slowly Brian sat up and gathered his tools of the trade. A grim, satanic smile had grown across his face.

"I've been waiting for this day to come. Finally she knows. It's so beautiful. My dear play toy doesn't even know that she is leading me to my prey and prize. Not even Rabecca will be able to refuse me once I have tasted the blood of an immortal!"

Brian pulled an old, and very worn, green duffel bag from under the bed. He then carefully placed each stake in the bag. Only afterward did he lay to rest a large wooden hammer on top of them. He ensured that a vial of holy water was emptied within his stomach. He placed the crucifix around his neck and then stuffed cloves of garlic into his pockets. As he walked for the door his hands felt of each pocket, followed by the duffel bag. When he had met his mental check list of materials, Brian started to walk out the door. He used one hand to close it behind himself, yet stopped before the door knob clicked— the sound that would have shown the door would not be opened again without a key.

"What does it matter?" Brian shoved the door open and caused it to crash against the wall.

"After all, when I become a god I can always get new things. Even a new place. That is, if I can find the right place where someone is dying to move."

He gave an evil chuckle that matched the smile he wore. It echoed through the hall as he walked out into the night.

"Please tell me that this isn't a dream. Or at least tell me that you're real and that I am not chasing only a ghost."

Rabecca found herself in new, yet familiar, surroundings as Rowan knelt over a gravestone. He turned his head and motioned her to his side. Rabecca quietly met his request as she slowly walked to his side. Without being asked, Rabecca knelt beside him upon the stone-cold earth. Her eyes locked upon the name carved upon the headstone as she tried to recall why it was so familiar.

"Kyra. She was my first and only wife. You met her here once before. That's why you know this place."

Rabecca's head turned to Rowan's lowered eyes. "You can hear my thoughts can't you?"

Rowan stood and offered his hand to help her upon her feet. "You can say that. But do not concern yourself with that right now. My dearest, you have already taken the first step of the most difficult journey of your life. He has started the trip to find you."

Rabecca took his hand and almost jerked away at his touch; however, it was not because of fear. It was because his hand was as cold as the earth that she had just knelt upon.

"Who are you? What are you? Why does Cliff act like he knows you but never says your name?"

Rowan tried to find a smile under his depressed face. Yet he found only enough of one to have made one corner of his mouth move upward.

"Who am I? Your heart already knows the answer to that question. I know you feel it each time you see me. The same as I feel it. What am I? Your mind holds the key. I would tell you, but I almost lost you the first time I did. I do not wish to chance it once again."

He held her hand gently and kissed it very lightly. The sensation caused cold chills to run up and down her spine. "But what about Cliff?"

"Yes, Clifford is one of the only two people I can trust besides you. He will keep you as safe as he possibly can. He will help you reclaim your memory no matter what length it requires you to go to."

Rabecca sighed deeply. "You could save us both a lot of trouble and just tell me what I'm supposed to remember."

"I could tell you of how I cannot bear to live without you. Or that I love you more than there are stars in the sky. But me confessing my love will not cause you to remember how we shared that love. After you can remember our love, if you have not remembered everything else, then I will tell you. Only then do I feel that the truth will not drive you away in fear. For you to leave of your own free will can only cause me heartache. Yet for you to run away out of fear, I could not live nor exist with that knowledge."

She lowered her eyes from his because somehow she knew that he was right. Then puzzlement caused her eyes to seek his again. The dark portals shone in pain; however, there was a hint of pure ecstasy that had been placed into his heart, only for it to be removed and hidden away from his possession. Images of a book flashed throughout her mind. A book that housed a sad tale that seemed timeless. She smelt the aroma of the coffee that had set before her. It mingled with the scent of stale, brittle pages and dusty leather.

The vision vanished and left her within the created world of night. Rowan still peered into her eyes, motionless. "You're not human, yet more humane than most who are."

A spark of hope fired within Rowan's eyes. It caused the depression to melt for a moment. It also caused a loving smile to appear upon his face.

"You are close. So very close to me and the answers you seek. When you find me a single touch will awaken me from my slumber. Do not rush to find your answers; however, you must hurry. The one who has caused you so much pain is following close in your steps. Remember."

Rabecca's eyes sprung open. She found that the night had been parted by a white light that poured from the exterior of the small gas station. She stretched as she rubbed her eyes to be rid of the tears that blurred her vision so she could only make out discolored images of people. Though she wondered how long she had slept, the dream that would not fade continued to replay within her mind.

Fighting to make her legs cooperate, Rabecca slowly opened the cab door and climbed out. After the first steps were made the pain of the cramps disappeared. Rabecca found herself behind Cliff who paid for various things.

"I see you finally woke up. I was beginning to think that you were going to sleep the whole way there. Here, have some coffee. I also got a whole sack full of snacks just in case. Oh, don't worry about them being drugged or anything."

Rabecca coughed to clear her throat. "I'm not worried about something like that, Clifford. I think I know you better than that."

She then looked at the cashier and said, "Give me a pack of your cheapest full-flavored, please."

Clifford stepped aside in silence. He watched Rabecca pay for her cigarettes and waste no time in opening them.

With a cigarette in hand awaiting to be lit Rabecca walked outside with Clifford who followed behind her. He walked to the car door as he searched for the words needed to question Rabecca without seeming intrusive. Both doors closed and left them shut off from the rest of the world almost. Clifford stared at her with a stern face as a cigarette met her lips. It caused the dim flame to become brighter as it touched the tip.

"What!?" Rabecca then realized she had lit the cigarette inside of the car. "Oh, I'm so sorry. I didn't ask you if it was okay to smoke in here." Her apologetic voice did not cause his expression to shift.

"I couldn't care less about you smoking in the car. He came to you again didn't he?"

Her eyes went from an ashamed look to bewilderment. "How did you know? I haven't said anything yet?"

"You called me Clifford. I told you my name was Cliff. The only other person who ever used my full name was Mr. Rasland."

A smile of confirmed satisfaction sprouted from her lips. "Yes! I knew that you were hinting about him! You know he's different don't you?"

The stern expression melted away. "Yes, he is different. But I can't give you the answer to that question."

Rabecca pouted in a playful manner as she looked at him. "Oh, come on. PPlleeaassee…?"

Clifford placed the car in gear and drove back to the main road. "I've been instructed not to tell you. I can't explain how he is coming to us. But there is probably another piece to the puzzle to find."

"You meant the other person I can trust besides you, right?"

His eyes cut back to Rabecca who sat beside him. He saw a sly smile before she inhaled the gray smoke. "Yes, as a matter of fact, I was talking about Norm. So what all did Mr. Rasland tell you?"

"Not enough for me to remember much. But for some reason he is afraid to tell me what he really is. That is, before I remember how I felt about him. When are we going to find Norman?" Rabecca paused and then looked at Clifford. "That's right, his name is Norman. He didn't want to…let me into the club the night I…"

"Met Mr. Rasland? It's amazing how your memory has been coming back. If he is right then this trip will do the trick. But if I'm right then Norm is already awaiting our arrival."

Rabecca tossed the cigarette out the window. "So how close are we?"

"We're as close to Heritage Landing as you are to remembering your past. Just in case you are wondering, I don't think you have very far to go."

Chapter Ten

Rabecca stared at the sign as she read *Java Rose 1/2 mile*. She spoke slowly as she asked, "I've been there before haven't I?"

Clifford smiled as he answered, "Yes. A long time ago after a secret was revealed to you. Now we're going there again."

"That's good. For some reason I think we should. It could just be another memory trying to resurface, but for some reason I think someone will be waiting for us there. I hope it is Rowan."

"It could be. Mr. Rasland does change his mind quickly. Well, that is if there is a good reason to do so."

Tension mounted within Rabecca and caused silence to fall between them. Her eyes began to search frantically as Clifford pulled into the parking lot and turned the engine off.

Before Clifford could unfasten his safety belt Rabecca had already jolted from the car. She stood in the center of the parking lot as if she waited for something or someone to jump from the shadows to surprise her.

From left to right her head jerked until he stepped around the corner of the building. Her eyes squinted. It made Rabecca look as if she were gazing into the sun while she studied his face. Suddenly she ran to him. With a jump her arms wrapped around his thick neck.

"Norman! I haven't seen you…" Her arms loosened as her feet dropped to the ground. "…since the night of the fight." Her eyes remained open, though the expression on her face told how deeply she dug through her mind.

"Now I feel jealous. She didn't act like that when she saw me. Come to think of it she didn't even remember me!"

Norman looked over the top of Rabecca's head with ease as he watched Clifford. He walked up as a smile grew across his face. "Cliff, aren't you a sight for sore eyes. Well, I'll tell you what. If it will make you feel better I'll run up to ya and jump in your arms."

They both started to laugh as their hands met firmly to greet each other. Norman looked back at Rabecca as she aimlessly walked inside the café. "I'm glad to see that I'm not losing my mind."

Clifford sighed. "I know what you mean. I thought I was, too, but I followed his instructions anyway and look who I found."

Norman looked back at Cliff. "Well, that answers my questions for you. But what about Rabecca?"

"Mr. Rasland has been coming to her as well. From what he has told me she lost her memory. That's the reason why she never returned."

Norman shook his head with disappointment. "Must have been caused by the accident. So we just take her to him and we're back in business."

"It's not that easy, Norm. Mr. Rasland wants her to at least remember what she felt for him. That way she won't run when she finds out his family secret."

"Great," Norman huffed as he looked back to check on Rabecca. "She obviously remembers some things. So what do we do now?"

"So far it seems that her memory can be triggered with places and even a face. She remembers a few things about Mr. Rasland. But nothing about their short-lived romance. So until more comes out I'm afraid that she is running this show."

With a shrug of the shoulders Norman walked to the door of the café. "Okay then, let's see if we can get this show started."

Rabecca found herself at a booth that had felt right to her. She continued to search deeper into the void as she tried to pull back a piece of her past. Norman and Clifford sat across from her as she continued looking through them as if they were not before her. The silence was broken as a waitress dressed in a multi-striped shirt said, "Welcome to the Java Rose. What can I get for you this evening?"

Before they could answer, Rabecca said, "Coffee, cream, and a spoon." Her eyes then focused upon Clifford and Norman. "Also one black and another with two sugars."

The waitress walked away quickly and left them alone. "Well she's remembering minor details at least," Norman said sarcastically. Rabecca glared at him. The look caused Norman to realize that he had made his comment out loud. Coffee was set before them. It sloshed a few drops out of the cup. "If you need anything else just let me know." As the waitress disappeared into the back room, Rabecca continued.

"No, there's more. A book. A book that I read at this very booth. A very sad, long book that Rowan gave me to read. He gave it to me so that I could make a choice of some kind."

Clifford took a sip of coffee, then nodded his head. "I brought you here so you could read it. It was one of Mr. Rasland's journals that told the events of his life."

Rabecca's eyes locked upon Clifford as she quoted, "I am born only sixteen short years after the Wars of the Roses had begun. It was a time of great turmoil in England; it was due to the houses of York and Lancaster and their ongoing fight to quench their thirsts for power." Her eyes then lowered as she said, "I remember."

Rabecca stopped as she thought over her own words. "August 1, 1471? How can it be right? I'm sorry, guys. I must be trying to remember something from a movie, or history class."

She started to light a cigarette; however, Rabecca then started to choke on the smoke as Norman said, "No, Rabecca. You're right, don't ask me how, but you are."

Rabecca then looked at Clifford. "A cemetery. He gave it to me in a cemetery."

Clifford nodded his head in agreement. The motion caused Rabecca to spring up from her seat. "What are we waiting for? If we go there now maybe I'll remember something else!"

The pay phone sat on the side of the lifeless road. The light flickered in the darkness. With the drop of a few coins he dialed the number and listened to the dull ring. He waited and hoped for an answer.

"Hello, Ms. Duffy, it's Brian. I know it's late and that you're not too happy with me but we have to put that aside for Rabecca's sake. After she found out what happened to Porter and Rachel she lost it. She was committed. I know she is a very fragile girl. I went to visit her today and she had escaped! I think she is coming to see you. I just don't want Rabecca to hurt herself. No, don't call the police. It may drive her over the edge. I'm only a few hours away. Let me come over and we will wait for her. Then I'll take her back. Thank you, Ms. Duffy. I'll see you soon."

The phone clicked as he hung up the receiver. His laughter echoed into the night, unheard by another.

The air seemed colder as Rabecca, Clifford, and Norman neared the spear point fence that surrounded the graveyard. Their breath poured from their mouths like fog that rolled in from the bay on a mild summer evening. The gate screeched as it swung open and then fell off one hinge. It left the cold sound of steel to echo through the colder night.

One by one Rabecca looked at each tombstone carefully. She then moved to one marked Kyra Rasland.

"This one here is real. So is the other one, but it still isn't right," she blurted as she walked past it. Rabecca then stopped at the headstone marked Rowan Rasland.

"This one is different somehow." Her eyes looked at the detailed knot work that was carved within the stone. Her eyes shifted between the two. She made sure each detail matched except for the given names. Then her eyes lowered to the dates that read: *December 11, 1925 – January 1, 1998.*

"The last time this wasn't here." She pointed an outstretched finger to the death date. "I can't forget that is a real grave, too. I don't think that he's there, though." Rabecca then turned and found that neither Clifford or Norman had an argument to offer.

Rabecca sighed. "Rowan gave me that book here. He wanted me to understand how different we were from each other."

She then smiled with a hint of love in her eyes. "He was afraid to tell me about something. He thought that even though I had fallen in love with him his secret would drive me away."

A warmth came over her body as she looked back at his head stone. "I loved him. Truly loved him because I knew it didn't matter."

"Loved or still love?" Clifford asked. It drew her attention back to Norman and himself.

Rabecca blushed slightly as she lowered her head to look at her feet. "Still love. I think. It seems like it was meant to be."

"You know fate has a way of bringing two people together. No matter what the odds may be." Clifford looked at Norman who tried to hide the tear that ran down his face. Rabecca looked up in enough time to see Norman turning his head while he mumbled, "Damn cold weather. Always makes my eyes water."

"Let's go, you two, before the sentimental memories here make us all cry." Rabecca led the way from the cemetery gates and through the small park. Then a familiar squeak caused her to freeze. Her eyes followed the direction of the sound. She traced it back to a small blue and red merry-go-round that gently turned due to the chilling breeze in the air.

"You okay?" Norman asked as he walked close beside her. Rabecca quickly shook the familiar feeling as she smiled at Norman. "I'm fine. It's just something else seems familiar. But I'm not sure what." Her stomach then growled loud enough so that Norman heard it. "I am sure that I am hungry. Where can we get something to eat this early in the morning?"

Clifford's eyes shown with more life as he heard food mentioned. "Tee's should be opening right about now!"

"Oh come on, Cliff. You know I can't stand Tee's," Norman groaned.

"Shut up," Clifford said as he guided Rabecca to the car. "Tee's has the best gravy and biscuits you have ever tasted in your life. Trust me!"

"Yeah trust him, Rabecca. If you don't mind so much grease in the place that you can skate across the floor," Norman grumbled.

"Don't mind him. It's not his fault that he wasn't given enough common sense to know good food. Even if he was smacked in the face with it. Now everyone in the car and across the street we will go!"

The car started. Before anyone could fasten their seatbelts the car darted across the street. As the car screeched to a halt beside the building, the wooden sign sprung to life as flood lights that faced the sign were turned on.

"Great! We're just in time," Clifford said as he cut off the engine and opened his door.

"Just in time? Like anyone else but you would be here just as this grease pit would open." Norman stepped out of the car. He still wore his face of opposition as he watched four more cars pull in and park.

"Only people with taste buds and brains enough to understand good country cookin'," Clifford said as he opened the door to the restaurant. "Maybe you should wait out here, Norm. I don't want you to get a headache. Or brain damage from trying to eat here."

"You're pushing it, old man. You're really pushing it!"

Rabecca watched as they both walked into the first set of doors as she thought, *They're worse than two little old women bickering at each other.* She chuckled as her hand reached blindly for her diary.

Her eyes looked at the cover as if she had just found a long-lost friend. *I think it's about time we get totally reacquainted.*

The sun had broke over the horizon as the late 1970s model pick up crossed the city limits of Heritage Landing. His eyes were bloodshot from lack of sleep as he forced himself to continue onward.

"I'm coming, Rabecca. You may not know it, but I am coming for you. After you lead me to that creature, I'll take what I deserve from it. Then things will be different. Then if you don't want me, well I think I will still have a purpose for you. You will always be a part of me then."

Chapter Eleven

December 19, 1999
Dear Diary,
    It's been a long time since we have seen each other. Since I last told you about my life. I wish that I could say that everything is perfect. But it's far from perfect. I'll try to fill you in and keep it short.
    I lost my memory a year ago. I'm just now starting to remember bits and pieces while having the image of Rowan haunt me while I sleep. But it gets better because Clifford and Norman, who used to work for him, are being haunted, too.
    I left Brian. I found out that I love Rowan to an extent I don't understand. Not to mention that two friends who I barely remember are dead. Other than that my life has been normal if you want to call it that.

    "Is everything okay here?" the balding man asked with a smile and a twinkle in his eye. His voice drew Rabecca's attention away from her diary.
    "Perfect," Clifford said as Rabecca studied his features, he then looked at Rabecca.
    "You're the young lady who was having a fight with your boyfriend the last time you were in here, right?" He continued to smile as Rabecca thought deeply before she answered.
    "Yes. Yes, that's what happened."

"I thought so. I never forget a face. So, did everything work out for you?"

"Actually I just left him for good," she said calmly as she folded her diary closed.

"I'm sorry. But you're still young. You'll find the right guy. Let me tell you from experience, when you do find the right one you'll know. No matter what they have done, or what kind of person they are you will still love them."

Rabecca smiled unlike what Clifford and Norman had seen before. "I know. I've already found him."

"That's good. I hope everything works out for you." He then turned and to visit other tables.

Rabecca stood from her seat and looked at Clifford and Norman with tear-filled eyes. "We need to go now."

Without disagreement they stood. Quickly Norman left money on the table before they followed her out the doors. As they climbed into the car Clifford looked at the tears that ran down her face. "What's wrong, Rabecca?"

She smiled as she used her sleeves to wipe away the tears. "Nothing is wrong. Everything is right. I want you to find out the phone number for a Ms. Carol Duffy. After I call her I want to go see her. After I pay my respects to her, then I want you to take me to Rowan."

Norman leaned forward from the back seat. "Are you sure that you are ready to see him?"

Rabecca laughed as she said, "Don't you see? I don't care who or what he is. I'm always going to love him because he is himself. Because he's not someone who pretends to be something other than what he is."

"Very well then. Give me just a minute, because if I'm not mistaken somebody in Tee's will know her." Clifford rushed from the car back into Tee's. Norman was left in silence as Rabecca continued to cry tears of happiness.

Clifford then ran back to the car only after a few moments. He moved as fast as he could and was somewhat out of breath. "I got the number from our waitress."

Norman pulled out his cell phone and gave it to Rabecca. "Here, give her a call and let her know you are coming. Then we can bring this love story to an end."

Rabecca smiled as she dialed the number. "No, not an end. But a new beginning."

The phone was then pressed against her ear just as a female voice answered. "Hello."

"Hi, Ms. Duffy, this is Rabecca. I'm in town...Brian and I broke up. It's a long story, but I lost my memory a year ago. It's just now starting to come back to me."

"Oh, that's fine, dear. Go ahead and drop by. I'll be waiting for you."

Ms. Duffy looked at Brian as she took a drink of coffee. "She said exactly what you said she would. I'll believe it for now, so you need to get ready because she's on her way."

Brian smiled devilishly. "Thank you, Ms. Duffy."

The cab turned the corner in the small suburban community. They all watched for the house numbered 1346.

"Here we are." Clifford slowed down in front of the house. Ms. Duffy opened the front door and waved as Rabecca opened the passenger door to step out.

"Ms. Duffy, how are you?" Rabecca's smile melted as Brian walked out of the house with a sadistic grin upon his face.

"Rabecca, honey, it's okay. Brian has told me everything. He's here to take you back to a safe place."

"The hell he is!" Rabecca jumped back into the cab and shouted, "Drive!"

The cab's tires screeched as Brian ran behind the house. Norman shouted, "What's going on?!"

Rabecca looked at him and said, "Rowan warned me that he was close. But I had no clue he was this close." Her eyes then looked out the back windshield. "Take me to Rowan as fast as you can! He's chasing us!"

Clifford's eyes looked into the rearview mirror. The brown, rusted pickup slid around the corner recklessly. Clifford stomped upon the accelerator as the pickup started to catch up to them.

The two cars wove throughout the early morning traffic. Traffic that was becoming more abundant with each minute that passed.

"Hang on, everybody!" Clifford continued to gain speed as the cab maneuvered its way through a busy intersection. Clifford looked back in his rearview mirror at the cars that had stopped in the middle of the intersection. "That should slow him down."

Suddenly a loud crash drew their attention away. They found that the truck had plowed through the two cars and had barely slowed. Clifford continued to speed off as he dodged traffic, slowly losing the unwanted tail. At last he could barely see the pickup.

The cab then made a sharp left turn as it darted through traffic onto a small road. After the car climbed a large hill it came to a halt at the bottom. Large double-steel gates that had been chained shut sat before the car.

"Mr. Rasland is in there sleeping! Go to him. We'll stay behind and take care of that mad man!"

Rabecca jumped out of the cab. Her heart pounded as she pushed the gates open enough so that she could duck under the chain. She ran up the cobblestone drive as she heard the familiar sound of Brian's loud pickup in the distance.

Her legs ached, but the sight of the mansion caused her to push onward. When she reached the front door a crashing echo of steel caused her to stop. She looked back and found that the truck had climbed over the cobblestone hilltop.

Frantically she reached for the door knob and twisted. It swung open and banged against the wall. Dust flew from the sheets that covered the furniture as Rabecca ran in.

Instinct caused her to run to the door on the left. She then ran down the dark stone hallway. As it became darker her hand felt along the wall. She touched each door until her heart screamed to open the door she stood before.

Her hand grasped the door knob as a bright flashlight flooded her eyes. She knew the anger-filled voice that screamed, "Rabecca!" Quickly she pushed the door open. It left her in complete darkness; however, the dim light from the hall grew with each step she heard.

"Rowan, help! Please, where are you?" Rabecca cried as Brian turned the corner and shined the flashlight into the center of the room.

Rabecca tried to run to Rowan's side as the light poured onto him. He lay motionless upon a dust-covered bed.

"I don't think so," Brian said as he grabbed her by the back of the hair and slung her against the wall. Pain shot through her body as she fell to the stone floor, crying. "Rowan, please wake up. Please…"

Brian smiled as he reached into his duffel bag. He pulled out a single wooden stake and hammer.

"With your death comes my rebirth, you blood-sucking bastard!" Brian drew back the hammer as he carefully aimed the stake over Rowan's pale, bear chest. Then as he swung with all of his might, Rabecca grabbed his arm while she screamed.

"No!" It threw Brian off balance and caused the stake to scrape his flesh.

Brian pulled his arm away and then looked back at Rowan. His eyes had opened and stared back at him. He then smiled, which exposed the two sharp, white fangs. Before Brian could draw back again with the hammer, Rowan grabbed the stake and sat up.

Brian stumbled backward as fear filled his body. The sound of the stake being broken echoed through the room, followed by Rowan's voice. "You've watched far too many movies, my dear boy. Far, far too many."

Brian grasped Rabecca's wrist firmly and drug her as he said, "We've got to get into the sunlight! He won't be able to do anything to us in the sunlight!"

Rabecca fought and pulled until she felt her wrist snap from the pressure it was under. But he did not care. He continued to drag her to the front door. The pain was outweighed by the desire to escape. She continued to scream and fight as Brian drug her from the house and under the cold, gray sky of winter. With his back to the door Brian doubled over and breathed hard. Though he shook greatly from fear, he kept his firm grip on Rabecca.

Then suddenly the voice caused him to turn.

"Far too many movies."

His eyes widened as Rowan stepped from beyond the shadows and into the sunlight. Each time Rabecca pulled, the fire of pain shot up her arm; however, she continued to pull and claw at his arm. Brian spun her around and smacked her with all of his strength. The blow caused her to land upon the cold ground. Her mouth and nose gushed forth blood.

As Brian glanced back toward Rowan his throat was met with a cold hand. It tightened enough to cut off his air supply.

"You've tried to make her fear me. You've tried to mold her into what you believe a woman should be. Now you hit her! All because, even though she has lost her memory, she still wishes to be with me! I hope whatever god you believe in takes mercy upon you, because I'm not."

Rowan snarled and with one clean jerk he ripped Brian's throat out. His body filled with shock as he fell upon the ground. The sound of air that escaped from his lungs was the last sound he made. The last sound he would ever hear.

Rowan then released the gob of flesh. He tasted a small trail of blood that ran down his hand. "Not even a good vintage year."

He then turned his attention to Rabecca. She looked at him from upon the ground with tears in her eyes.

"Shh, don't be afraid. It's all over. You're safe with me now. He'll never be able to hurt you again."

Rowan extended his hand to her. Rabecca continued to cry while she attempted to say, "You're a… you're a…"

"Blood drinker? Yes. It is the one thing I learned to hate about myself when I first met you."

Her hand gently met his as she allowed him to help her stand. Gently he wiped away her tears. "I will understand if you cannot take knowing this. I will understand if you want to leave now."

Rabecca sniffled as she wiped away the blood from her nose. "No. It doesn't matter. With love, true love, nothing ever matters."

They leaned close to each other. With Rabecca's blood-covered lips they kissed more deeply than anyone in history had ever kissed before. They felt as if nothing could ever end this one kiss. However, a voice asked, "Boss, does this mean we're back in business?"

Rowan turned his head and found Clifford and Norman smiling.

"Yes. I do think we are."

Chapter Twelve

May 11, 2000
Dear Diary,

It's been five months since I fell back into Rowan's arms. I've never been this happy, and I know Rowan feels the same way about me. We love each other for who we are. Also, thanks to him, I've recovered most of my memories, good and bad.

It's so great. I've seen things with him that I thought I would never see before. All I have to do is mention that I want to go some place. That same night we are on a flight there.

London, Paris, Rome, New York, my fairy tale has come true. Even though my knight in shining armor is, well, you know what I mean.

That reminds me. I finally made a choice he still doesn't know about. But if I don't do it now I'll probably never get the nerve to do it again.

Rabecca

Rabecca closed her diary and placed it on the night stand of the luxurious bedroom. She tried to hide the smile upon her face as she put on a white silk gown. The length easily dragged across the marble floor.

Slowly she walked out of the bedroom and found Rowan. He sat in a chair near the large bay window as he read a volume of poetry. As he turned the page Rabecca said, "Dear, we need to talk."

Rowan closed the book and set it upon the chair-side table. "What is it, my love? Are the room accommodations not what you had in mind? We could remodel the mansion a second time if needed."

Rabecca smiled as she pulled out a small knife. Quickly she drug the blade across her wrist. Rowan smiled as the scent of her fresh blood filled his nose.

"Rowan, my love, show me the beauty within darkness. I never want to be without you in life, nor in death."

Rowan stood and walked over to her. He gently stroked his hand against the soft skin of her face before he kissed Rabecca one last time.